# Aluminum and Aluminum Alloys

REVIEWED BY A COMMITTEE CONSISTING OF:

D. V. WILCOX
   *Reynolds Metals Company—Chairman*
H. E. ADKINS
   *Kaiser Aluminum & Chemical Sales, Inc.*
P. B. DICKERSON
   *Aluminum Company of America*
W. C. SCHULTZ
   *Ordnance Div. F.M.C. Corp.*

M. J. WAITE
   *Arcos Corporation*
A. R. PFLUGER
   *Lockheed Missiles & Space Company*
J. HASSLER
   *Euclid Division, General Motors Corp.*
P. G. PARKS
   *Marshall Space Flight Center*

*Edited by Arthur L. Phillips*

Published by AMERICAN WELDING SOCIETY

United Engineering Center

345 East 47th St., New York, N.Y. 10017

*Reprinted from the Welding Handbook*

American Welding Society
Fifth Edition Copyright 1966

First Printing 1966

Printed in the United States of America

# Contents

| | |
|---|---|
| Commercial Forms | 3 |
| Selection of Joining Method | 14 |
| Design for Welding | 18 |
| Filler Metal Selection | 27 |
| Gas Metal-Arc Welding | 32 |
| Gas Tungsten-Arc Welding | 44 |
| Square Wave AC Welding | 49 |
| Gas Welding | 54 |
| Shielded Metal-Arc Welding | 56 |
| Shielded Carbon-Arc Welding | 57 |
| Atomic Hydrogen Welding | 57 |
| Stud Welding | 58 |
| Electron-Beam Welding | 59 |
| Arc Cutting | 60 |
| Shop Practices | 63 |
| Weld Defects | 70 |
| Repair Welding | 72 |
| Properties and Performance of Weldments | 72 |
| Welding of Aluminum Alloy Castings | 88 |
| Resistance Welding | 89 |
| Solid State Bonding | 112 |
| Brazing | 117 |
| Soldering | 120 |
| Adhesive Bonding | 126 |
| Joining to Other Metals | 126 |
| Quality Control | 127 |
| Bibliography | 130 |

THE MATERIAL IN THIS BOOK HAS BEEN REPRINTED FROM SECTION FOUR OF THE FIFTH EDITION OF THE WELDING HANDBOOK

# Aluminum and Aluminum Alloys

## INTRODUCTION

ALUMINUM IS READILY JOINED by welding, brazing, soldering, adhesive bonding or mechanical fastening. In many instances, aluminum is joined with the conventional equipment and techniques used with other metals. Sometimes, however, specialized equipment or techniques may be required. The alloy, joint configuration, strength required, appearance and cost are factors dictating the choice of process. Each process has certain advantages and limitations for joining aluminum, which are pointed out in this chapter to aid the designer in the choice of joining method. Individual processes are discussed in detail in Sections 2 and 3.

## GENERAL CHARACTERISTICS OF ALUMINUM

Aluminum is light in weight, yet some of its alloys have strengths comparable to mild steel. It retains good ductility at subzero temperatures, has high resistance to corrosion, forms no colored salts and is not toxic. Aluminum has good electrical and thermal conductivity and high reflectivity to both heat and light. It is nonsparking and nonmagnetic.

Aluminum is easy to fabricate. It can be cast, rolled, stamped, drawn, spun, stretched or roll-formed (Fig. 69.1). The metal may also be hammered, forged, or extruded into a wide variety of shapes. Machining ease and speed is one of the important factors in using aluminum parts. Aluminum may also be given a wide variety of mechanical, electrochemical, chemical or paint finishes.

## CHARACTERISTICS INFLUENCING JOINING

Pure aluminum melts at 1220°F, whereas the aluminum alloys have an approximate melting range of from 900° to 1220°F, depending upon the alloying constituents. There is no color change in aluminum when heated to the welding or brazing range. This makes it difficult to judge when the metal is near the melting point.

The high thermal conductivity as compared to steel necessitates high heat input for fusion welding. Heavy sections may require preheating.

The high electrical conductivity of aluminum requires higher currents and shorter weld time in resistance welding as compared to steel and more precise control of the welding variables.

Aluminum and its alloys rapidly develop a tenacious, refractory oxide film when exposed to air. The oxide film must be removed or broken up during welding to permit proper coalescence of the base and filler material in fusion welding or to permit flow in brazing or soldering. The oxide film may be removed by fluxes, by the action of a welding arc in an inert gas atmosphere, or by mechanical or chemical means.

Fig. 69.1.—*Welded aluminum tank constructed of flat plate and roll formed plate sections*

## COMMERCIAL FORMS

Pure aluminum can be alloyed readily with many other metals to produce a wide range of physical and mechanical properties. Table 69.1 describes the major alloying elements in the wrought aluminum alloys. The means by which the alloying elements strengthen aluminum is used as a basis to classify the alloys into two categories: nonheat treatable and heat treatable.

Wrought alloys in the form of sheet and plate, tubing, extruded and rolled shapes and forgings have similar joining characteristics regardless of the form. Aluminum alloys are also produced as castings in the form of sand, permanent mold or die castings. Substantially the same welding, brazing or soldering practices are used on both cast and wrought metal. Die castings have not been widely used where welded construction is required; however, they have been adhesively bonded and, to a limited extent, soldered. Recent developments in vacuum die casting have improved the quality of the castings to the point where they may be satisfactorily welded for some applications.

Table 69.1—Designations for alloy groups*

| Major Alloying Element | Designation |
|---|---|
| 99.0% minimum aluminum and over | 1xxx |
| Copper | 2xxx |
| Manganese | 3xxx |
| Silicon | 4xxx |
| Magnesium | 5xxx |
| Magnesium and Silicon | 6xxx |
| Zinc | 7xxx |
| Other element | 8xxx |
| Unused Series | 9xxx |

* Aluminum Association designations.

## 4/Commercial Forms

**Table 69.2—Nominal compositions and properties of nonheat-treatable wrought aluminum alloys**

| ASA Alloy Designation | Nominal Composition (% Alloying Elements) ||| Forms Available |||||||| Typical Applications |
| --- | --- | --- | --- | --- | --- | --- | --- | --- | --- | --- | --- |
| | Mn | Mg | Cr | Sheet/plate | Clad sheet/plate | Wire | Rod/bar | Extrusions | Tubing/pipe | Forgings | |
| EC | 99.45% min. aluminum ||| X | | X | X | X | X | | Electrical conductor wire, bus conductor. Also for display racks, shelving and tie wire. |
| 1060 | 99.6% min. aluminum ||| X | | X | X | X | X | | Chemical process equipment, tanks, piping. |
| 1100 | 99.0% min. aluminum ||| X | | X | X | X | X | X | Architectural and decorative applications, furniture, kitchen equipment, plumbing fixtures, piping, deep drawing applications, spun hollow ware. |
| 3003 | 1.2 | | | X | X | X | X | X | X | X | General purpose applications similar to those for 1100, where slightly higher strength is required. Processing industries and food handling equipment, chemical and petroleum drums and tanks. |
| 3004 | 1.2 | 1.0 | | X | X | | | | | | Sheet metal work requiring higher strength than 3003. Roofing, siding, gutters, pressure vessels, and irrigation pipe. |
| 5005 | | 0.8 | | X | | X | X | | | | Electrical conductor applications similar to 3003. Finishes clearer and lighter than 3003 and matches 6063 extrusions more closely. Particularly desirable for architectural applications. |
| 5050 | | 1.4 | | X | | X | X | | X | | Applications similar to 3003 and 5005 but requiring greater strength. Excellent finishing qualities. |
| 5052 5652 | | 2.5 | 0.25 | X | | X | X | X | X | | Higher strength alloy than 5050, corrosion resistance very good, and readily formed in the intermediate tempers. Sheet metal parts, storage tanks, boats, home appliances and utensils, automotive and truck body uses, electronic mounting plates, panels and cabinets, ladders and irrigation tubing. Alloy 5652 is a higher purity version acceptable for $H_2O_2$ service. Hydraulic pressure tube. |
| 5083 | 0.65 | 4.45 | 0.15 | X | | | X | X | X | X | Structures, tanks, unfired pressure vessels, marine components, railroad cars, cryogenics, drilling rigs. |
| 5086 | 0.45 | 4.0 | 0.1 | X | | | X | X | X | X | Marine components, tanks, tankers, truck frames. |

Commercial Forms/5

Table 69.2—Nominal compositions and properties of nonheat-treatable wrought aluminum alloys (continued)

| | | | | | | | | | |
|---|---|---|---|---|---|---|---|---|---|
| 5154 5254 | 3.5 | 0.25 | X | X | X | | X | | Unfired pressure vessels, tankers. Alloy 5254 is a higher purity version acceptable for $H_2O_2$ service. |
| 5252 | 2.5 | | X | | | | | | Bright finishing alloys for auto and appliance trim, architectural finishes. |
| 5257 | 0.40 | | X | | | | | | Bright finishing alloys for auto and appliance trim, architectural finishes. |
| 5454 | 2.8 | 0.10 | X | | X | X | X | X | Structural applications and tanks for sustained elevated temperature service. |
| 5456 | 5.2 | 0.10 | X | | X | X | | X | Structures, tanks, unfired pressure vessels, marine components. |
| 5457 | 1.0 | | X | | | | | | Bright finishing alloys for auto and appliance trim, architectural finishes. |
| 5557 | 0.6 | | X | | | | | | Bright finishing alloys for auto and appliance trim, architectural finishes. |
| 5657 | 0.8 | | X | | | | | | Bright finishing alloys for auto and appliance trim, architectural finishes. |

Column headers for composition: Mg 0.8, 0.8, 0.30, 0.25 (partial, as transcribed from leftmost numeric column).

**6**/*Commercial Forms*

Table 69.2—Nominal compositions and properties of nonheat-treatable wrought aluminum alloys (continued)

| ASA* Alloy Designation | Weldability[1,3] Gas | Arc with flux | Arc with inert gas | Resistance | Pressure | Brazing | Soldering with flux | Density, lbs/cu. in. | Melting range (approximate), °F | Thermal conductivity at 25°C, CGS units | Electrical conductivity, % IACS, equal volume at 68°F | Temper | Tensile strength, psi x 10³ | Yield strength (0.2% offset), psi x 10³ | Elongation % in 2 Inches 1/16 in. Sheet | Elongation 1/2 in. Dia. Round | Shear strength,[2] psi x 10³ | Fatigue strength, psi x 10³ | Hardness, Brinell (500 kg load, 10 mm ball) |
|---|---|---|---|---|---|---|---|---|---|---|---|---|---|---|---|---|---|---|---|
| EC | A | A | A | B | A | A | A | 0.098 | 1195-1215 | 0.57 / 0.56 | 63 / 62.5 | —O / —H19 | 10 / 27 | 4 / 24 | .. / .. | 2.3† / 2.5† | 8 / 15 | .. / 7 | .. / 19 / 35 |
| 1060 | A | A | A | B | A | A | A | 0.098 | 1195-1215 | 0.56 / 0.55 | 62 / 61 | —O / —H18 | 10 / 19 | 4 / 18 | 43 / 6 | .. / .. | 7 / 11 | 3 / 6 | 19 / 35 |
| 1100 | A | A | A | A | A | A | A | 0.098 | 1190-1215 | 0.53 / 0.53 | 59 | —O / —H14 / —H18 | 13 / 18 / 24 | 5 / 17 / 22 | 35 / 9 / 5 | 45 / 20 / 15 | 9 / 11 / 13 | 5 / 7 / 9 | 23 / 32 / 44 |
| 3003 | A | A | A | A | A | A | A | 0.099 | 1190-1210 | 0.42 / 0.42 / 0.42 | 46 | —O / —H14 / —H18 | 16 / 22 / 29 | 6 / 21 / 27 | 30 / 8 / 4 | 40 / 16 / 10 | 11 / 14 / 16 | 7 / 9 / 10 | 28 / 40 / 55 |
| 3004 | B | A | A | A | B | B | B | 0.098 | 1165-1205 | 0.39 | 42 | —O / —H34 / —H38 | 26 / 35 / 41 | 10 / 29 / 36 | 20 / 9 / 5 | 25 / 12 / 6 | 16 / 18 / 21 | 14 / 15 / 16 | 45 / 63 / 77 |
| 5005 | A | A | A | A | A | B | B | 0.097 | 1160-1205 | 0.49 | 54 | —O / —H14 / —H18 / —H34 / —H38 | 18 / 23 / 29 / 23 / 29 | 6 / 22 / 28 / 20 / 27 | 30 / 6 / 4 / 8 / 5 | .. | 11 / 14 / 16 / 14 / 16 | .. | 28 / .. / 41 / .. / 51 |
| 5050 | A | A | A | A | A | B | B | 0.097 | 1160-1205 | 0.46 | 50 | —O / —H34 / —H38 | 21 / 28 / 32 | 8 / 24 / 29 | 24 / 8 / 6 | .. | 15 / 18 / 20 | 13 / 16 / 18 | 36 / 53 / 63 |
| {5052 / 5652} | A | A | A | A | B | C | C | 0.097 | 1100-1200 | 0.33 | 35 | —O / —H34 / —H38 | 28 / 38 / 42 | 13 / 31 / 37 | 25 / 10 / 7 | 30 / 14 / 12 | 18 / 21 / 24 | 16 / 18 / 20 | 47 / 68 / 77 |
| 5252 | A | A | A | A | B | C | C | 0.096 | 1125-1200 | 0.33 | 35 | —H25 / —H28 | 35 / 41 | 27 / 35 | 18 / 8 | .. | 21 / 23 | .. | 68 / 75 |

## Commercial Forms / 7

Table 69.2—Nominal compositions and properties of nonheat-treatable wrought aluminum alloys (continued)

| | | | | | | | | | | | | | | | | | | | |
|---|---|---|---|---|---|---|---|---|---|---|---|---|---|---|---|---|---|---|---|
| 5257 | A | A | A | A | A | A | A | A | A | 0.097 | 1185–1215 | .... | .. | –H25<br>–H28 | 19<br>23 | 16<br>19 | 14<br>8 | .. | 11<br>12 | .. | 32<br>43 |
| 5457 | B | A | A | A | A | A | A | B | B | 0.098 | 1165–1210 | 0.42 | 46 | –H26<br>–H38 | 19<br>32 | 24<br>30 | 10<br>7 | .. | 17<br>18 | .. | 52<br>55 |
| 5557 | A | A | A | A | A | A | A | A | A | 0.098 | 1180–1215 | 0.45 | 49 | –H25<br>–H28 | 26<br>28 | 20<br>24 | 12<br>7 | .. | 16<br>15 | .. | 40<br>50 |
| 5657 | A | A | A | A | A | A | A | B | B | 0.098 | 1175–1210 | 0.45 | 49 | –H25<br>–H28 | 23<br>28 | 20<br>24 | 12<br>24 | .. | 14<br>15 | .. | 40<br>50 |
| 5083 | C | A | A | A | C | A | A | X | X | 0.096 | 1070–1185 | 0.28 | 29 | 0<br>–H321<br>–H323<br>–H343<br>–H113 | 40<br>46<br>47<br>52<br>46 | 21<br>33<br>36<br>41<br>33 | 22<br>16<br>10<br>8<br>16 | 25<br>16<br>..<br>..<br>.. | 25<br>28<br>27<br>30<br>27 | 22<br>22<br>..<br>..<br>23 | 67<br>82<br>84<br>92<br>84 |
| 5086 | C | C | A | A | A | A | A | X | X | 0.096 | 1085–1185 | 0.30 | 32 | 0<br>–H34<br>–H112 | 38<br>47<br>39 | 17<br>37<br>19 | 22<br>10<br>14 | 30<br>14 | 23<br>28<br>25 | 21<br>23<br>.. | 60<br>82<br>68 |
| 5154<br>5254 | B | A | A | A | B | A | B | X | X | 0.096 | 1100–1190 | 0.30 | 32 | 0<br>–H34<br>–H38<br>–H112 | 35<br>42<br>48<br>35 | 17<br>33<br>39<br>17 | 27<br>13<br>10<br>25 | 30<br>16<br>..<br>.. | 22<br>24<br>28<br>22 | 17<br>20<br>21<br>17 | 58<br>76<br>87<br>63 |
| 5454 | B | B | A | A | B | A | B | X | X | 0.097 | 1115–1195 | 0.32 | 34 | 0<br>–H34<br>–H112<br>–H311 | 36<br>44<br>36<br>38 | 17<br>35<br>18<br>26 | 22<br>10<br>18<br>14 | 25<br>16<br>..<br>.. | 23<br>26<br>23<br>23 | 20<br>21<br>..<br>.. | 60<br>81<br>62<br>70 |
| 5456 | C | C | A | A | C | A | C | X | X | 0.096 | 1055–1180 | 0.28 | 29 | 0<br>–H112<br>–H311<br>–H321 | 45<br>45<br>47<br>51 | 23<br>24<br>33<br>37 | 24<br>22<br>18<br>16 | 20<br>..<br>..<br>18 | 27<br>27<br>27<br>30 | 22<br>..<br>24<br>23 | 70<br>70<br>75<br>90 |

\* Aluminum Association, ASA and ASTM are same designation. † 10 inch gauge length.

Noted: ¹ Weldability rating (based on most weldable temper):
    A—Readily weldable.
    B—Weldable in most applications; may require special technique or preliminary trials to establish welding procedure and/or performance.
    C—Limited weldability.
    X—Particular joining method not recommended.
² All alloys can be adhesive bonded, ultrasonic welded or mechanically fastened. Some alloys can be ultrasonic or abrasive soldered.
³ Fatigue strength—for round specimens and 500 million cycles.

**8**/*Commercial Forms*

To increase the corrosion resistance of some alloys, they are often clad with high purity or other special aluminum alloys. The cladding, usually from 2-1/2 to 15% of the total thickness on one or both sides, not only protects the composite due to its inherent corrosion resistance, but generally exerts a galvanic effect which further protects the core material. Special composites are also produced for brazing, soldering or finishing purposes.

## WROUGHT ALLOYS

### Nonheat-Treatable Aluminum Alloys

The initial strengths of the nonheat-treatable alloys depend primarily upon the hardening effect of elements such as silicon, iron, manganese and magnesium. These elements effect increases in strength, either as dispersed phases or by solid solution strengthening. The nonheat-treatable alloys are mainly found in the 1000, 3000, 4000 or 5000 series (Table 69.2) depending upon their major alloying elements. Iron and silicon are the major impurities in commercially pure aluminum and add strength to alloys in the 1000 series. Magnesium is the most effective solution strengthening element in the nonheat-treatable alloys. Aluminum-magnesium alloys of the 5000 series have relatively high strength in the annealed condition. All of the nonheat-treatable alloys are work hardenable.

To remove the effects of cold working and improve ductility, the nonheat-treatable alloys may be annealed by heating to a uniform temperature. The exact annealing schedule used will depend upon the alloy and the temper of the alloy being annealed.

Basic temper designations applicable to the nonheat-treatable aluminum alloys are indicated in Table 69.3.

Upon fusion welding, the nonheat-treatable alloys may lose the effects of

**Table 69.3—Basic temper designations applicable to the nonheat-treatable aluminum alloys**

| Designation | Description | Application |
|---|---|---|
| –0 | Annealed, recrystallized | Softest temper of wrought products. |
| –F | As fabricated | Applies to products which acquire some temper from shaping processes not having special control over the amount of strain hardening or thermal treatment. |
| –H1 | Strain hardened only | Applies to those products which have some temper from shaping processes without special control over the amount of strain hardening or thermal treatment. The number following this designation indicates the degree of strain hardening. |
| –H2 | Strain hardened and then partially annealed | Applies to products which are strain hardened more than the desired final amount and then reduced in strength to the desired level by partial annealing. |
| –H3 | Strain hardened and then stabilized | Applies to products which are strain hardened and then stabilized by a low temperature heating to slightly lower their strength and increase ductility. This designation applies only to the magnesium containing alloys which, unless stabilized, gradually age-soften at room temperature. |

Note: The degree of strain hardening is indicated by the number following either the –H1, –H2 or –H3 designations shown above. The hardest commercially practical temper is designated by the numeral 8 (full hard). Tempers between –0 (annealed) and 8 (full hard) are designated by numerals 1 through 7. Thus numeral 2 designates "quarter hard," numeral 4 "half hard," and numeral 6 "three-quarter hard." Numeral 9 designates extra hard tempers. Reference should be made to ASTM B296 and ASA H35.1 for full description of temperature designations.

strain hardening in a narrow zone adjacent to the weld, and thus their strength in this zone may approach that of the annealed condition. The nominal compositions, properties and related joining characteristics of the more widely used nonheat-treatable alloys are listed in Table 69.2.

## HEAT-TREATABLE ALUMINUM ALLOYS

The initial strength of alloys in this group depends only upon the alloy composition, just as in the nonheat-treatable alloys. However, since elements such as copper, magnesium, zinc and silicon, either singly or in various combinations, show a marked increase in solid solubility in aluminum with increasing temperature, it is possible to subject them to thermal treatments which will impart pronounced strengthening. Heat-treatable aluminum alloys develop their properties by solution heat treating and quenching, followed by either natural or artificial aging. Cold working may add additional strength. The heat-treatable alloys may also be annealed to attain maximum ductility if desired. This treatment involves holding at an elevated temperature and controlled cooling to achieve maximum softening. Basic temper designations are indicated in Table 69.4.

Table 69.4—Basic temper designations applicable to the heat-treatable aluminum alloys

| Designation* | Description | Application |
|---|---|---|
| –0 | Annealed, recrystallized | Softest temper of wrought products. |
| –F | As fabricated | |
| –W | Solution heat treated | An unstable temper applicable only to alloys which spontaneously age at room temperature after solution heat treatment. This designation is specific only when the period of natural aging is indicated (for example, –W ½ hour). |
| –T1 | Modified solution heat-treated and then cold worked | Applies to certain extruded material. |
| –T3 | Solution heat treated and then cold worked | |
| –T4 | Solution heat treated and naturally aged to a substantially stable condition. | |
| –T5 | Artificially aged after a modified solution heat-treatment | Applies to certain extruded products. |
| –T6 | Solution heat treated and then artificially aged | |
| –T7 | Solution heat treated and then stabilized | |
| –T8 | Solution heat treated, cold worked and then artificially aged | |
| –T9 | Solution heat treated, artificially aged and then cold worked | |
| –T10 | Artificially aged and then cold worked | Applies to products which are artificially aged after an elevated-temperature rapid-cool fabrication process, such as casting or extrusion and then cold worked to improve strength. |

* Reference should be made to ASTM B296 and ASA H35.1 for full description of temperature designations.

**Table 69.5—Nominal compositions and properties of heat-treatable wrought aluminum alloys**

| ASA Alloy Designation | Cu | Si | Mn | Mg | Zn | Ni | Cr | Sheet/plate | Clad sheet/plate | Wire | Rod/bar | Extrusions | Tube | Forgings | Typical Applications |
|---|---|---|---|---|---|---|---|---|---|---|---|---|---|---|---|
| 2014 | 4.4 | 0.8 | 0.8 | 0.4 | | | | X | X | | X | X | X | X | Structures, structural fittings, and heavy-duty forgings for aircraft or automotive uses, hydraulic fittings, hardware. |
| 2017 | 4.0 | | 0.8 | 0.8 | | | | | | X | X | | | X | Same as 2014, also screw machine parts. Combines machinability with high strength and forgeability. |
| 2024 | 4.5 | | 0.0 | 1.5 | | | | X | X | X | X | X | X | | Structural applications, standard sheet alloy for aircraft construction, truck wheels. Clad 2024 sheet provides strength with maximum corrosion resistance. |
| 2219 | 6.2 | | 0.30 | | | | | X | X | | X | X | X | X | Structural applications where strength at elevated temperatures is required. Good fusion weldability of high strength, heat treatable alloys. Tanks. |
| 2618* | 2.3 | | | 1.5 | | 1.1 | | | | | | | | X | Forging alloy; engine pistons and parts that require hardness and good strength at elevated temperatures. |
| 2218 | 4.0 | | | 1.8 | | 2.0 | | | | | | | | X | Forging alloy: engine cylinder heads, pistons and parts requiring good strength and hardness at elevated temperatures. |
| 6061 | 0.25 | 0.6 | | 1.0 | | | 0.20 | X | X | X | X | X | X | X | Structural and architectural, automotive, railway and marine applications. Pipe and pipe fittings. Good formability, weldability, corrosion resistance and strength after heat treatment. |
| 6063 | | 0.4 | | 0.7 | | | | | | | | X | X | | Pipe, railings, hardware, architectural applications. |

Commercial Forms/**11**

Table 69.5—Nominal compositions and properties of heat-treatable wrought aluminum alloys (continued)

| | | | | | | | | | | |
|---|---|---|---|---|---|---|---|---|---|---|
| 6070 | 0.27 | 1.35 | 0.7 | 0.85 | | | | | X | X | Structural applications, pipe lines. |
| 6071 | 0.27 | 1.35 | 0.7 | 1.1 | | X | | | | | Structural |
| 6101 | 0.5 | | 0.55 | | | | | | X | X | Electrical conductors. |
| 6201 | | 0.7 | | 0.75 | | | X | | | | Electrical conductors. |
| 6951 | 0.25 | 0.35 | | 0.6 | | X | | | | | Brazing sheet core alloy. |
| 7039 | 0.10 | 0.30 | 0.3 | 2.8 | 4.0 | X | | | X | | Armor plate, cryogenic, applications. |
| 7075 | 1.6 | | | 2.5 | 5.6 | X | X | | X | X | Aircraft and other applications where the highest strength is required. Cladding gives good corrosion resistance. |
| 7079 | 0.6 | | 0.2 | 3.3 | 4.3 | | 0.20 | | X | | Large or massive parts for aircraft and allied construction. Strongest aluminum alloy where section thicknesses are greater than 3 inches. Similar to 7075 alloy in most respects. |
| 7178 | 2.0 | | | 2.7 | 6.8 | X | | 0.30 | | | Aircraft construction, slightly higher strength than 7075. |

**12**/*Commercial Forms*

Table 69.5—Nominal compositions and properties of heat-treatable wrought aluminum alloys (continued)

| ASA Alloy Designation | Weldability[1,2] Gas | Arc with flux | Arc with inert gas | Resistance | Pressure | Brazing | Soldering with flux | Density, lbs/cu in. | Melting range, °F, (Approximate) | Thermal conductivity at 25°C, CGS units | Electrical conductivity, % IACS, equal volume at 68°F. | Temper | Ultimate Tensile Strength, psi x 10³ | Yield Strength (0.2% offset) psi x 10³ | Elongation % in 2 In. 1/16 In. Sheet | Elongation % in 2 In. 1/2 In. Dia. Round | Shear Strength psi x 10³ | Fatigue Strength psi x 10³ | Brinell hardness (500 kg load) |
|---|---|---|---|---|---|---|---|---|---|---|---|---|---|---|---|---|---|---|---|
| 2014 | X | C | C | A | C | X | C | 0.101 | 950–1180 | 0.46 0.32 0.37 | 50 34 40 | -O- -T4 -T6 | 27 63 70 | 14 40 63 | 22 18 10 | 18 20 13 | 18 38 42 | 13 20 18 | 45 105 135 |
| 2017 | X | C | C | A | C | X | C | 0.101 | 955–1185 | 0.46 0.32 | 50 34 | -O- -T4 | 26 62 | 10 40 | ... ... | 22 22 | 18 38 | 13 18 | 45 105 |
| 2024 | X | C | C | A | C | X | C | 0.100 | 935–1180 | 0.46 0.29 0.29 0.29 | 50 30 30 30 | -O- -T3 -T4 -T36 | 27 70 68 72 | 11 50 47 57 | 20 20 20 13 | 22 ... 19 ... | 18 41 41 42 | 13 20 20 18 | 47 120 120 130 |
| 2218 | X | C | B | A | C | X | C | 0.102 | 940–1175 | 0.37 | 40 | -T72 | 48 | 37 | ... | 11 | 30 | ... | 95 |
| 2219 | X | C | C | A | C | X | C | 0.102 | 1010–1190 | 0.41 0.27 0.30 | 44 28 32 | -O- -T31 -T81 -T62 | 25 52 66 60 | 11 34 50 42 | 18 16 10 0 | 22 20 12 ... | 32 39 37 | ... 15 15 | 96 123 115 |
| 2618 | X | C | C | A | C | X | B | 0.100 | 1040–1185 | 0.36 | 39 | -T61 | 64 | 54 | ... | 10 | 38 | 18 | 115 |
| 6061 | A | A | A | A | B | A | B | 0.098 | 1080–1200 | 0.43 0.37 0.40 | 47 40 43 | -O- -T4 -T6 | 18 35 45 | 8 21 40 | 25 22 12 | 30 25 17 | 12 24 30 | 9 13 14 | 30 65 95 |

## Commercial Forms/13

Table 69.5—Nominal compositions and properties of heat-treatable wrought aluminum alloys (continued)

| | | | | | | | | | | | | | | | | | | |
|---|---|---|---|---|---|---|---|---|---|---|---|---|---|---|---|---|---|---|
| 6063 | A | A | B | A | A | A | B | 0.098 | 1140-1205 | 0.52 / 0.50 / 0.48 | 58 / 50 / 55 / 53 | —0 / —T4 / —T5 / —T6 | 13 / 25 / 27 / 35 | 7 / 13 / 21 / 31 | . / 22 / 12 / 12 | . / 22 / 22 / 18 | 10 / 16 / 17 / 22 | 8 / . / 10 / 10 | 25 / . / 60 / 73 |
| 6070 | C | B | A | C | A | A | B | 0.098 | 1070-1200 | 0.47 / 0.41 | 52 / 44 | —0 / —T6 | 21 / 55 | 10 / 51 | 25 / 10 | . . . | 14 / 34 | 9 / 14 | . . . |
| 6071 | C | B | A | C | A | A | B | 0.098 | 1055-1195 | 0.47 / 0.40 | 51 / 43 | —0 / —T6 | 21 / 54 | 8 / 51 | 25 / 10 | . . . | 14 / 34 | 9 / 14 | . . . |
| 6101 | A | A | A | A | A | A | A | 0.098 | 1150-1210 | . . / 0.52 | . . / 57 | —H111 / —T6 | 14 / 32 | 11 / 28 | . . / 15 | . . / 19 | . . / 20 | . . / 9 | . . / 71 |
| 6201 | A | A | A | A | A | A | B | 0.097 | 1130-1205 | 0.49 | 54 | —T81 | 50 | . . | . . | 6* | . . | 13 | . . |
| 6951 | A | A | A | A | A | A | A | 0.098 | 1140-1210 | 0.51 / 0.52 | 56 / 58 | —0 / —T6 / —T61 | 16 / 39 / 58 | 6 / 33 / 48 | 30 / 13 / . | . / . / 13 | 11 / 26 / 33 | . . . | 28 / 82 / 105 |
| 7039 | X | X | A | A | A | A | B | 0.099 | 1070-1180 | 0.37 | 34 | —T64 | 65 | 55 | 13 | 10 | 38 | . . | 120 |
| 7075 | X | X | A | C | C | C | C | 0.101 | 890-1175 | . . / 0.31 | . . / 33 | —0 / —T6 / —T73 | 33 / 83 / 73 | 15 / 73 / 63 | 17 / 11 / . | 16 / 11 / 13 | 22 / 48 / 44 | . / 22 / 22 | 60 / 150 |
| 7079 | X | X | A | C | X | A | C | 0.099 | 900-1180 | 0.30 / . . | . . / 32 | —0 / —T6 | . . / 78 | . . / 68 | . . | . . / 14 | . . / 45 | . . / 22 | . . / 145 |
| 7178 | X | X | A | C | X | A | C | 0.102 | 890-1165 | 0.32 / . . | . . / 31 | —0 / —T6 | 33 / 88 | 15 / 78 | 15 / 10 | 16 / 11 | 22 / 55 | . . / 22 | 60 / 160 |

* Gauge length 10 in.

Notes:
[1] Weldability rating (based on most weldable temper):
  A—Readily weldable.
  B—Weldable in most applications; may require special technique or preliminary trials to establish welding procedure and/or performance.
  C—Limited weldability.
  X—Particular joining method not recommended.
[2] All alloys can be adhesive bonded, ultrasonic welded or mechanically fastened.
[3] Fatigue strength—for round specimens and 500 million cycles.

**14**/*Joining Methods*

The heat-treatable alloys are found in the 2000, 4,000, 6000 and 7000 series, depending on their major alloying elements. Some of the more widely used heat-treatable alloys are listed in Table 69.5 with their nominal composition, physical and mechanical properties and relative ease of joining.

## CAST ALLOYS

Although the commercial aluminum casting alloys are designated by a number, they do not follow a definite alloy grouping system. A letter preceding the number simply means that the alloy is a modification of the basic composition indicated by the number. Casting alloys like the wrought alloys are either nonheat-treatable or heat-treatable. A second classification may be made according to the type of casting method for which the alloy is suitable, such as sand casting, permanent mold casting or die casting. Tables 69.6 and 69.7 give the characteristics of nonheat-treatable and heat-treatable casting alloys, respectively.

The temper designation system for castings generally follows that for wrought aluminum products. Basic temper designations applicable to cast aluminum alloys are detailed in Table 69.8.

## SELECTION OF JOINING METHOD

Applications and service environment of the weldment often determine alloy and temper selection as well as joining method. Neither should be selected without regard for the other (Tables 69.2,5,6,7 and 9).

Joint design is important in selecting the joining method. If butt joints are required, the choice is limited preferably to a gas shielded-arc welding process, depending upon the thickness. In some applications, gas welding may also be considered. More specialized processes adaptable to butt joints are pressure welding, flash welding and electron-beam welding. Resistance spot and seam welding as well as ultrasonic and pressure welding, adhesive bonding and mechanical fastening are applicable to lap joints. Lap, tee or line contact joints are widely used in brazing or soldering. Where joints are relatively inaccessible, adhesive bonding and furnace or dip brazing may be used to advantage.

The choice of method may also depend upon whether the joint will be made in the shop or in the field, and whether the part is small enough to be brought to the welding equipment.

Another consideration is the performance of the part after joining. Here the important considerations are joint strength, impact, fatigue and corrosion resistance, and performance under special service conditions. The quality of the joint and the possibility of using nondestructive testing are often important considerations as are pressure tightness requirements.

Since most joining methods use heat to effect joining, the allowable amount of softening of the base material adjacent to the joint is another consideration. Moreover, the heat of joining may affect corrosion resistance of some materials in the immediate vicinity. The processes involving the least amount of heat are resistance, pressure and ultrasonic welding, adhesive bonding, and mechanical fastening. Soldering may be carried out at relatively low temperatures. Where the minimum width of the heat-affected zone and maximum properties across a groove weld are desired, the more rapid welding processes such as the gas shielded-arc welding processes are preferred. When applicable, the electron beam, induction and flash welding processes provide the minimum heat-affected zones (Fig. 69.2).

Appearance is often of primary importance in selecting a joining method.

Joining Methods/ **15**

**Table 69.6—Nominal compositions and properties of nonheat-treatable cast aluminum alloys**

| Alloy Designation | | Nominal Composition (% Alloying Element) | | | | Types of Castings | | | Typical Applications |
|---|---|---|---|---|---|---|---|---|---|
| ASTM | Commercial | Cu | Si | Mg | Zn | Sand | Permanent Mold | Die | |
| S12A | 13–F | | 12.0 | | | | | X | General purpose die casting alloy for large, intricate parts with thin sections, as typewriter frames, instrument cases, etc. Excellent casting characteristics, very good corrosion resistance. |
| S5A S5B | 43–F | | 5.0 | | | X X | X X | | General purpose alloy, cooking utensils, architectural and marine applications, pipe fittings. Excellent castability and pressure tightness. |
| CS43A | 108–F | 4.0 | 3.0 | | | X | | | General purpose alloy, manifolds, valve housings, and applications requiring pressure tightness. |
| SC64A | A108–F | 4.5 | 5.5 | | | | X | | General purpose alloy, ornamental grills, reflectors, and parts requiring pressure tightness. |
| CS104A CS104B | 138–F. | 10.0 | 4.0 | 0.3 | | | X X | | High as-cast hardness. Sole plates for electric hand irons. |
| G4A | 214–F | | | 4.0 | | X | | | Chemical process fittings, special food handling equipment, marine hardware. Excellent corrosion resistance. |
| GZ42A | A214–F | | | 4.0 | 1.8 | | X | X | Cooking utensils and ornamental hardware, takes uniform anodic finish. |
| GS42A | B214–F | | 1.8 | 4.0 | | X | | | Cooking utensils and pipe fittings. |
| | F214–F | | 0.5 | 4.0 | | X | | | Anodically treated architectural parts and ornamental hardware. Takes uniform anodic finish. |
| | 344–F | | 7.0 | | | | X | | (Same as A214). |
| SG100A SG100B | 360–F | | 9.5 | 0.5 | | | | X | General purpose die castings, cover plates and instrument cases. Excellent casting characteristics. |
| SC84B | 380–F | 3.5 | 9.0 | | | | | X | General purpose use. Good casting characteristics and mechanical properties. |
| ZG61B | A612–F | 0.5 | | 0.7 | 6.5 | X | | | General purpose sand castings for subsequent brazing. Good machinability. |
| ZC60A | C612–F | 0.5 | | 0.35 | 6.5 | | X | | Torque converter blades and brazed parts. Good machinability. |
| | D612 | | | 0.6 | 5.8 | X | | | Same as A612 (above), good corrosion resistance. |

* Also contains 0.50% Cr.

# 16/Joining Methods

**Table 69.6—Nominal compositions and properties of nonheat-treatable cast aluminum alloys (continued)**

| Alloy Designation ASTM | Commercial | Gas | Arc with flux | Arc with inert gas | Resistance | Pressure | Brazing | Soldering with flux[2] | Density, lbs/cu in. | Melting range of (approximate), °F | Thermal conductivity at 25°C, CGS Units | Electrical conductivity, % IACS equal volume at 68°F. | Tensile strength, psi x 1000 | Yield strength (0.2% offset), psi x 1000 | Elongation, % in 2 inches; ½ in. dia. round | Shear strength, psi x 1000 | Fatigue strength,[2] psi x 1000 | Hardness, Brinell (500 kg load, 10mm ball) |
|---|---|---|---|---|---|---|---|---|---|---|---|---|---|---|---|---|---|---|
| S5A S5B | 43-F | A | A | A | A | X | C | C | 0.097 | 1065-1170 | 0.34 | 37 | 19 | 8 16 | 8.0 9.0 | 14 21 | 8 17 | 40 60 |
| CS43A | 108-F | C | B | B | B | X | X | C | 0.101 | 970-1160 | 0.30 | 31 | 21 | 14 | 2.5 | 17 | 11 | 55 |
| CS72A | 112-F | C | C | C | C | X | X | C | 0.105 | 985-1165 | 0.29 | 30 | 24 | 15 | 1.5 | 20 | 9 | 70 |
| CS72A | 113-F | C | C | B | C | X | X | C | 0.106 | 965-1160 | 0.29 | 30 | 24 | 15 | 1.5 | 20 | 9 | 70 |
| | 212-F | C | C | C | B | X | X | C | 0.104 | 965-1160 | 0.29 | 30 | 23 | 14 | 2.0 | 20 | 9 | 65 |
| G4A | 214-F | C | C | A | B | X | X | X | 0.096 | 1110-1185 | 0.33 | 35 | 25 | 12 | 9.0 | 20 | 7 | 50 |
| GS42A | B214-F | C | C | B | B | X | X | X | 0.096 | 1090-1170 | 0.36 | 38 | 20 | 13 | 2.0 | 17 | 8.5 | 50 |
| | F214-F | C | C | A | B | X | X | X | 0.096 | 1090-1185 | 0.34 | 36 | 21 | 12 | 3.0 | 17 | 8 | 50 |
| ZG61B | A612-F | C | C | B | C | X | A | B | 0.102 | 1105-1195 | 0.33 | 35 | 35 | 25 | 5.0 | 26 | 8 | 75 |
| | D612-F | C | C | B | C | X | A | B | 0.100 | 1135-1200 | 0.25 | 25 | 35 | 25 | 5.0 | 26 | .. | 75 |

**Sand Castings**

Joining Methods/**17**

Table 69.6—Nominal compositions and properties of nonheat-treatable cast aluminum alloys (continued)

**Permanent Mold Castings**

| | | | | | | | | | | | | | | | | | |
|---|---|---|---|---|---|---|---|---|---|---|---|---|---|---|---|---|---|
| S5A<br>S5B | 43–F | A | A | A | A | X | C | C | 0.097<br>0.097 | 1065–1170<br>1065–1170 | 0.34 | 37<br>37 | 23<br>33 | 9<br>16 | 10.0<br>9.0 | 16<br>21 | 8<br>17 | 45<br>60 |
| SC64A | A108–F | B | B | B | B | X | X | X | 0.101 | 970–1135 | 0.35 | 37 | 28 | 16 | 2.0 | 22 | 13 | 70 |
| CS104A<br>CS104B | 138–F | X | X | C | C | X | X | X | 0.107 | 945–1110 | 0.25 | 25 | 30 | 24 | 1.5 | 24 | .. | 100 |
| GZ42A | A214–F | C | C | A | B | X | X | X | 0.097 | 1075–1180 | 0.32 | 34 | 27 | 16 | 7.0 | 22 | .. | 60 |
| 344–F | C | C | B | C | X | A | B | 0.103 | 1120–1190 | 0.37 | 40 | 35 | 18 | 8.0 | .. | 11 | 70 |
| ZC60A | C612–F | A | A | A | A | X | B | C | 0.097 | 1065–1145 | .... | .. | 28 | 10 | 10.0 | .. | .. | 50 |

**Die Castings**

| | | | | | | | | | | | | | | | | | |
|---|---|---|---|---|---|---|---|---|---|---|---|---|---|---|---|---|---|
| S12A | 13–F | B | B | B | C | X | X | X | 0.096 | 1065–1080 | 0.30 | 31 | 43 | 21 | 2.5 | 28 | 19 | 80 |
| GZ42A | A214–F | C | C | A | B | X | X | X | 0.097 | 1075–1180 | 0.32 | 34 | 40 | 22 | 10.0 | 26 | 18 | 60 |
| G8A | 218–F | X | X | B | C | X | X | X | 0.093 | 995–1150 | 0.24 | 24 | 45 | 27 | 8.0 | 29 | 20 | 75 |
| SG100A<br>SG100B | 360–F | X | X | B | B | X | X | X | 0.095 | 1035–1105 | 0.27 | 28 | 47 | 25 | 3.0 | 30 | 19 | 80 |
| SC84B | 380–F | X | X | B | C | X | X | C | 0.098 | 1000–1100 | 0.23 | 23 | 48 | 24 | 3.0 | 31 | 21 | 85 |

Notes: [1] Weldability rating (based on most weldable temper):
    A—Readily weldable.
    B—Weldable in most applications; may require special technique or preliminary trials to establish welding procedure and/or performance.
    C—Limited weldability.
    X—Particular joining method not recommended.
[2] All alloys can be adhesive bonded, ultrasonic welded or mechanically fastened.
[3] Fatigue strength—for round specimens and 500 million cycles.
[4] Weldability ratings are based upon the assumption of acceptable casting structure for welding die castings.

**18**/*Joining Methods*

*Fig. 69.2.—World's largest welded aluminum railroad car, represents an application in which joint strength, impact, fatigue and corrosion resistance are design considerations*

Among the fusion welding processes, gas tungsten-arc and gas metal-arc produce the best as-welded appearance. Resistance spot and seam and ultrasonic welding may mar the surface. Brazing and adhesive bonding form joints of excellent appearance which require little or no finishing. Pressure welding causes large deformations and cannot be used where a good surface appearance is necessary. Pressure butt welds, flash welds or stud welds may have flash removed to enhance appearance.

Welded parts may be given a chemical or electrochemical surface treatment. Resistance, ultrasonic and pressure welds are least noticeable after treatment, but require attention to rinsing operations to show less color change and avoid trapping chemical solutions in the lapped joints.

Brazing filler metals darken in anodic treatment. Solders also darken and can be dissolved into the solutions to attack the joints and contaminate the solutions. Complete flux removal from brazed, soldered and welded joints is necessary prior to anodic treatment.

Some adhesives can be subjected to chemical and electrochemical treatment. In addition, adhesive bonding can be used successfully on pretreated parts.

Economic considerations include equipment cost, skill and amount of labor required, and cost of related operations such as preparation and finishing. The volume required, probability of repeat business and availability of equipment influence process selection. Where the same size and shape assemblies are produced at high production rates, automation is desirable.

## DESIGN FOR WELDING

Sound design will eliminate joints and reduce the amount of welding without affecting the product requirements. A reduction in the number of welded joints will minimize heating and the possibility of distortion, and usually results in an improvement in the appearance and function of the product. To eliminate joints the designer may often use castings, extrusions, forgings or bent or roll formed shapes to replace complex assemblies. Figure 69.3 shows an all-welded 165 foot aluminum gunboat constructed from sheet, plate and extrusions.

Another method of reducing cost is to minimize edge preparation by use of special extrusions, as shown in Fig. 69.4. Machining is eliminated by extruding the edge preparation on the sections.

When thin aluminum sheets are to be welded to heavier sections, it is always

## Design for Welding / 19

**Table 69.7—Nominal compositions and properties of heat-treatable cast aluminum alloys**

| Alloy Designation Commercial | Nominal Composition (% Alloying Element) |      |      |     | Types of Castings |               | Typical Applications |
|---|---|---|---|---|---|---|---|
|   | Cu | Si | Mg | Ni | Sand | Permanent Mold |   |
| 122 | 10.0 |  | 0.2 |  | X |  | Bushings, bearing caps and meter parts. Air cooled cylinder heads. Retains strength at elevated temperatures. |
| A132 | 1.0 | 12.0 | 1.0 | 2.5 |  | X | Heady-duty diesel pistons. Good strength at elevated temperatures. |
| F132 | 3.0 | 9.5 | 1.0 |  |  | X | Automotive pistons. Good properties at operating temperatures. |
| 142 | 4.0 |  | 1.5 | 2.0 | X | X | Heavy-duty pistons and air-cooled cylinder heads. Good strength at elevated temperatures. |
| A142[1] | 4.1 |  | 1.5 | 2.0 | X |  | Heavy-duty pistons and air-cooled cylinder heads. Good strength at elevated temperatures. |
| 195 | 4.5 |  | 0.8 |  | X |  | Machinery and aircraft structural members, crankcases, wheels. |
| 220 |  |  | 10.0 |  | X |  | Sand. castings requiring strength and shock resistance, such as aircraft structural members. Excellent corrosion resistance. Not recommended for use over 250°F. |
| 319 | 3.5 | 6.0 |  |  | X |  | General purpose, engine parts, automobile cylinder heads, piano plates. |
| 333 | 3.5 | 9.0 |  |  |  | X | Engine parts, gas meter housing, regulator parts, general purpose. |
| 354 | 1.8 | 9.0 | 0.50 |  |  | X | Aircraft, missile and other applications requiring premium strength castings. |
| 355 | 1.3 | 5.0 | 0.5 |  | X | X | General purpose castings, crankcases, accessory housings and aircraft fittings. |
| C355 | 1.3 | 5.0 | 0.5 |  |  | X | Aircraft, missile and other structural applications requiring high strength. |
| 356 |  | 7.0 | 0.30 |  | X | X | General purpose castings, transmission cases, truck-axle housings and wheels, cylinder blocks, railway tank car fittings, marine hardware, bridge railings parts, architectural uses. |
| A356 |  | 7.0 | 0.30 |  | X | X | Aircraft, missile and other structural applications and aircraft fittings. |
| A357[5] |  | 7.0 | 0.50 |  |  | X | Aircraft, missile and other structural applications requiring high strength. |
| 359 |  | 9.0 | 0.6 |  |  | X | Aircraft, missile and other structural applications requiring high strength |

Notes: [1] Weldability rating (based on most weldable temper):
    A—Readily weldable.
    B—Weldable in most applications; may require special technique or preliminary trials to establish welding procedure and/or performance.
    C—Limited weldability.
    X—Particular joining method not recommended.
[2] All alloys can be adhesive bonded, ultrasonic welded or mechanically fastened.
[3] Fatigue strength—for round specimens and 500 million cycles.
[4] Also contains 0.20% Cr.
[5] Also contains 0.50% Be.

**20**/Design for Welding

**Table 69.7—Nominal compositions and properties of heat-treatable cast aluminum alloys (continued)**

| Alloy Designation | | Weldability[1,2] | | | | | | Physical Properties | | | | Typical Mechanical Properties | | | | | |
|---|---|---|---|---|---|---|---|---|---|---|---|---|---|---|---|---|---|
| ASTM | Commercial | Gas | Arc with flux | Arc with inert gas | Resistance | Pressure | Brazing | Soldering with flux[2] | Density, lbs/cu in. | Melting range of (approximate), °F | Thermal conductivity at 25°C CGS units | Electrical conductivity % IACS, equal volume at 68°F | Temper | Tensile strength, psi x 1000 | Yield strength (0.2% offset), psi x 1000 | Elongation, % in 2 inches: ½ in. dia. round | Shear strength, psi x 1000 | Fatigue strength,[3] psi x 1000 | Hardness, Brinell (500 kg load, 10mm ball) |

**Sand Castings**

| CG100A | 122 | C | C | C | C | X | X | X | 0.107 | 965–1155 | 0.31 | 33 | –T61 | 41 | 40 | ... | 32 | 8.5 | 115 |
| CN42A | 142 | C | C | C | C | X | X | X | 0.102 | 990–1175 | 0.32 0.36 | 34 38 | –T571 –T77 | 32 30 | 30 23 | 0.5 2.0 | 26 24 | 11 10.5 | 85 75 |
| C4A | A142 | C | C | C | C | X | X | X | 0.102 | 990–1175 | ... | ... | –T75 | 31 | ... | 2.0 | ... | 7.5 | 7.5 |
| C4A | 195 | C | C | C | C | X | X | C | 0.102 | 970–1190 | 0.33 0.33 | 35 35 | –T4 –T6 | 32 36 | 16 24 | 8.5 5.0 | 26 30 | 7 7.5 | 60 75 |
| G10A | 220 | X | X | B | C | X | X | X | 0.093 | 840–1120 | 0.21 | 21 | –T4 | 48 | 26 | 16.0 | 34 | 8 | 75 |
| 319 | | C | B | B | B | X | X | X | 0.101 | 960–1120 | ... | ... | –T5 –T6 | 30 36 | 26 24 | 1.5 2.0 | 24 29 | 11 11 | 80 80 |
| SC51A | 355 | B | B | B | B | X | X | X | 0.098 | 1015–1150 | 0.40 0.34 | 43 36 | –T51 –T6 –T71 | 28 35 35 | 23 25 29 | 1.5 3.0 1.5 | 22 28 26 | 8 9 10 | 65 80 75 |
| SG70A | 356 | A | A | A | A | X | C | C | 0.097 | 1035–1135 | 0.40 0.36 | 43 39 | –T51 –T6 –T71 | 25 33 28 | 20 24 21 | 2.0 3.5 3.5 | 20 26 20 | 8.0 8.5 8.5 | 60 70 60 |

Design for Welding/**21**

Table 69.7—Nominal compositions and properties of heat-treatable cast aluminum alloys (continued)

**Permanent Mold Castings**

| | | | | | | | | | | | | | | | | | | |
|---|---|---|---|---|---|---|---|---|---|---|---|---|---|---|---|---|---|---|
| CG100A | 122 | C | C | C | C | X | X | X | 0.107 | 965–1155 | 0.31 | 33 | –T65 | 48 | 36 | … | 36 | 9.5 | 140 |
| SN122A | A132 | C | C | B | C | X | X | X | 0.098 | 1000–1050 | 0.28 | 29 | –T551 | 36 | 28 | 0.5 | 28 | 13.5 | 105 |
| | F132 | C | C | C | B | X | X | X | 0.100 | 970–1080 | 0.25 | 26 | –T5 | 36 | 28 | 1.0 | … | 13.5 | 105 |
| CN42A | 142 | C | C | C | C | X | X | X | 0.102 | 990–1175 | 0.32 / 0.31 | 34 / 33 | –T571 / –T61 | 40 / 47 | 34 / 42 | 1.0 / 0.5 | 30 / 35 | 10.5 / 9.5 | 105 / 110 |
| | 333 | C | B | C | C | X | B | X | 0.100 | 960–1085 | 0.28 / 0.28 / 0.33 | 29 / 29 / 35 | –T5 / –T6 / –T7 | 34 / 42 / 37 | 25 / 30 / 28 | 1.0 / 1.5 / 2.0 | 27 / 33 / 28 | 12 / 15 / 12 | 100 / 105 / 90 |
| | 354 | B | B | B | B | X | X | X | 0.098 | 1000–1105 | 0.30 | 32 | –T62 | 57 | 46 | 3.0 | 40 | … | 110 |
| | C355 | B | B | B | B | X | X | X | 0.098 | 1015–1150 | 0.36 | 39 | –T61 | 46 | 34 | 6.0 | 32 | 14 | 100 |
| SC51A | 355 | B | B | B | B | X | X | X | 0.098 | 1015–1150 | 0.40 / 0.34 | 43 / 36 | –T51 / –T6 / –T71 | 30 / 42 / 36 | 24 / 27 / 31 | 2.0 / 4.0 / 3.0 | 24 / 34 / 27 | … / 10 / 10 | 75 / 90 / 85 |
| SG70A | 356 | A | A | A | A | X | C | C | 0.097 | 1035–1135 | 0.36 / 0.37 | 39 / 40 | –T6 / –T7 | 32 / 38 | 27 / 24 | 5.0 / 6.0 | 30 / 25 | 13 / 11 | 80 / 70 |
| | A356 | A | A | A | A | X | C | C | 0.097 | 1035–1135 | 0.36 | 39 | –T61 | 41 | 30 | 1.0 | 28 | 13 | 90 |
| | A357 | B | A | A | B | X | B | C | 0.096 | 1035–1135 | 0.36 | 39 | –T61 | 52 | 42 | 5.0 | … | … | … |
| | 359 | B | B | B | B | X | B | C | 0.097 | 1045–1115 | 0.33 | 35 | –T61 | 47 | 37 | 7.0 | 32 | … | … |

## 22/Design for Welding

Table 69.8—Basic temper designations applicable to cast aluminum alloys

| Designation | Temper |
|---|---|
| –T2 | Annealed |
| –T4 | Solution heat treated and naturally aged to a substantially stable condition |
| –T5 | Artificially aged only |
| –T6 | Solution heat treated and then artificially aged |
| –T7 | Solution heat treated and then stabilized by heating at a temperature above the aging temperature to go beyond the point of maximum hardness and provide control of growth and/or residual stress |

Table 69.9—Practical ranges by process for joining aluminum

| Joining Process | Minimum Thickness, In. | Maximum Thickness, In. |
|---|---|---|
| Gas metal-arc | 0.062 | No limit |
| Gas tungsten-arc | 0.020 | 1 |
| Gas welding | 0.032 | 1 |
| Metal-arc | 0.125 | 1 |
| Resistance spot | Foil | 0.187 |
| Resistance seam | 0.010 | 0.187 |
| Flash welding | 0.032 | 3 sq. |
| Stud welding | 0.020 | No limit |
| Pressure—butt | 0.015 | 3 sq. |
| Pressure—lap | Foil | ¼ |
| Ultrasonic welding | Foil | 0.093 |
| Electron-beam welding | 0.025 | 5.00 |
| Brazing | 0.006 | No limit (Preheated) |

difficult to obtain adequate penetration in the heavy section without burning away the lighter section. This difficulty can be overcome by extruding or machining a lip on the heavy section equal in thickness to that of the thinner part. Since extruded sections of almost any geometry can be readily obtained in aluminum, it is possible to have a welding lip extruded on the thicker section (Fig. 69.4). This facilitates welding and increases welding speeds while materially reducing costs.

The five basic joints, butt, lap, tee, edge and corner may be used in aluminum design. For structural applications, however, edge and corner joints should be avoided as they are harder to fit, weaker, and more prone to fatigue failure.

## BUTT JOINTS

Butt joints are easy to design, use a minimum of base material, present good appearance, and perform better under fatigue loading than other types of joints. However, they require accurate alignment and edge preparation, and usually require joint preparation on thicknesses above 1/4 inch to permit satisfactory

Fig. 69.3.—An all-welded 165 foot aluminum gunboat constructed from sheet, plate and extrusions

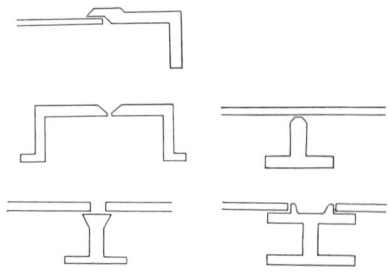

Fig. 69.4.—Typical extruded sections which minimize edge preparation or facilitate joint fit-up

root pass penetration. In addition, back chipping plus a back pass is recommended to ensure complete fusion on these thicker sections.

Sections with different thicknesses may be butt welded, but it is a good practice, particularly for fatigue loading, to bevel the thicker section before welding (Fig. 69.5).

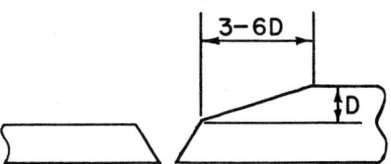

*Fig. 69.5.—Preferred practice for butt joints in plates of different thicknesses*

Tube to tube sheet applications usually represent extreme differences in thicknesses. Figure 69.6 represents a suitable joint design for these applications. In weldable aluminum alloys butt joint efficiencies range from about 60 to 100% depending on the base alloy and temper. To obtain maximum joint strength the designer must make suitable allowances and provide joint reinforcement where necessary. Doubler plates of the shape shown in Fig. 69.7 are effective in increasing the static strength and do not adversely affect the fatigue strength of joints in the heat-treated or work-hardened alloys.

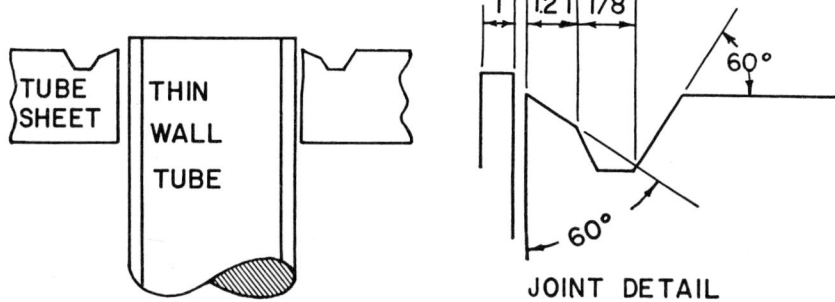

*Fig. 69.6.—Preferred joint design employed when welding thin wall tubes to tube sheet or headers*

## FILLET WELDS

### Lap Joints

Lap joints are more universally used on aluminum alloys than is customary with most other materials. The gas metal-arc process is widely used for making fillet welds in aluminum.

In thicknesses of aluminum up to one-half inch (Fig. 69.8) it is more economical to use double-welded single lap joints than double-welded butt joints. Lap joints require no edge preparation, are easy to fit, and require less jigging than butt joints. The efficiency of lap joints ranges from 70 to 100% depending upon the base alloy and temper. Preferred types of lap joints are shown in Fig. 69.9.

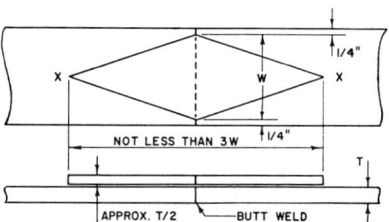

*Fig. 69.7.—Preferred doubler plate design for reinforcing butt joints, X indicates points of weld termination*

# 24/Design for Welding

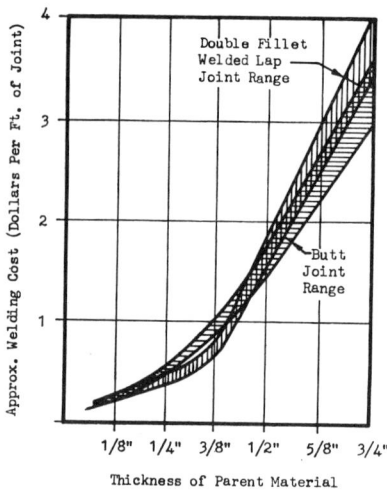

Fig. 69.8.—Comparative welding costs of gas metal-arc welded butt and lap joints in aluminum

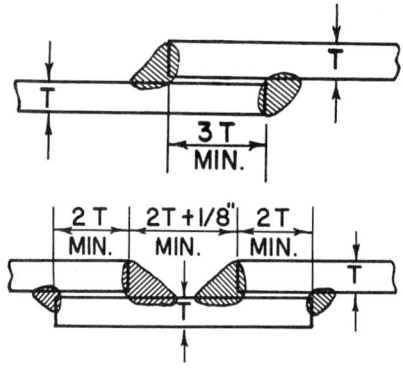

Fig. 69.9.—Preferred types of lap joints

## Tee Joints

Tee joints have a number of the advantages of lap joints. They seldom require edge preparation because fillet welds on tee joints, as on lap joints, are termed fully penetrated if the weld is fused into the root of the joint. Edge penetration may be used on thick material to reduce welding costs and minimize distortion (Fig. 69.4). Tee joints are easily fitted and normally require no back chipping. Any necessary jigging is usually quite simple. Welding a tee joint on one side only is not ordinarily recommended. Although the joint may have adequate shear and tensile strength, it is very weak when loaded so that the weld acts as a hinge. It is better to use a small continuous fillet weld on each side of the joint, rather than a large weld on one side or intermittent welding on both sides. Continuous fillet welding is recommended over intermittent welding for better fatigue life.

### JOINT ACCESSIBILITY

In choosing the joint design, accessibility must always be kept in mind. Because of the very high arc travel speeds employed for aluminum welding it is important that all joints have excellent accessibility and that they do not require abrupt changes in welding direction. If welding can be mechanized by rotating the part or the torch, welds, such as circumferential welds in pipe, can be speedily effected (Fig. 69.10). However, when welded manually much slower weld travel speeds are required. It is frequently advantageous to employ transi-

Fig. 69.10.—Welding a circumferential joint in a section of piping using the U-groove technique

tion pieces so that rapid changes in weld direction can be avoided (Figs. 69.11 and 69.12).

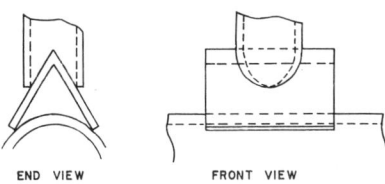

Fig. 69.11.—Illustrates the use of a transition section to facilitate welding and to minimize heat effect and distortion

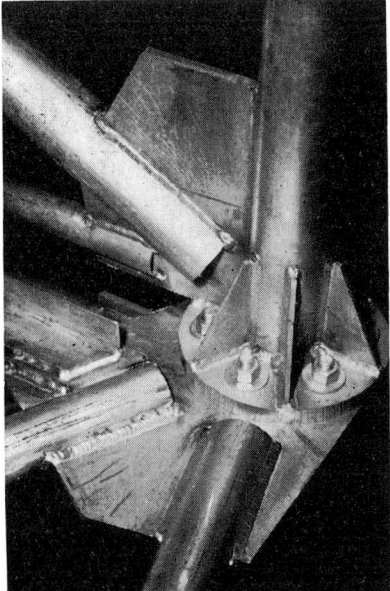

Fig. 69.12.—Typical joint array indicating the use of transition sections to minimize rapid changes in weld direction

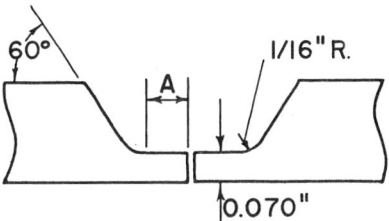

Fig. 69.13.—Typical joint design for complete and controlled penetration for all-position welding. A is 1/8 in. minimum for gas tungsten arc welding and 1/16 in. minimum for gas metal-arc welding

The designer should strive to use material with the best mechanical properties consistent with adequate corrosion resistance, weldability and other desirable features. Since welding costs vary approximately as the square of the thickness, use of a thinner gage in a higher strength alloy may result in cost savings much greater than the saving in weight alone.

EDGE PREPARATION

In general, the design of welded joints for aluminum is quite consistent with the recommendations for steel joints in Chapter 8, Section 1. However, because of the higher fluidity of aluminum under the welding arc, some important general principles should be kept in mind. In the lighter gages of aluminum sheet, less groove spacing is advantageous when weld dilution is not a factor. The controlling criterion is joint preparation. Joint design should assume complete penetration.

A special joint design that is applicable to aluminum is shown in Fig. 69.13. It is typical of joints where welding can be done from one side only and where a smooth, penetrating bead is desired. The effectiveness of this particular design is dependent upon surface tension. To accomplish this a U-groove is employed on all material thicknesses over 1/8 inch. The bottom of the "U" must be wide enough to contain the root pass completely. This necessitates adding a relatively large amount of filler alloy to fill the groove, but it results in excellent control of penetration and sound root pass welds. This technique has been employed with outstanding success in welding circumferential joints in aluminum pipe.

**26**/*Design for Welding*

This edge preparation can be employed for welding in all positions with elimination of suckback difficulties in the overhead and horizontal welding positions. It is applicable to all weldable base alloys and all filler alloys.

STRESS DISTRIBUTION

In most cases, the efficiency of a welded aluminum assembly depends on the location and orientation of the welds, since with all aluminum alloys in other than the annealed condition, the heat of welding reduces the mechanical properties in localized regions around the welds. Thus a designer should generally avoid locating welds in areas of maximum stress.

When welded joints must be located in critical areas, there is little to be gained by welding strain-hardened alloys in the harder tempers, as the joints in H18 tempers will not be stronger than those in H14 temper even when welded at high speeds. When using the heat treatable alloys it may be preferable to employ the T4 temper and age harden only, to obtain maximum strength without the probability of distortion from quenching during reheat treating.

However, in many weldments it is possible to locate the welds where they will not be subjected to maximum stresses. If the design is such that the maximum stresses in the structure occur at points remote from welding, it is possible to take advantage of the stronger tempers. It is frequently possible to make connections between a main member and such accessories as braces by welding at the neutral axis, or other point of low stress. Joints of low efficiency may be reinforced, but only at additional cost.

Where welds are located in critical areas but do not cover the entire cross section, the strength of the section depends on the relative amount of the cross-sectional area affected by the heat of welding. Thus when members must be joined at locations of high stress, it is desirable that the welds be longitudinal to the principal member and parallel to the direction of main stresses in the principal member. Transverse welds should be avoided. For example, longitudinal welds used to join a web to a flange of an I-beam frequently have very little effect on the strength of the aluminum structural member because most of the cross section has original base metal properties.

Frequently the ends of welds are more highly stressed than the central portions. To avoid using heavier thicknesses, it is desirable that areas of high stresses in the welds be eliminated or minimized. This can easily be accomplished by the use of sniping. This preferable type of member termination is illustrated in Fig. 69.14.

In general, channel stiffeners in one form or another are most attractive for

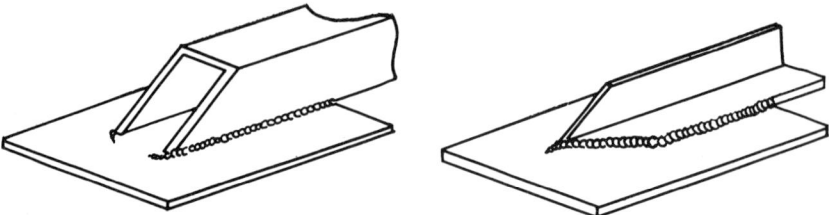

*Fig. 69.14.—Typical end-connection details showing sniping of angles and channels to give maximum efficiency*

# Design for Welding/27

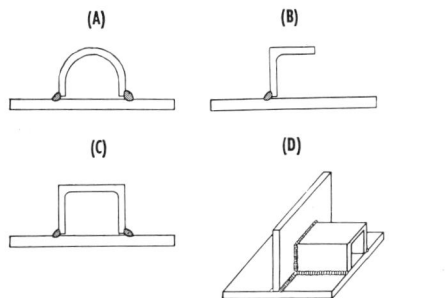

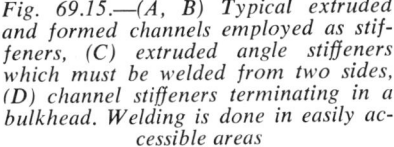

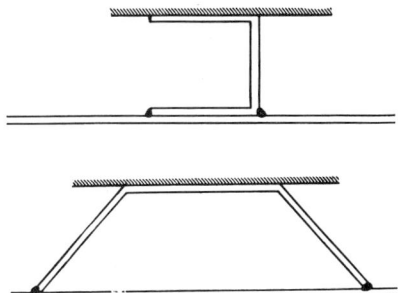

Fig. 69.15.—(A, B) Typical extruded and formed channels employed as stiffeners, (C) extruded angle stiffeners which must be welded from two sides, (D) channel stiffeners terminating in a bulkhead. Welding is done in easily accessible areas

Fig. 69.16.—The use of trapezoidal stiffeners (lower) results in a reduced unsupported span and does not require sway bracing; use of conventional channel stiffeners (upper) requires sway bracing

aluminum designs. They form box sections which are more effective than angles or tees under compressive or torsional loading. They can be formed to fit a curved surface more easily, and fit-up is greatly facilitated. Welding accessibility is best with a hat-shaped section. Welding of channels is over a greater area, since the welds are spaced further apart. The versatility of formed channels permits the designer to choose the most appropriate strength and distribution of stiffeners. Typical examples are illustrated in Fig. 69.15. The unsupported floor span can be halved by the use of channel stiffeners placed so as to weld both toes to the floor.

Forming may give rigidity to flat surfaces for easier handling and may provide some self-jigging in assembling. Bending may also aid fit-up, as when a trapezoidal channel stiffener is used (Fig. 69.16). Here, intimate contact with the flat surface is automatically afforded when the stiffener is pressed into place under a slight pressure. The same technique can be used to replace heavier angle sections to reinforce the corners of a box or structure. Typical examples of this type of design are shown in Fig. 69.17, which illustrates methods of obtaining improved performances of weldment while decreasing weight and welding costs. An additional feature of this type of design is the improved appearance of the weldment.

## FILLER METAL SELECTION

### WELD METAL DILUTION

When a filler metal is used, the weld deposit is an alloy formed of a mixture of the filler metal and the base metal. The properties of this alloy will largely determine the properties of the joint. Strength, ductility, resistance to weld cracking, corrosion resistance, heat treatability and other properties may be greatly influenced by the degree of dilution between the base alloy and filler metal. Refer to the filler metal supplier for detailed information on the influence of percentages of dilution on properties. The extent of fusion and dilution of the base metal with the filler metal depends upon joint design, welding process

# 28/Filler Metal Selection

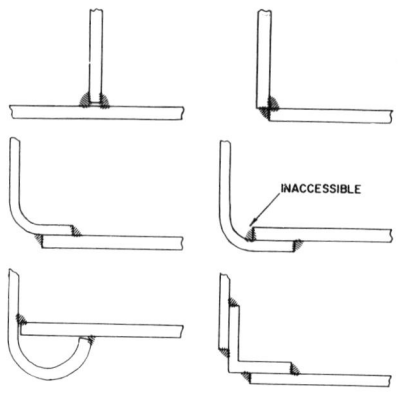

Fig. 69.17.—Preferred and unsatisfactory types of corner joints

used, and welding procedure. Weld cracking tendencies are generally reduced by keeping the base alloy dilution to a minimum.

## CRACKING

One of the most important factors to be considered in the choice of a filler alloy is freedom from weld cracking. Weld cracking is generally minimized by using a filler alloy of higher alloy content than the base metal. For example, alloy 6061 is extremely crack-sensitive when welded with 6061 filler metal, but it is readily welded with 4043 filler metal which contains more silicon (5%). Increased weld ductility can be obtained with the 5000 series filler alloys such as 5154, 5356, etc. The use of a higher alloy content filler metal often imparts increased weld strength and ductility, as well as decreased crack sensitivity. An example would be the application of 5356 filler metal to weld 5052 base material. In this case, the filler alloy contains twice as much magnesium as the base material.

## CORROSION RESISTANCE

Assemblies, vessels and drums for use in certain corrosive environments or with certain chemicals may require special filler alloys. These alloys may be of higher purity or may have closer composition limits on some of the alloying constituents. Aluminum-magnesium filler alloys are highly resistant to corrosion but tend to be anodic to many other nonheat-treatable alloys, particularly in joints with low dilution. For this reason they should be used with base alloys possessing a similar electrical potential whenever the weld and base metal are to be continuously or cyclically exposed to an electrolyte.

## ELEVATED-TEMPERATURE SERVICE

Elevated-temperature service influences the choice of both base material and filler metal. In general, aluminum alloys of over 3% magnesium content are not recommended for sustained service at temperatures of 150°F and above.

## ANODIC TREATMENTS

Chemical treatments, and particularly anodic treatments, of a weldment will often influence the choice of aluminum filler alloy because of the change in appearance and color of the weld zone. Welds made with filler alloys containing silicon, such as 4043, turn dark gray with these treatments, and contrast greatly with most base metals. In general, the pure aluminum and the aluminum-magnesium filler alloys will produce a good color match.

## SELECTION

The filler metal for joining a particular base alloy for a given application should be selected after consideration of all the abovementioned factors. For suggested filler metals see Table 69.10.

## Filler Metal Selection / 29

**Table 69.10—Suggested fillers for commonly welded aluminum alloys**

| Material Welded | Strength | Ductility | Color Match after Anodizing | Salt Water Corrosion Resistance |
|---|---|---|---|---|
| 1100 | 4043 | 1100 | 1100 | 1100 |
| 2219 | 2319 | 2319 | 2319 | 2319 |
| 6061 | 5356 | 5356 | 5154 | 4043 |
| 6063 | 5356 | 5356 | 5356 | 4043 |
| 3003 | 5356 | 1100 | 1100 | 1100 |
| 5052 | 5356 | 5356 | 5356 | 4043 |
| 5086 | 5556 | 5356 | 5356 | 5183 |
| 5083 | 5183 | 5356 | 5356 | 5183 |
| 5454 | 5356 | 5554 | 5554 | 5554 |
| 5456 | 5556 | 5356 | 5556 | 5556 |
| 7039 | 5039 | 5356 | 5039 | 5039 |

Recommended filler metals for general-purpose welding of various aluminum alloy combinations are given in Table 69.11. In repair of castings, the filler alloy is generally chosen to match the composition of the casting, and is often cast from the same heat of material (Fig. 69.18). Additional filler alloys for repair of castings are given in Table 69.12.

### STORAGE AND USE OF ALUMINUM FILLER METAL

A major step toward producing good aluminum welds is the use of high quality filler metal of the correct size and alloy. It should be free of gas and nonmetallic impurities, with a clean, smooth surface free of moisture, lubricant or other contaminants. Care must be taken during storage and use to prevent contamination of the filler which might result in poor welds.

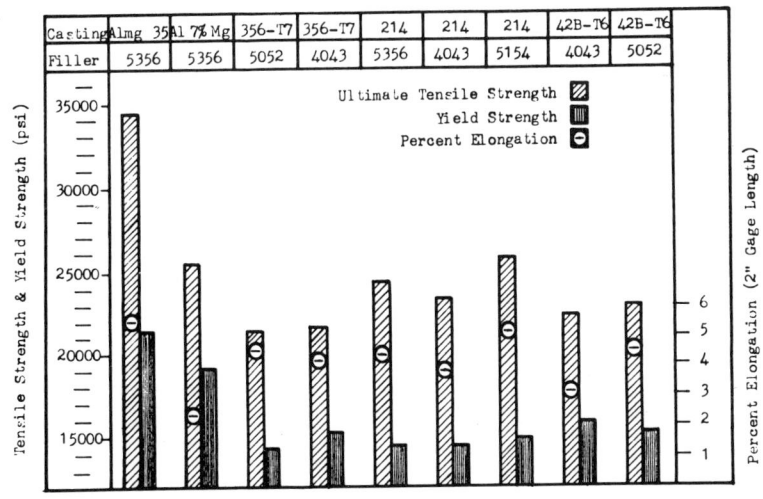

Average tensile data on transverse-weld specimens removed from 3/8-in. thick castings joined to 3/8-in. thick 5086 wrought alloy; each weldment was machined to 1/4-in. thickness before the specimens were removed

*Fig. 69.18.—Average tensile data on transverse-weld specimens from 3/8 in. castings*

**30**/Filler Metal Selection

**Table 69.11—Guide to the choice of aluminum filler metal for general purpose welding**

| Base Metal | 319, 333 354, 355 C355 | 13, 43, 344 356, A356 A357, 359 | 214, A214 B214, F214 | 7039 A612, C612 D612 | 6070 6071 | 6061, 6063 6101, 6151 6201, 6951 | 5456 | 5454 | 5154 5254[a] |
|---|---|---|---|---|---|---|---|---|---|
| 1060, EC | 4145[c] | ER4043 | ER5356[e] | ER4043 | ER4043 | ER4043 | ER5356[e] | ER5356[e,e] | ER5356[e,c] |
| 1100, 3003 Alclad 3003 | 4145[c] | ER4043 | ER5356[e] | ER4043 | ER4043 | ER4043 | ER5356[e] | ER4043[e] | ER4043[e] |
| 2014, 2024 | 4145[g] | 4145 | .... | .... | 4145 | 4145 | .... | .... | .... |
| 2219 | 4145[g] | 4145[c] | .... | ER4043 | ER4043[f] | ER4045[f] | ER4043 | ER4043 | ER4043 |
| 3004 Alclad 3004 | ER4043 | ER4043 | ER5356[e] | ER4043[e] | ER4043 | ER4043[b] | ER5356[e] | ER5356[e,e] | ER5356[e] |
| 5005, 5050 | ER4043 | ER4043 | ER5356[e] | ER5356[e] | ER4043[e] | ER4043[b] | ER5356[e] | ER5356[e,e] | ER5356[e,e] |
| 5052, 5652[a] | ER4043 | ER4043[e] | ER5356[e] | ER5356[e,h] | ER4043[e] | ER5356[b,e] | ER5356[b,e] | ER5356[b,e] | ER5356[b] |
| 5083 | .... | ER5356[e,e] | ER5356[e] | ER5183[e,h] | ER5356[e] | ER5356[e] | ER5183[e] | ER5356[e] | ER5356[e] |
| 5086 | .... | ER5356[e,e] | ER5356[e] | ER5356[e,h] | ER5356[e] | ER5356[e] | ER5356[e] | ER5356[b] | ER5356[b] |
| 5154, 5254[a] | .... | ER4043[e] | ER5356[b] | ER5356[b,h] | ER5356[b,e] | ER5356[b,e] | ER5356[b] | ER5356[b] | ER5356[a,b] |
| 5454 | .... | ER4043[b] | ER5356[e] | ER5356[b,h] | ER5554[e,e] | ER5356[b,e] | ER5356 | ER5554[e,e] | |
| 5456 | .... | ER5356[e,e] | ER5356[h] | ER5556[h] | ER5356[h] | ER5356[e] | ER5556[h] | | |
| 6061, 6063, 6101, 6151, 6931 | ER4043[f,i] | ER4043[e,i] | ER5356[b,e] | ER5356[b,e,h] | ER4043[b,i] | ER4043[b,i] | | | |
| 6070, 6071 | ER4043[f,i] | ER4043[e,i] | ER5356[e,e] | ER5356[e,h] | 4643[e,e] | | | | |
| 7039 A612, C612 D612 | ER4043 | ER4043[e,h] | ER5356[e,h] | 5039[e] | | | | | |
| 214, A214 B214, F214 | .... | ER4043[e] | ER5356[e,d] | | | | | | |
| 13, 43, 344 355, C355 356, A356 A357, 359 | ER4043[d,f] | ER4043[d,i] | | | | | | | |
| 319, 333 354 | 4145[d,f] | | | | | | | | |

## Filler Metal Selection / 31

**Table 69.11—Guide to the choice of aluminum filler metal for general purpose welding (continued)**

| Base Metal | 5086 | 5083 | 5052 5652[a] | 5005 5050 | 3004 Alc. 3004 | 2219 | 2014 2024 | 1100 3003 Alc. 3003 | 1060 EC |
|---|---|---|---|---|---|---|---|---|---|
| 1060, EC | ER5356[e] | ER5356[e] | ER4043 | ER1100 | ER4043 | 4145 | 4145 | ER1100[e] | ER1260 |
| 1100, 3003 Alclad 3003 | ER5356[e] | ER5356[e] | ER4043[e] | ER4043[e] | ER4043[e] | 4145 | 4145 | ER1100[e] | |
| 2014, 2024 | .... | .... | .... | .... | .... | 4145[g] | 4145[g] | | |
| 2219 | ER4043 | ER4043 | ER4043 | ER4043 | ER4043[e] | 2319[e,f] | | | |
| 3004 Alclad 3004 | ER5356[e] | ER5356[e] | ER5356[e,e] | ER4043[e] | ER4043[e] | | | | |
| 5005, 5050 | ER5356[e] | ER5356[e] | ER4043[e] | ER4043[d,e] | | | | | |
| 5052, 5652[a] | ER5356[e] | ER5356[e] | ER5356[a,b,e] | | | | | | |
| 5083 | ER5356[e] | ER5183[e] | | | | | | | |
| 5086 | ER5356[e] | | | | | | | | |

NOTE: 1—Service conditions such as immersion in fresh or salt water, exposure to specific chemicals or a sustained high temperature (over 150°F) may limit the choice of filler metals.
NOTE: 2—Recommendations in this table apply to gas shielded-arc welding processes. For gas welding, only R1100, R1260 and R4043 filler metals are ordinarily used.
NOTE: 3—Filler alloys designated with ER prefix are listed in AWS specification A5.10. Alloys not possessing the prefix letters are not included in the AWS specification.
  [a] Base metal alloys 5652 and 5254 are used for hydrogen peroxide service. ER5254 filler metal is used for welding both alloys for low-temperature service (150°F and below). ER5652 filler metal can be used for welding 5652 for high-temperature service (150°F and above).
  [b] ER5154, ER5254, ER5183, ER5356 and ER5556 may be used. In some cases they provide: (1) improved color match after anodizing treatment, (2) highest weld ductility, and (3) higher weld strength. ER5554 is suitable for elevated temperature service.
  [c] ER4043 may be used for some applications.
  [d] Filler metal with the same analysis as the base metal is sometimes used.
  [e] ER5356, ER5183 or ER5556 may be used.
  [f] 4145 may be used for some applications.
  [g] 2319 may be used for some applications.
  [h] 5039 may be used for some applications.
  [i] 4643 may be used and is often desirable to provide highest strength in postweld heat-treated assemblies.
NOTE: 4—Where no filler metal is listed, the parent alloy combination is not recommended for welding.

**32**/*Filler Metal Selection*

**Table 69.12—The following filler alloys are primarily used for repair of castings**

| AWS-ASTM Classification | Percentage of Alloying Elements ||||||||
|---|---|---|---|---|---|---|---|---|
| | Si | Cu | Mg | Mn | Cr | Ni | Zn | Ti |
| R–C4A |  | 4.5 |  |  |  |  |  |  |
| R–CN42A |  | 4.0 | 1.5 |  |  | 2.0 |  |  |
| R–SC51A | 5.0 | 1.3 | .50 |  |  |  |  |  |
| R–SG70A | 7.0 |  | .30 |  |  |  |  |  |
| R–ZG61A |  |  | .58 |  | 0.5 |  | 5.6 |  |
| B Al Si-3 | 10.0 | 4.0 |  |  |  |  |  |  |

The quality of the filler is particularly important in producing sound welds with the gas metal-arc welding process. In this consumable electrode process a relatively small diameter filler wire feeds through the welding gun at a high rate of speed. To feed properly the electrode wire must be uniform in diameter, of a suitable temper, free from slivers, scratches, inclusions, kinks, waves or sharp bends, and spooled so that it is free to unwind without restriction. Proper pitch and cast is also important to prevent wandering of the wire as it emerges from the contact tube. The small diameter and high rate of feed of the wire can carry a relatively large amount of foreign material into the weld pool if the surface is not clean. This may cause weld porosity or poor quality welds.

To avoid contamination, filler metal supplies should be kept covered, and stored in a dry place at relatively uniform temperature. Wire spools temporarily left unused on the welding machine, as between work shifts, should be covered with a clean cloth or a plastic bag if the feed unit does not have its own cover. If a spool of wire will not be used for a considerable length of time, it should be returned to its carton and tightly sealed. Original electrode or wire containers should not be opened until the contents are to be used. The basic filler metal compositions are outlined in Table 69.13.

Information on selection, manufacture, packaging and availability of aluminum filler metals is covered in the AWS Filler Metal Specifications series.

## GAS METAL-ARC WELDING

### CHARACTERISTICS OF PROCESS

This fast, adaptable process is used with direct current reverse polarity, and an inert gas to weld aluminum alloys from 1/16 inch to several inches thick (Fig. 69.19). With good jigging and proper equipment, some types of joints can be welded in thicknesses as low as 0.040 inches. The process is well adapted to welding in all positions. Further information can be found in Chapter 27, Section 2.

### POWER SUPPLY AND EQUIPMENT

Most direct current welding power supplies may be used for gas metal-arc welding of aluminum. A detailed discussion of the power supply for this process is given in Chapter 29, Section 2.

Gas Metal-Arc Welding/**33**

*Fig. 69.19.—Gas metal-arc welding process was used extensively in fabrication of these tank truck trailers*

The wire driving equipment for aluminum must be capable of driving the electrode through the gun at a uniform speed. All wire passages must be clean and free of excessive wear. Any sharp edges or burrs that might gouge the aluminum wire must be eliminated.

SHIELDING GAS

Welding grade argon or helium or a mixture of these shielding gases is used for aluminum welding. Argon produces a smoother and more stable arc than helium. At a specific current and arc length helium provides deeper penetration and a hotter arc than argon. Arc voltage is higher with helium, and a given change in arc length results in a greater change in arc voltage. Conversely, in automatic welding a fluctuating voltage from the power supply will have less effect on arc length with helium. The bead profile and penetration pattern of aluminum welds made with argon and helium differ (Fig. 69.20).

The bead profile with argon is narrower and more convex than with helium. The penetration pattern shows a deep central section. Helium results in a flatter, wider bead, and has a broader underbead penetration pattern.

A mixture of approximately 75% helium and 25% argon provides the advantages of both shielding gases with none of the undesirable characteristics of

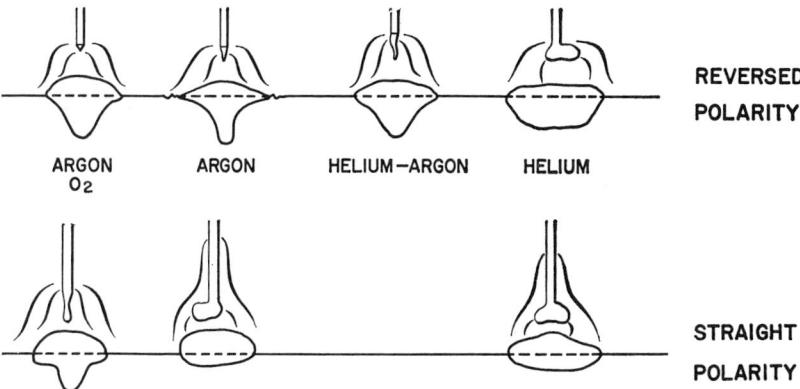

*Fig. 69.20.—Bead contour and penetration pattern for various shielding gases*

## Table 69.13—Composition of aluminum welding rods and electrode material for gas metal-arc and gas tungsten-arc welding

| Type[2] | Copper, % | Magnesium, % | Manganese, % | Chromium, % | Silicon, % | Iron, % | Zinc, % | Titanium, % | Zirconium, % | Vanadium, % | Beryllium, % | Other Each, % | Other Total, % | Aluminum, % |
|---|---|---|---|---|---|---|---|---|---|---|---|---|---|---|
| ER1100 | 0.20 | ..... | 0.05 | ..... | [3] | [3] | 0.10 | ..... | ..... | ..... | ..... | 0.05 | 0.15 | 99.0–99.5 |
| 2319 | 5.8–6.8 | 0.02 | 0.20–0.40 | ..... | 0.20 | 0.30 | 0.10 | 0.10–0.20 | 0.10–0.25 | 0.05–0.15 | 0.0008 | 0.05 | 0.15 | Remainder |
| ER4043 | 0.03 | 0.05 | 0.05 | ..... | 4.5–6.0 | 0.8 | ..... | 0.20 | ..... | ..... | 0.0008 | 0.05 | 0.15 | Remainder |
| 5039 | 0.03 | 3.3— | 0.30— | 0.10— | 0.10 | 0.40 | 2.4— | 0.10 | ..... | ..... | 0.0008 | 0.05 | 0.10 | Remainder |
| 4643 | 0.10max. | 0.10–0.30 | 0.50 | 0.20 | 3.6–4.6 | 0.8 | 0.10 | ..... | ..... | ..... | ..... | 0.05 | 0.15 | Remainder |
| 4145 | 3.3–4.7 | 0.15 | 0.05 | 0.15 | 9.3–10.7 | [4] | 0.20 | 0.15 | ..... | ..... | 0.0008 | 0.05 | 0.15 | Remainder |
| ER5154 | 0.10 | 3.1–3.9 | 0.10 | 0.15–0.35 | [4] | [4] | 0.20 | 0.20 | ..... | ..... | 0.0008 | 0.05 | 0.15 | Remainder |
| ER5183 | 0.10 | 4.3–5.2 | 0.50–1.0 | 0.05–0.25 | 0.40 | 0.40 | 0.25 | 0.15 | ..... | ..... | 0.0008 | 0.05 | 0.15 | Remainder |
| ER5254 | 0.05 | 3.1–3.9 | 0.01 | 0.15–0.35 | [4] | [4] | 0.20 | 0.05 | ..... | ..... | 0.0008 | 0.05 | 0.15 | Remainder |
| ER5356 | 0.10 | 4.5–5.5 | 0.05–0.20 | 0.05–0.20 | [5] | [6] | 0.10 | 0.06–0.20 | ..... | ..... | 0.0008 | 0.05 | 0.15 | Remainder |
| ER5554 | 0.10 | 2.4–3.0 | 0.50–1.0 | 0.05–0.20 | [6] | [6] | 0.25 | 0.05–0.20 | ..... | ..... | 0.0008 | 0.05 | 0.15 | Remainder |
| ER5556 | 0.10 | 4.7–5.5 | 0.50–1.0 | 0.05–0.20 | [6] | [6] | 0.25 | 0.05–0.20 | ..... | ..... | 0.0008 | 0.05 | 0.15 | Remainder |

\* Nominal composition.
[1] Values shown are maximum percentages except where otherwise specified.
[2] The alloy designations are in accordance with the system approved by the Aluminum Association.
[3] Iron plus silicon = 1.0 percent maximum.
[4] Iron plus silicon = 0.45 percent maximum.
[5] Iron plus silicon = 0.50 percent maximum.
[6] Iron plus silicon = 0.40 percent maximum.

either. Penetration pattern and bead contour show the characteristics of both gases. Arc stability is comparable to argon. Mixtures of argon and helium ranging between 50% to 80% helium are widely used.

The purity of the shielding gas is of utmost importance. Only gases of welding grade or better should be used, and care must be taken to prevent contamination. Dust, dirt and moisture can accumulate in the cylinder fitting, which should be carefully cleaned and blown out before use. Rubber hose, if used, should be thoroughly blown out before use. Plastic hose is recommended. All hose connections and other gas fittings must be pressure tight, since aspiration of air or escape of shielding gas will invariably affect welding adversely.

## WELDING TECHNIQUE

Correct electrode wire alloy and size must be selected and the wire threaded through the wire drive unit. Shielding gas flow, power supply, and wire feed speed should be adjusted for the welding procedure employed. When setting up new equipment it is advisable to start with high wire feed speed with conventional power type welding machines to avoid burnbacks. Wire feed can then be reduced until the desired voltage and arc length is obtained. Voltage, current and wire feed are interdependent with a constant power supply. Adjustment of any one may require readjustment of the others.

The arc is struck with the electrode wire protruding about one-half inch from the cup, employing either a scratch start or a running start. Running starts are usually used with constant potential power sources. This type of start tends to be too cold at the beginning of the weld, which may cause poor bead contour, lack of penetration and porosity at this point.

A technique frequently employed to ensure good weld starts is to strike the arc approximately an inch ahead of the beginning of the weld and then quickly bring the arc to the weld starting point, reverse the direction of travel, and proceed with normal welding. Alternatively, the arc may be struck outside the weld groove on a starting tab. When finishing or terminating the weld, a similar practice may be followed by reversing the direction of welding and simultaneously increasing the speed of welding to taper the width of the molten pool prior to breaking the arc. This helps to avert craters and crater cracking. Runoff tabs are commonly used.

Having established the arc, the welder moves the electrode along the joint while maintaining a 70 to 85 degree forehand angle relative to the work (Fig. 69.21). A string bead technique is normally preferred. Care should be taken

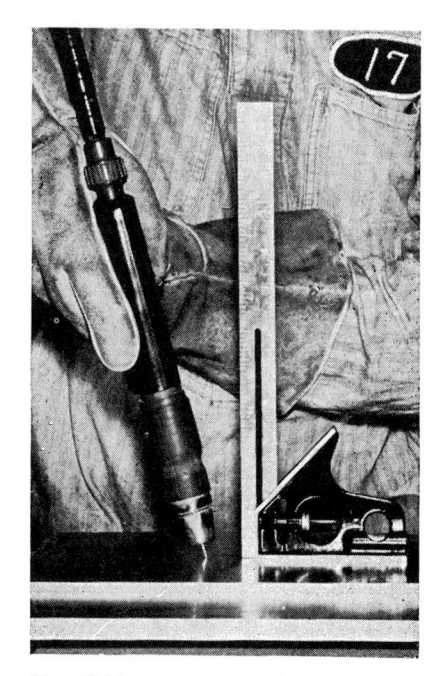

*Fig. 69.21.—Illustration showing proper electrode angle for gas metal-arc welding of aluminum*

**36**/*Gas Metal-Arc Welding*

Table 69.14—Approximate groove welding procedures for the gas metal-arc welding of aluminum

| Metal Thickness (Inches) | Weld Position* | Edge Preparation† | Joint Spacing (Inches) | Weld Passes | Electrode Diameter (Inches) | DC (Amps) | Arc Voltage (Volts) | Argon Gas Flow (Cfh) | Arc Travel Speed (Ipm) | Approximate Electrode Consumption (lb/100 feet) |
|---|---|---|---|---|---|---|---|---|---|---|
| 1/16 | F | A | None | 1 | .030 | 70–110 | 15–20 | 25 | 25–45 | 1.5 |
|  |  | G | 1/32 | 1 | .030 | 70–110 | 15–20 |  | 25–45 | 2 |
| 3/32 | F, V, H, O | A | None | 1 | .030–3/64 | 90–150 | 18–22 | 30 | 25–45 | 1.8 |
|  |  | G | 1/8 | 1 | .030 | 110–130 | 18–23 | 30 | 23–30 | 2 |
| 1/8 | F, V, H, O | A | 0–3/32 | 1 | .030–3/64 | 120–150 | 20–24 | 30 | 24–30 | 2 |
|  | F, V, H, O | G | 3/16 | 1 | .030–3/64 | 110–135 | 19–23 | 30 | 18–28 | 3 |
| 3/16 | F, V, H | B | 0–1/16 | 1F, 1R | .030–3/64 | 130–175 | 22–26 | 35 | 24–30 | 4 |
|  | F, V, H | F | 0–1/16 | 1 | 3/64 | 140–180 | 23–27 | 35 | 24–30 | 5 |
|  | O, V | F | 0–1/16 | 2F | 3/64 | 140–175 | 23–27 | 60 | 24–30 | 5 |
|  | F, V | H | 3/32–3/16 | 2 | 3/64–1/16 | 140–185 | 23–27 | 35 | 24–30 | 8 |
|  | H, O | H | 3/16 | 3 | 3/64 | 130–175 | 23–27 | 60 | 25–35 | 10 |
| 1/4 | F | B | 0–3/32 | 1F, 1R | 3/64–1/16 | 175–200 | 24–28 | 40 | 24–30 | 6 |
|  | F | F | 0–3/32 | 2 | 3/64–1/16 | 185–225 | 24–29 | 40 | 24–30 | 8 |
|  | V, H | F | 0–3/32 | 3F, 1R | 3/64 | 165–190 | 25–29 | 45 | 25–35 | 10 |
|  | F, V | F | 0–3/32 | 3F, 1R | 3/64–1/16 | 180–200 | 25–29 | 60 | 24–30 | 10 |
|  | F, V | H | 1/8–1/4 | 2–3 | 3/64–1/16 | 175–225 | 25–29 | 40 | 24–30 | 12 |
|  | O, H | H | 1/4 | 4–6 | 3/64–1/16 | 170–200 | 25–29 | 60 | 25–40 | 12 |
| 3/8 | F | C–90° | 0–3/32 | 1F, 1R | 1/16 | 225–290 | 26–29 | 50 | 20–30 | 16 |
|  | F | F | 0–3/32 | 2F, 1R | 1/16 | 210–275 | 26–29 | 50 | 24–35 | 18 |
|  | V, H | F | 0–3/32 | 3F, 1R | 1/16 | 190–220 | 26–29 | 55 | 24–30 | 20 |
|  | F, V | F | 0–3/32 | 5F, 1R | 1/16 | 200–250 | 26–29 | 80 | 25–40 | 20 |
|  | O, H | H | 1/4–3/8 | 4 | 1/16 | 210–290 | 26–29 | 50 | 24–30 | 35 |
|  |  | H | 3/8 | 8–10 | 1/16 | 190–260 | 26–29 | 80 | 25–40 | 50 |
| 3/4 | F | C–60° | 0–3/32 | 3F, 1R | 3/32 | 340–400 | 26–31 | 60 | 14–20 | 50 |
|  | F | F | 0–1/8 | 4F, 1R | 1/16–3/32 | 325–375 | 26–31 | 60 | 16–20 | 70 |
|  | V, H, O | F | 0–1/16 | 8F, 1R | 1/16 | 240–300 | 26–30 | 80 | 24–30 | 75 |
|  | F | E | 0–3/32 | 3F, 3R | 1/16 | 270–330 | 26–30 | 60 | 16–24 | 70 |
|  | V, H, O | E | 0–1/16 | 6F, 6R | 1/16 | 230–280 | 26–30 | 80 | 16–24 | 75 |

* F = Flat; V = Vertical; H = Horizontal; O = Overhead.
† Refer to Fig. 69A.18.

## Gas Metal-Arc Welding/37

that the forehand angle is not changed or increased as the end of the weld is approached. Arc travel speed controls the bead size. When welding aluminum with this process it is most important that the exceptionally high travel speeds indicated in the procedure be maintained or exceeded.

When welding uniform thicknesses, the electrode-to-work angle should be equal on all sides. When welding in the horizontal position, best results are obtained by pointing the gun upward slightly. When welding thick-to-thin joints it is helpful to direct the arc toward the heavier section. A slight back-hand angle is sometimes helpful when welding thin to thick sections.

The root pass of a joint usually requires a short arc to provide the desired penetration. Slightly longer arcs and higher arc voltages may be used on subsequent passes.

Burnbacks are caused by insufficient or unsteady electrode wire feed, slippage of the drive rolls, bends or kinks in the electrode wire, insufficient, improper or misaligned wire guides, or excessive clearance in the contact tube. To facilitate the wire-driving operation, the flexible electrode conduit should be as short as possible, and the welder should keep it reasonably straight, avoiding sharp bends or loops. This is particularly important when pushing small diameter electrodes of the softer aluminum alloys.

The welder may be confronted with the problem of insufficient cleaning action by the arc, resulting in dirty welds and poor wetting of the base metal by the filler metal. Major causes of this difficulty are insufficient current, incomplete oxide removal prior to welding, and inadequate gas shielding. This problem may be alleviated by increasing welding current, using a smaller electrode or providing greater gas flow. The inside of the gas cup should be kept free of spatter. Maintenance of the proper forehand angle by the welder is also important.

The foregoing discussion of gas metal-arc welding of aluminum has been confined to welding with high current densities which produce a spray-type of welding arc. Recent modifications in power supplies have made welding possible at much lower current densities and low arc voltage, with a resultant change to a globular-type metal transfer. This technique employs argon shielding with amperages and voltage below the spray transition values, and requires the use of electrodes 3/64 inch diameter or less. This practice is often used to advantage when limited heat input is desired, and for welding thin sections.

Welding is accomplished by touching the electrode to the work, causing a short circuit. Localized resistance heating of the electrode causes the electrode wire to melt. Surface tension and the electromagnetic pinch effect cause the molten metal to be wiped off the electrode, breaking contact with the weld pool. When this happens a relatively high arc pressure against the weld pool is established because of the inductance in the welding circuit. This pressure causes the weld pool to be forced away from the electrode. The arc force supplied by the inductive energy decays. This allows the depressed pool to rise toward the advancing electrode that again contacts the weld pool and the process is repeated.

Penetration and heat input are limited. Typical welding conditions for 0.040-0.064 in. thick aluminum are: 12-15 volts, 60-100 amps, 0.030 inch diameter electrode fed at 300-400 inch per minute, 40-60 inch per minute travel speed.

## JOINT DESIGN

Edges may be prepared for welding by sawing, machining, rotary planing, routing or arc cutting. The edge preparations and joint designs discussed and

# 38/Gas Metal-Arc Welding

illustrated in this section have been established by production experience. Acceptable joint designs are shown in detail in Fig. 69.22.

The use of high welding currents and current densities may, with experience, permit narrower welding grooves. This applies particularly to machine welding. A decrease in filler metal requirements, however, does not normally result in decreased welding costs. More often a higher deposition rate can be employed when welding in a properly prepared and fitted groove.

## WELDING VARIABLES

It is not possible to cover all of the welding variables in detail. They are affected by base alloy, filler alloy, temperature of the metal, shielding gas and welding equipment, as well as other factors. The basic welding procedures are outlined in Tables 69.14 and 69.15.

The deposition rate for any electrode alloy is roughly proportional to the welding current. Poor welds frequently result from the use of electrode wire that is too large. High current densities using smaller electrode wire sizes frequently result in faster welding with a decrease in total welding cost, even though the smaller electrode is more expensive in first cost. At high current, particular attention must be given to the maintenance of the gas shield and uniform arc travel.

Arc voltage is of extreme importance to the satisfactory use of this welding process. It controls penetration, bead contour, and to some degree such defects as undercutting, porosity and weld discontinuities. An abnormally long arc is smoother and quieter, and is frequently employed to the detriment of quality and economy, especially when welding with an argon gas shield. The arc should be on the threshold of being noisy for most applications. The voltages indicated in Table 69.14 have been found most acceptable. It should be noted that the voltages given are based on measurement from the contact tube to the work. Because of voltage drop in the leads, voltages measured at the power source are often misleading.

## AUTOMATIC WELDING

The gas metal-arc process is well adapted to fully automatic welding. Points to receive particular attention in automatic welding operations are those affecting the uniformity of electrode wire drive speed, electrode contact in the welding torch and maintenance of a constant welding current. A high quality electrode with uniform surface resistance is necessary to provide a uniform current pick-up in the contact tube, since high welding currents are preferred for automatic welding operations. Automatic arc voltage control may be used in the conventional manner by governing the electrode feed speed, or using a constant-potential type power source. Proper operation with either type requires uniform and dependable electrode feeding.

The electrode drive motor must have ample power to drive the wire at a uniform speed. Wire passages must be free of sharp bends or discontinuities and perfectly aligned. Grooved drive rolls are preferred over serrated rolls as they do not mark the wire. The grooves must be perfectly aligned, and there should be a minimum of friction or eccentricity. Drive roll pressure is critical, and means for accurate and fixed adjustment must be provided. Drive rolls should be located as close to the arc as practical, thus affording a minimum electrode wire column to the tip of the contact tube to assure good transfer of current at the end of the tube. Wire straighteners are sometimes used to reduce

*Gas Metal-Arc Welding*/**39**

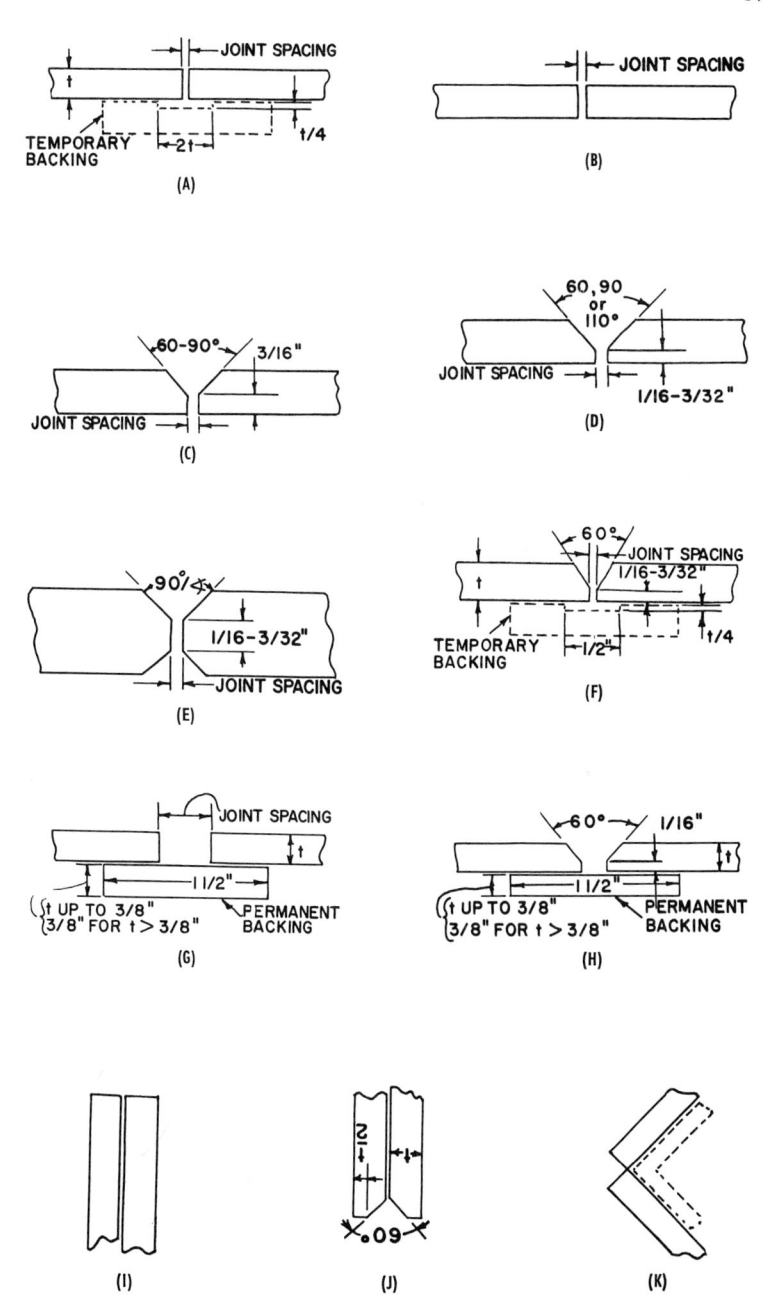

Fig. 69.22.—Recommended joint designs for the gas metal-arc and gas tungsten-arc welding of aluminum (see Tables 69.14, 16 and 18). Joints shown in (C), (D), (E) and (F) should be backchipped to solid weld metal before applying the root pass

## 40/Gas Metal-Arc Welding

**Table 69.15—Approximate fillet and lap welding procedures for the gas metal-arc welding of aluminum**

| Metal Thickness (Inches)* | Weld Position† | Weld Passes‡ | Electrode Diameter (Inches) | DC (Amps) | Arc Voltage (Volts) | Argon Gas Flow (Cfh) | Arc Travel Speed (Ipm) | Approximate Electrode Consumption (lb./100 feet) |
|---|---|---|---|---|---|---|---|---|
| 3/32 | F, V, H, O | 1 | 0.030 | 100–130 | 18–22 | 30 | 24–30 | 1.8 |
| 1/8 | F<br>V, H<br>O | 1<br>1<br>1 | 0.030–3/64<br>0.030<br>0.030–3/64 | 125–150<br>110–130<br>115–140 | 20–24<br>19–23<br>20–24 | 30<br>30<br>40 | 24–30<br>24–30<br>24–30 | 2<br>2<br>2 |
| 3/16 | F<br>H, V<br>O | 1<br>1<br>1 | 3/64<br>0.030–3/64<br>0.030–3/64 | 180–210<br>130–175<br>130–190 | 22–26<br>21–25<br>22–26 | 30<br>35<br>45 | 24–30<br>24–30<br>24–30 | 4.5<br>4.5<br>4.5 |
| 1/4 | F<br>H, V<br>O | 1<br>1<br>1 | 3/64<br>3/64<br>3/64–1/16 | 170–240<br>170–210<br>190–220 | 24–28<br>23–27<br>24–28 | 40<br>45<br>60 | 24–30<br>24–30<br>24–30 | 7<br>7<br>7 |
| 3/8 | F<br>H, V<br>O | 1<br>3<br>3 | 1/16<br>1/16<br>1/16 | 240–300<br>190–240<br>200–240 | 26–29<br>24–27<br>25–28 | 50<br>60<br>85 | 18–25<br>24–30<br>24–30 | 17<br>17<br>17 |
| 3/4 | F<br>H, V<br>O | 4<br>4–6<br>10 | 3/32<br>1/16<br>1/16 | 360–380<br>260–310<br>275–310 | 26–30<br>25–29<br>25–29 | 60<br>70<br>85 | 18–25<br>24–30<br>24–30 | 66<br>66<br>66 |

\* Metal thickness of 3/4 in. or greater for fillet welds sometimes employs a double vee bevel of 50 deg. or greater included vee with 3/32 to 1/8 in. land thickness on the abutting member.
† F = Flat; V = Vertical; H = Horizontal; O = Overhead.
‡ Number of weld passes and electrode consumption given for weld on one side only.

## Gas Metal-Arc Welding / 41

**Table 69.16—Typical butt welding procedure for the gas tungsten-arc welding of aluminum***

| Aluminum Thickness, Inch | Weld Position† | Edge Preparation‡ | Joint Spacing, (Inch) | Preheat,§ °F | Weld Passes | Filler Diameter, (Inch) | Electrode Diameter, (Inch) | Cup Diameter, Inch | Argon (cfh) | A-C (Amps) | Arc Travel Speed (Ipm) | Approximate Wire Consumption (lb./100 feet) |
|---|---|---|---|---|---|---|---|---|---|---|---|---|
| 1/16 | F, V, H | B | 0–1/16 | None | 1 | 3/32 | 1/16–3/32 | 3/8 | 20 | 70–100 | 8–10 | 0.5 |
|  | O | B | 0–1/16 | None | 1 | 3/32 | 1/16 | 3/8 | 25 | 60–75 | 8–10 | 0.5 |
| 3/32 | F | B | 0–3/32 | None | 1 | 1/8 | 3/32–1/8 | 3/8 | 20 | 95–115 | 8–10 | 1 |
|  | V, H | B | 0–3/32 | None | 1 | 3/32–1/8 | 3/32–1/8 | 3/8 | 20 | 85–110 | 8–10 | 1 |
|  | O | B | 0–3/32 | None | 1 | 3/32–1/8 | 3/32–1/8 | 3/8 | 25 | 90–110 | 8–10 | 1 |
| 1/8 | F | B | 0–1/8 | None | 1–2 | 1/8 | 1/8 | 7/16 | 20 | 125–150 | 10–12 | 2 |
|  | V, H | B | 0–3/32 | None | 1–2 | 1/8–5/32 | 1/8 | 7/16 | 20 | 110–140 | 10 | 2 |
|  | O | B | 0–3/32 | None | 1–2 | 1/8–5/32 | 1/8 | 7/16 | 25 | 115–140 | 10–12 | 2 |
| 3/16 | F | D–60° | 0–1/8 | None | 2 | 5/32–3/16 | 5/32–3/16 | 7/16–1/2 | 25 | 170–190 | 10–12 | 4.5 |
|  | V | D–60° | 0–3/32 | None | 2 | 5/32 | 5/32 | 7/16 | 25 | 160–175 | 10–12 | 4.5 |
|  | H | D–90° | 0–3/32 | None | 2 | 5/32 | 5/32 | 7/16 | 25 | 155–170 | 10–12 | 5 |
|  | O | D–110° | 0–3/32 | None | 2 | 5/32 | 5/32 | 7/16 | 30 | 165–180 | 10–12 | 6 |
| 1/4 | F | D–60° | 0–1/8 | None | 2 | 3/16 | 3/16–1/4 | 1/2 | 30 | 220–275 | 8–10 | 8 |
|  | V | D–60° | 0–3/32 | None | 2 | 3/16 | 3/16 | 1/2 | 30 | 200–240 | 8–10 | 8 |
|  | H | D–90° | 0–3/32 | None | 2–3 | 5/32–3/16 | 5/32–3/16 | 1/2 | 30 | 190–225 | 8–10 | 9 |
|  | O | D–110° | 0–3/32 | None | 2 | 3/16 | 3/16 | 1/2 | 35 | 210–250 | 8–10 | 10 |
| 3/8 | F | D–60° | 0–1/8 | Optional up to 350°F Max. | 2 | 3/16–1/4 | 1/4 | 5/8 | 35 | 315–375 | 8–10 | 15.5 |
|  | F | E | 0–3/32 |  | 2 | 3/16–1/4 | 3/16–1/4 | 5/8 | 35 | 340–380 | 8–10 | 14 |
|  | F | D–60° | 0–3/32 |  | 3 | 3/16 | 3/16–1/4 | 5/8 | 35 | 260–300 | 8–10 | 19 |
|  | V, H, O | E | 0–3/32 |  | 2 | 3/16 | 3/16–1/4 | 5/8 | 35 | 240–300 | 8–10 | 17 |
|  | H | D–90° | 0–3/32 |  | 3 | 3/16 | 3/16–1/4 | 5/8 | 35 | 240–300 | 8–10 | 22 |
|  | O | D–110° | 0–3/32 |  | 3 | 3/16 | 3/16–1/4 | 5/8 | 40 | 260–300 | 8–10 | 32 |

\* See also "Recommended Practices for Gas Shielded-Arc Welding of Aluminum and Aluminum Alloy Pipe," AWS D10.7-60.
† F = Flat; V = Vertical; H = Horizontal; O = Overhead.
‡ Refer to Fig. 69A.18.
§ Preheating at excessive temperatures or for extended periods of time will reduce weld strength. This is particularly true for alloys in heat-treated tempers.

## 42/Gas Metal-Arc Welding

**Table 69.17—Typical fillet and lap welding procedures for the gas tungsten-arc welding of aluminum**

| Aluminum Thickness (Inches) | Weld* Position | Preheat† °F | Weld Passes | Filler Diameter (Inches) | Electrode Diameter Inches | Gas Cup Diameter (Inches) | Argon Flow (cfh) | A-C (Amps) | Arc Travel Speed (Ipm) | Approximate Wire Consumption (lb./100 feet) |
|---|---|---|---|---|---|---|---|---|---|---|
| 1/16 | F, H, V | None | 1 | 3/32 | 1/16–3/32 | 3/8 | 16 | 70–100 | 8–10 | 0.5 |
|  | O | None | 1 | 3/32 | 1/16–3/32 | 3/8 | 20 | 65–90 | 8–10 | 0.5 |
| 3/32 | F | None | 1 | 3/32–1/8 | 1/8–5/32 | 3/8 | 18 | 110–145 | 8–10 | 1 |
|  | H, V | None | 1 | 3/32 | 3/32–1/8 | 3/8 | 18 | 90–125 | 8–10 | 1 |
|  | O | None | 1 | 3/32 | 3/32–1/8 | 3/8 | 20 | 110–135 | 8–10 | 1 |
| 1/8 | F | None | 1 | 1/8 | 1/8–5/32 | 7/16 | 20 | 135–175 | 10–12 | 2 |
|  | H, V | None | 1 | 1/8 | 3/32–1/8 | 3/8 | 20 | 115–145 | 8–10 | 2.5 |
|  | O | None | 1 | 1/8 | 3/32–1/8 | 7/16 | 25 | 125–155 | 8–10 | 2 |
| 3/16 | F | None | 1 | 5/32 | 5/32–3/16 | 1/2 | 25 | 190–245 | 8–10 | 4.5 |
|  | H, V | None | 1 | 5/32 | 5/32–3/16 | 1/2 | 25 | 175–210 | 8–10 | 5.5 |
|  | O | None | 1 | 5/32 | 5/32–3/16 | 1/2 | 30 | 185–225 | 8–10 | 4.5 |
| 1/4 | F | None | 1 | 3/16 | 3/16–1/4 | 1/2 | 30 | 240–295 | 8–10 | 7 |
|  | H, V | None | 1 | 3/16 | 3/16 | 1/2 | 30 | 220–265 | 8–10 | 9 |
|  | O | None | 1 | 3/16 | 3/16 | 1/2 | 35 | 230–275 | 8–10 | 7 |
| 3/8 | F | Optional 350°F Maximum | 2 | 3/16 | 1/4 | 5/8 | 35 | 325–375 | 8–10 | 17 |
|  | V |  | 2 | 3/16 | 3/16–1/4 | 5/8 | 35 | 280–315 | 8–10 | 20 |
|  | H |  | 3 | 3/16 | 3/16–1/4 | 5/8 | 35 | 270–300 | 8–10 | 20 |
|  | O |  | 3 | 3/16 | 3/16–1/4 | 5/8 | 40 | 290–335 | 8–10 | 17 |

* F = Flat; V = Vertical; H = Horizontal; O = Overhead.
† Preheating at excessive temperatures of extended periods of time will reduce weld-strength. This is particularly true for alloys in heat-treated tempers.

**Table 69.18—Typical edge and corner weld procedure for the gas tungsten-arc welding of aluminum**

| Metal Thickness (Inches) | Edge Preparation§ | Weld Passes | Filler Diameter (Inches) | Electrode Diameter (Inches) | Gas Cup Diameter (Inches) | Argon Flow (cfh) | A-C*‡ (Amps) | Arc Travel Speed (Ipm) | Approximate Wire† Consumption (lb./100 feet) |
|---|---|---|---|---|---|---|---|---|---|
| 1/16 | I, K | 1 | 3/32 | 1/16 | 3/8 | 20 | 60-85 | 10-16 | 0.5 |
| 3/32 | I, K | 1 | 1/8 | 3/32 | 3/8 | 20 | 90-120 | 10-16 | 1 |
| 1/8 | I, K | 1 | 1/8-5/32 | 1/8 | 3/8 | 20 | 115-150 | 10-16 | 2 |
| 3/16 | J, K | 1 | 5/32 | 5/32 | 7/16 | 25 | 160-210 | 10-16 | 4.5 |
| 1/4 | J, K | 2 | 3/16 | 3/16 | 1/2 | 30 | 200-250 | 8-12 | 7 |

\* Higher currents and welding speeds can be employed if a temporary backing is used for corner joints.
† For corner joints.
‡ Use low side of current range for horizontal and vertical welds.
§ Refer to Fig. 69A.18.

**44**/*Gas Metal-Arc Welding*

the cast in the electrode wire as it comes off its spool, and keep the electrode and arc directed properly.

Bent or spring-loaded contact tubes will provide most uniform electrical contact with the electrode, but straight contact tubes are equally satisfactory when of sufficient length and if the electrode wire retains zero pitch and a uniform cast after passing through the torch. When spool, drive rolls and electrode holder are suitably oriented and aligned, wire should feed uniformly without wandering.

## GAS TUNGSTEN-ARC WELDING

### ALTERNATING CURRENT

### *Characteristics of Process*

The welding of aluminum by the gas tungsten-arc welding process using alternating current produces an oxide cleaning action. Conventional a-c equipment with high current capacity and maximum arc stabilization is satisfactory for aluminum welding.

Argon shielding gas is used with the same precautions outlined in the previous section on gas metal-arc welding. The same importance is attached to the condition of the gas cup on the torch, but smaller cups are generally employed. (See Tables 69.16, 17 and 18). Either copper or ceramic cups are satisfactory, but copper is more rugged, easier to maintain, and may be used in smaller sizes. All torches used for this process should have their electrode holder designed so that the gas cups are electrically insulated from the electrode.

Better results are obtained when welding aluminum with alternating current by using equipment designed to produce a balanced wave or equal current in both directions. Unbalance will result in loss of power and a reduction in the cleaning action of the arc. Characteristics of a stable arc are the absence of snapping or cracking, smooth arc starting, and attraction of added filler to the weld puddle rather than a tendency to repulsion. A stable arc results in fewer tungsten inclusions.

Arc starting and reignition during welding is accomplished by superimposing high frequency current across the arc as a continuous pilot arc. This is usually done with a spark gap type oscillator with power output adjusted by the spark spacing or with high open-circuit voltage. The density of the arc must be relatively high for adequate gas ionization and to form a ready conductor to start the welding current flowing smoothly on the instant of current reversal. Means of achieving balanced flow are discussed in Chapter 29, Section 2.

Pure or zirconiated tungsten electrodes are satisfactory for welding aluminum with this process. The zirconiated electrode is less liable to electrode contamination by aluminum and has a slightly higher current rating. Thoriated tungsten electrodes are not generally recommended for welding aluminum with alternating current.

When welding aluminum the end of the electrode should be hemispherical as shown in Figure 69.23. Using an electrode one size larger than required for the welding current, and tapered, assists in maintaining this desired hemispherical molten end.

Fully automatic controls are effective in increasing welding output, quality of welds, and decreasing welding costs. For manual welding, a foot operated heat control is available on some power sources which helps in preventing craters, adjusting the current as the work heats up, or adjusting for change in section thickness.

## Welding Technique

For manual welding of aluminum with this process, the electrode holder is held in one hand and filler rod (if used) in the other. An initial arc is struck on a starting block to heat the electrode. The arc is then broken and reignited in the joint. This technique reduces the tendency for tungsten inclusions at the start of the weld, which may occur when starting the joint with a cold electrode. The arc is held at the starting point until the metal liquifies and a weld pool is established. Establishment and maintenance of a suitable weld pool is important and welding must not proceed ahead of the puddle.

If filler metal is required, it may be added to the front or leading edge of the pool, but to one side of the center line. Both hands are moved in unison, with a slight backward and forward motion along the joint. The tungsten electrode should not touch the filler rod and the hot end of the filler rod should not be withdrawn from the argon shield (Fig. 27.3, Chapter 27, Section 2).

A short arc length must be maintained to obtain sufficient penetration and avoid undercutting, excessive width of the weld bead, and consequent loss of control of penetration and weld contour. One rule is to use an arc length approximately equal to the diameter of the tungsten electrode.

The arc and puddle must be seen by the welder. Because this is more difficult with shorter arcs, the gas cup should be as small as possible while providing adequate shielding of the weld puddle.

The torch should be vertical to the center line of the joint, at a forehand angle of about 75-85 degrees from the plane of the work. When welding unequal sections the arc should be directed more toward the heavier section.

Welding speed and frequency of adding filler metal are governed by the skill of the welder. When using the correct current travel speed is higher with less heat dissipation into the part. This promotes progressive solidification and better weld bead control.

When the arc is broken, shrinkage cracks may occur in the weld crater, resulting in a defective weld. This defect can be prevented by gradually lengthening the arc while adding filler metal to the crater, quickly breaking and restriking the arc several times while adding additional filler metal into the crater, or by using a foot control to reduce the current at the end of a weld. Crater filling devices may be used if properly adjusted and timed.

When the electrode has been contaminated with aluminum it must be replaced or cleaned. Minor contamination can be burned off by increasing the current while holding the arc on a piece of scrap metal. Severe contamination can be removed on a grinding wheel or by breaking off the contaminated portion of the electrode and reforming the correct electrode contour on a piece of scrap aluminum. The arc should never be struck on a piece of carbon.

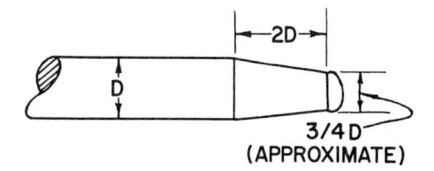

Fig. 69.23.—*Taper grinding of tungsten electrode for gas tungsten-arc welding of aluminum. Taper is ground and hemisphere is formed by welding for a few seconds at 20 amps excess current with electrode vertical*

## 46/Gas Tungsten-Arc Welding

Tacking before welding is helpful in controlling distortion. Tack welds should be of ample size and strength, and should be chipped out or tapered at the ends before welding over.

### Joint Designs

The joint designs in Figure 69.22 and in the accompanying Tables 69.16, 17 and 18 are applicable to the gas tungsten-arc welding process with minor exceptions. Inexperienced welders who cannot maintain a very short arc may require a wider edge preparation, included angle or joint spacing.

Joints may be fused with this process without the addition of filler metal if the base metal alloy also makes a satisfactory filler alloy. Edge and corner welds are rapidly made without addition of filler metal and have a good appearance, but a very close fit is essential. Such joints are not recommended in 6061, 6063, 3004 or similar alloys that tend to hot-shortness.

### Welding Variables

Welding variables for the gas metal-arc welding process apply to the gas tungsten-arc welding process, except those related to feeding the electrode wire. Proper gas shielding is indicated by a bright silvery band bordering each side of the weld bead and a bright shiny bead. Poor cleaning action may be caused by an unstable arc, low welding current, incomplete gas shielding or an abnormally long arc. Correct welding procedures combined with welding equipment capable of providing a stable arc results in excellent control of the welding operation and good wetting of the base metal by the advancing molten weld puddle.

### Automatic Welding

Automatic gas tungsten-arc welding is a direct mechanization of the manual technique. Manual or special machine welding electrode holders are mounted and the work moved past them, or the holder is moved uniformly along the joint by mechanical means. Automatic gas tungsten-arc welding usually employs shorter arc lengths, higher welding current and travel speed, and achieves deeper penetration than manual welding. Additional gas tungsten-arc welding electrode holders may be installed for cleaning or preheating in advance of the main welding arc.

If filler metal is used to fuse joint edges it is normally added mechanically by cold wire feed units. Joint fitup, joint cleanliness and filler metal cleanliness must be stressed when machine welding with this process. Weld contamination by dirty joint edges or burrs will appear as voids in the weld. Joint edge cleaning must be thorough and should immediately precede welding.

Portable equipment such as shown in Figure 69.24 is commercially available for field use in gas metal-arc, gas tungsten-arc and stick electrode welding, along with power tools for preparation and finishing of surfaces.

## DIRECT CURRENT, STRAIGHT POLARITY

### Characteristics of Process

Formerly d-c straight polarity (DCSP) current was considered unsuitable for welding aluminum because of the absence of any arc cleaning action. Today this process, using helium and thoriated tungsten electrodes has proved

## Gas Tungsten-Arc Welding / 47

*Fig. 69.24.—Portable equipment for use with gas metal-arc, gas tungsten-arc and stick electrode welding*

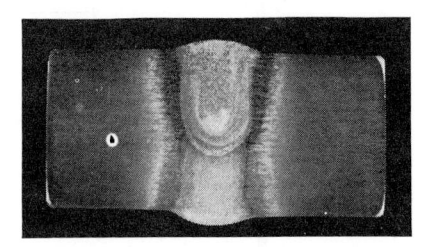

*Fig. 69.25.—Typical weld contour for gas tungsten-arc weld in aluminum with DCSP*

advantageous for many automatic welding operations, especially in the welding of heavy sections. Since there is less tendency to heat the electrode, smaller electrodes can be used for a given welding current which will contribute to keeping the weld bead narrow. The use of d-c straight polarity (DCSP) provides a greater heat input than can be obtained with a-c current. Greater heat is developed in the weld pool which is consequently deeper and narrower (Fig. 69.25).

The greater heat input produces rapid melting of the base metal and excellent penetration. It is not necessary to preheat before welding even heavy sections, and edge preparation can be eliminated or the groove reduced in size so that less filler metal is required. As the heating rate is more rapid with DCSP the welding puddle is formed immediately and there is less distortion of the base metal.

The surface appearance of d-c straight polarity welds differs from a-c current welds and welders accustomed to a-c aluminum welding expect to see clean bright metal on the weld surface during welding. Using DCSP, the weld surface is dulled by a film which is easily removed by light wire brushing. The surface oxide does not indicate lack of fusion, porosity, or inclusions in the weld.

As there is no arc cleaning action, thorough preweld cleaning of the base metal is very necessary. This normally involves chemical cleaning plus scraping or filing of the joint area.

## Joint Designs

The joint designs illustrated in Fig. 69.26 are applicable to the automatic gas tungsten-arc (DCSP) welding process with minor exceptions. For manual DCSP the concentrated heat of the arc gives excellent root fusion. Root face

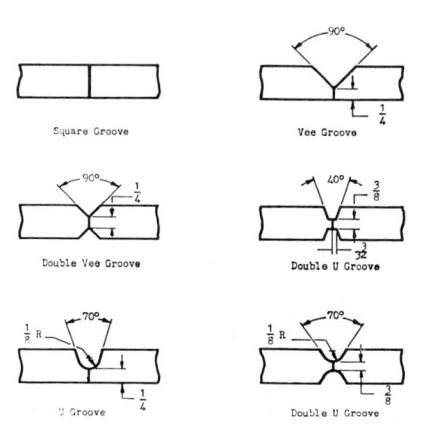

*Fig. 69.26.—Typical joint designs applicable to the DCSP gas tungsten-arc welding of aluminum*

**48**/*Gas Tungsten-Arc Welding*

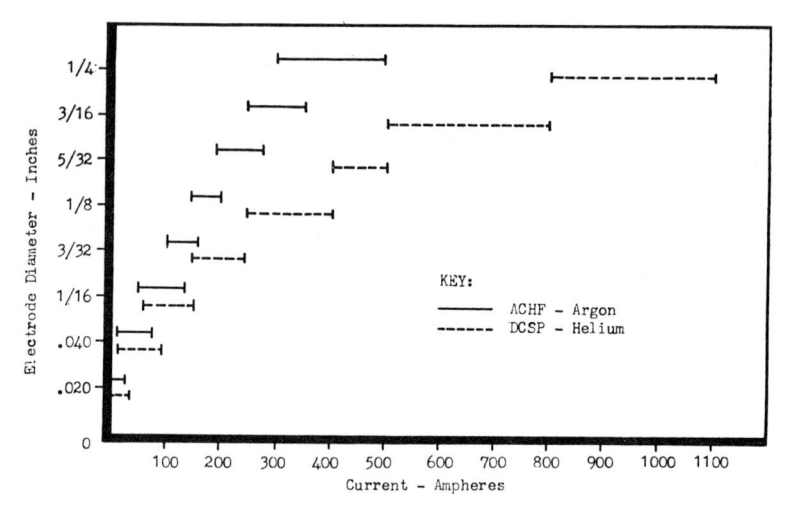

*Fig. 69.27.—Current range for standard tungsten electrodes with both DCSP and alternating current*

will be thicker, grooves narrower and build-up can be easily controlled by varying filler wire size and travel speed. The edge preparations and joint designs discussed and illustrated in this section have been established by production experience.

## Electrodes

Thoriated tungsten electrodes should be used as they withstand heat better and are less apt to be contaminated. Figure 69.27 shows current range for standard tungsten electrodes with both DCSP and alternating current while Fig. 69.28 covers thoriated tungsten electrodes.

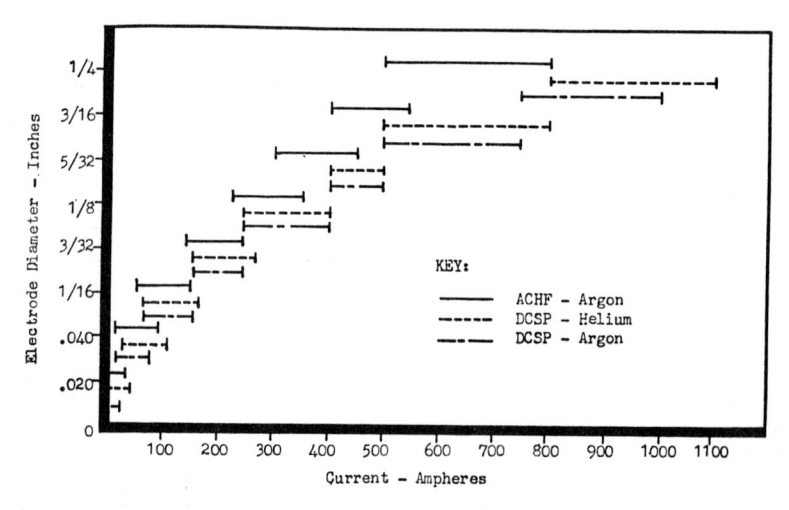

*Fig. 69.28.—Current range for thoriated tungsten electrodes with alternating current and DCSP*

## Manual Welding Technique

The technique for manual DCSP welding of aluminum is somewhat different than a-c welding of aluminum (Tables 69.19 and 69.20). It is advisable to use high frequency current to initiate the arc as touch starting will contaminate the tungsten electrode. It is not necessary to form a puddle as in a-c welding since melting occurs the instant the arc is struck. Care should be taken to strike the arc within the weld area to prevent undesirable marking of the material. Standard techniques such as run-out tabs and foot-operated heat controls are used. These are advantageous in preventing or filling craters, for adjusting the current as the work heats, and to adjust for a change in section thickness. In DCSP the torch movement and the feeding of filler rod differs from a-c welding. The torch is moved steadily forward in DCSP welding and the filler wire is fed evenly into the leading edge of the weld puddle or laid on the joint and melted as the arc moves forward. In all cases the crater should be filled to a point above the weld bead to eliminate crater cracks. The fillet can be controlled by varying filler wire size. DCSP welding is adaptable to repair work. Preheat is not required even for heavy sections and the heat-affected zone will be smaller with less distortion.

## Automatic Welding Technique

Special precision welding equipment has been designed for fully mechanized automatic welding with DCSP current (Tables 69.21 and 69.22). Since there is no preweld cleaning by arc action it is very important to clean the weld joint and adjacent area mechanically by methods such as scraping and draw filing. Modern equipment has up slope of current, start delay, wire feed start delay, prepurge, weld current, stop delay, wire feed stop delay, down slope of current, post purge, and may have a programmer to control head movement, current and voltage. Infrared penetration control is also available.

In welding square groove butt joints a very short arc is used with the tip of the tungsten electrode below the plate surface. Starting and stopping tabs are recommended on circumferential welds and craters should be filled and built-up 1/8 inch above the base metal to eliminate crater cracks.

With the proper machine schedule it is not necessary in most cases to use back-up bars when welding square groove butt joints from one side. In multi-pass V-groove welding the groove can be narrow and the root face thicker than in a-c welding.

Figure 69.29 shows a 33 foot diameter aluminum Y-ring being welded by the gas tungsten-arc welding process and DCSP.

## SQUARE WAVE AC WELDING

Square wave gas tungsten-arc welding with alternating current differs from conventional a-c balanced wave gas tungsten-arc welding in the type of welding current wave form used. With a square wave the time of current flow in either direction is adjustable from 20 to 1. In square wave gas tungsten-arc welding with alternating current there are the advantages of surface cleaning produced by positive ionic bombardment during the reversed polarity cycle, and the greater weld depth to width ratio, produced by the straight polarity cycle. Sufficient aluminum surface cleaning action has been obtained with a setting of approximately 10% DCRP and penetration equal to DCSP with 90% DCSP current.

**50**/*Square Wave AC Welding*

Table 69.19—Typical procedure for manual welding of butt joints in aluminum using the gas tungsten-arc welding process (DCSP)

| Metal Thickness, In. | Joint | Filler Rod Dia. (In.) | Thoriated Tungsten Electrode Dia. (In.) | Travel Speed, (ipm) | DSCP Current Amps | Arc Voltage, V | Helium Flow, cfh |
|---|---|---|---|---|---|---|---|
| 0.030 | Square groove 1 Pass | 3/64 | .040 | 17 | 20 | 21 | 20 |
| 0.040 | Square groove 1 Pass | 1/16 | .040 | 16 | 26 | 20 | 20 |
| 0.060 | Square groove 1 Pass | 1/16 | .040 | 20 | 44 | 20 | 20 |
| 0.090 | Square groove 1 Pass | 3/32 | 1/16 | 11 | 80 | 17 | 30 |
| 0.125 | Square groove 1 Pass | 1/8 | 1/16 | 16 | 118 | 15 | 20 |
| 0.250 | Square groove 1 Pass | 5/32 | 1/8 | 7 | 250 | 14 | 30 |
| 0.500 | 90° incl. angle bevel 1/4" nose 2 Passes | 5/32 | 1/8 | 5½ | 310 | 14 | 40 |
| 0.750 | 90° Double bevel 3/16" nose 2 Passes | 5/32 | 1/8 | 4 | 300 | 17 | 50 |
| 1 | 90° Double bevel 5 Passes | 1/4 | 1/8 | 1½ | 360 | 19 | 50 |

Notes: Helium is the recommended gas for DCSP gas tungsten-arc welding of aluminum.
1. Helium arc voltage is 40% greater than argon arc voltage per unit of arc length, resulting in a hotter arc, deeper penetration, greater travel speeds, and in some instances, minimization of heat effects on work.
2. For a given change in arc length the helium arc voltage changes more than the argon arc voltage. This makes possible more sensitive control of automatic welding with helium shielding gas.
3. Aluminum, because of its high thermal conductivity, requires the high rate of heat input which helium gas produces.

### Table 69.20—Typical procedure for manual fillet welds in aluminum using the gas tungsten-arc process (DSCP)

| Plate Thickness, Inches | Weld Position | Filler Rod Diameter, Inches | Fillet Size, Inches | Travel Speed In. per Min. | Arc Voltage | DCSP Current, Amps | Thoriated Tungsten Electrode Dia., In. | Helium* Flow, Cu Ft/Hr |
|---|---|---|---|---|---|---|---|---|
| .090 | Horizontal | 3/32 | 1/8 | 21 | 14 | 130 | 3/32 | 40 |
| .125 | Horizontal | 3/32 | 1/8 | 18 | 14 | 180 | 3/32 | 40 |
| .250 | Horizontal | 5/32 | 3/16 | 15 | 14 | 255 | 1/8 | 40 |
| .250 | Vertical | 5/32 | 3/16 | 10 | 14 | 230 | 1/8 | 40 |
| .375 | Horizontal | 1/4 | 5/16 | 7 | 14 | 290 | 1/8 | 50 |
| .375 | Horizontal | 5/32 | 3/16 | 14 | 14 | 335 | 1/8 | 50 |
| .500 | Horizontal | 1/4 | 5/16 | 7 | 16 | 315 | 1/8 | 50 |
| .500 | Vertical | 1/4 | 5/16 | 6 | 16 | 315 | 1/8 | 50 |

* Nozzle diameter ½ inch.

**52**/*Square Wave AC Welding*

Table 69.21—Typical procedures used for automatic welding of square butt joints in 2219 Al using the DCSP gas tungsten-arc welding process

| Metal Thickness, In. | Welding Position | Filler Wire 1/16 In. Dia. Wire Feed, (ipm) | Thoriated Tungsten Electrode Dia. In. | Travel Speed ipm | Current DCSP Amps | Arc Voltage Volts | Helium cfh |
|---|---|---|---|---|---|---|---|
| 0.250 | F V 2 Passes H one side | 36 | 1/8—0.100 TIP | 8 10 | 145 135 | 11.5-12.5 | 100 |
| 0.375 | F 2 Passes V one side H | 32 | 1/8—0.100 TIP | 8 10 | 220 180 | 11.5-12.5 | 120 |
| 0.500 | V 2 Passes H one each side | 10 10 | 1/8—0.100 TIP | 8 | 250 | 11.5-12.5 | 100 |
| 0.625 | V 2 Passes H one each side | 5-7 5-7 | 1/8—0.100 TIP | 7 | 300 | 11.5-12.5 | 120 |
| 0.750 | V 2 Passes H one each side | 5-7 5-7 | 1/8—0.100 TIP | 6 | 340 | 11.5-12.5 | 125 |
| 0.875 | V 2 Passes H one each side | 4-6 4-6 | 5/32—0.125 TIP | 5 | 385 | 11.5-12.5 | 125 |
| 1.000 | V 2 Passes H one each side | 3-5 3-5 | 3/16—0.156 TIP | 4 | 425 | 11.5-12.5 | 120 |

## Square Wave AC Welding / 53

Table 69.22—Typical procedure for automatic welding square butt joints in aluminum using the gas tungsten-arc process (DCSP)*

| Metal Thickness, Inches | Filler Wire Feed,† In. per Min. | Travel Speed‡ In. per Min. | Current, Amps | Filler Wire Diameter, Inches | Arc Voltage (Volts) | Helium Flow, Cu Ft/Hr |
|---|---|---|---|---|---|---|
| 0.041 | 60 | 54 | 65 | 1/16 | 14 | 30 |
| 0.090 | 75 | 54 | 180 | 1/16 | 13 | 30 |
| 0.125 | 55 | 40 | 240 | 1/16 | 11 | 30 |
| 0.250 | 40 | 15 | 350 | 1/16 | 11 | 30 |
| 0.375 | 30 | 8 | 430 | 1/16 | 11 | 40 |

\* Direct current straight polarity, thoriated tungsten electrodes.
† Automatic wire feed.
‡ Flat position, single pass welds.

### JOINT GEOMETRY

Square wave a-c welding offers substantial savings in weld joint preparation, over convential a-c balanced wave gas tungsten-arc welding. Smaller V-grooves, U-grooves and a thicker root face can be used and the greater depth to width weld ratio is conducive to less weldment distortion, more favorable welding residual stress distribution and less use of filler wire. With some slight modification the same joint geometry can be used as in DCSP gas tungsten-arc welding.

### WELDING TECHNIQUE

The welding technique is very similar to conventional a-c welding. It is necessary to have either superimposed high frequency or high open circuit voltage as the arc is extinguished every half cycle as the current decays toward zero and must be re-started each time. Thoriated tungsten electrodes should be used with this process and they should be precision shaped as in DCSP welding. Argon should be used to start the arc and can be used as the shielding gas but helium will give deeper penetration. A combination of the two gases may be used with the application deciding the shielding gas to be used.

This process is in the development stage and welding parameters will have to be developed for each application.

*Fig. 69.29.—Aluminum Y-ring, 33 ft in diameter, being welded by the gas tungsten-arc welding process with DCSP*

# GAS WELDING

Gas welding was one of the earliest processes used in welding aluminum and is still used for welding products such as aluminum cooking utensils and furniture, where smoothness and appearance are important. The equipment for gas welding is simple, relatively inexpensive and highly portable. A flux is used to remove the oxide coating on the aluminum. All flux residues must be removed after welding to prevent corrosion.

The most commonly used gas welding processes for use on aluminum and aluminum alloys are oxyacetylene and oxyhydrogen. Natural gas and propane are also used for groove welding although speed is decreased.

Standard torches, hoses and regulators are suitable for welding aluminum and aluminum alloys. This equipment is described in more detail in Chapter 23, Section 2.

Aluminum from about 1/32 to 1 inch thick may be gas welded. Heavier material is seldom gas welded as heat dissipation is so rapid that it is difficult to apply sufficient heat to melt the metal with a torch. Tip sizes, gas pressures and filler rod sizes for welding various thicknesses of aluminum are given in Table 69.23.

Hydrogen may be burned with oxygen in the same tips used with acetylene, but flame temperature is lower and larger tip sizes are necessary. Oxyhydrogen welding permits a wider range of gas pressures than acetylene without losing the desired, slightly reducing flame.

When gas welding, the freezing rate of the weld metal is very slow compared with arc welding. The heat input in gas welding is not as concentrated as in the other welding processes and may result in greater distortion unless precautions are taken. Minimum distortion is obtained with edge or corner welds.

## EDGE PREPARATION

Sheet or plate edges must be properly prepared to obtain gas welds of maximum strength. Edges are usually prepared the same as for similar thicknesses of steel. However, on thin material up to 1/16 inch thick the edges can be formed to a 90° flange about the same height as the thickness of the material or higher. The flanges prevent excessive warping and buckling and serve as filler metal during welding. Welding without filler rod is normally limited to the pure aluminum alloys, since weld cracking can occur in the higher strength alloys. In gas welding thicknesses over 3/16 inch the edges should be bevelled to secure complete penetration. The included angle of bevel may be 60° to 120°.

After the edges of the pieces have been properly prepared, the surface to be welded should be cleaned of grease, oil, and dirt. This may necessitate the use of solvent to complete the cleaning. If the edges are heavily oxidized it may be necessary to use a chemical or mechanical cleaning means, such as a clean rustfree wire brush.

Tack welds are placed 1 to 2 inches apart on materials up to 1/16 inch thick, depending upon the length of seam. This spacing can be increased proportionately up to about 10 inches on material 3/8 inch thick and over.

Preheating of the parts is recommended for all castings and plate 1/4 inch thick or over to avoid severe thermal stresses, insure good penetration and satisfactory welding speeds. Common practice is to preheat to a temperature

*Gas Welding*/**55**

**Table 69.23—Approximate conditions for gas welding of aluminum**

| Metal Thickness, In. | Filler rod diameter, In. | Oxy-hydrogen ||| Oxyacetylene |||
|---|---|---|---|---|---|---|---|
| | | Diameter of orifice in tip, In. | Oxygen pressure, psi | Hydrogen pressure, psi | Diameter of orifice in tip, In. | Oxygen pressure, psi | Acetylene pressure, psi |
| 0.032 | 3/32 | 0.045 | 1 | 1 | 0.035 | 1 | 1 |
| 0.064 | 3/32 | 0.065 | 2 | 1 | 0.045 | 2 | 2 |
| 0.081 | 1/8 | 0.075 | 2 | 1 | 0.055 | 3 | 3 |
| 0.125 | 1/8 or 5/32 | 0.095 | 3 | 2 | 0.065 | 4 | 4 |
| 0.250 | 3/16 | 0.105 | 4 | 2 | 0.075 | 5 | 5 |
| 0.325 | 3/16 | 0.115 | 4 | 2 | 0.085 | 5 | 5 |
| 0.375 | 3/16 | 0.125 | 5 | 3 | 0.095 | 6 | 6 |

of 300° to 500°F. Thin material should be warmed with the welding torch prior to welding. Even this slight preheat helps to prevent cracks. Heat treated alloys such as 6061-T6 should not be preheated above 300°F unless they are to be postweld heat treated. Pyrometric equipment or temperature indicating crayons should be used to check the preheat temperature.

### WELDING FLAME

A neutral or slightly reducing flame is recommended for welding aluminum for greatest speed and economy and to assure a sound weld. Oxidizing flames will cause the formation of aluminum oxide, resulting in poor fusion and a defective weld.

### FILLER MATERIAL

Filler alloys 1100, 1260 and 4043 may be used for gas welding.

Other filler metals, with the exception of some cast filler alloy rods, are

**Table 69.24—Methods for flux removal after welding or brazing aluminum**

| Method | Procedure | Rinse |
|---|---|---|
| Nitric-hydrofluoric cleaning | Immerse part for 3 to 5 minutes in cold acid.<br>1 gal. technical nitric acid (58-62% $HNO_3$) (39.5°Be)<br>½ pt. technical hydrofluoric acid (48% HF) (1.15 Sp.Gr.)<br>9 gal. water | Water rinse— hot or cold |
| Sulfuric cleaning | Immerse part for 10 to 15 minutes in cold acid or 4 to 6 minutes in acid held at 150°F.<br>1 gal. technical sulfuric acid (93% $H_2SO_4$) (66°Be)<br>19 gal. water | Water rinse— hot or cold |
| Nitric cleaning | Immerse part for 5 to 10 minutes in cold acid.<br>1 gal. technical nitric acid (58-62% $HNO_3$) (39.5° Be)<br>1 gal. water | Water rinse— hot or cold |
| Nitric-dichromate cleaning | Immerse part 5 to 10 minutes in hot acid.<br>1 pt. technical nitric acid (58-62% $HNO_3$) (39.5° Be)<br>14 oz. sodium dichromate ($Na_2Cr_2O_2$)<br>1 gal. water | Water rinse— hot or cold |

Note: To check effectiveness of flux removal, drops of distilled water may be placed on the part where flux is suspected. This is collected and dropped into a small tube containing a 5% silver nitrate solution. A white precipitate indicates the presence of flux.

not recommended for gas welding because of their susceptibility to cracking during welding. The recommended filler rod sizes ofr various thicknesses of aluminum are given in Table 69.23.

## WELDING FLUXES

Aluminum welding flux is designed to remove the aluminum oxide film and exclude oxygen from the vicinity of the weld pool.

Aluminum flux is generally in powder form. It is best prepared by mixing the powder with water to form a thin, freely flowing paste. The paste should be kept in aluminum, glass or earthenware vessels rather than steel or copper containers, as these metals tend to contaminate the mixture. The rod should be uniformly fluxed either by dipping or painting. It can be advantageous to apply flux to the prepared edges of the sheet or plate to prevent additional oxidation of these surfaces during the preheating and welding operations.

Care must be taken to remove all traces of adhering flux after welding. Common methods of removing flux after gas welding aluminum are shown in Table 69.24.

## WELDING TECHNIQUE

After the material to be welded has been properly prepared, fluxed, and preheated, the flame is passed in small circles over the starting point until the flux melts. The filler rod should be scraped over the surface at three or four second intervals permitting the filler rod to come clear of the flame each time. The scraping action will reveal when welding can be started without overheating the aluminum. After the flux melts, the base metal must be melted before the filler rod is applied.

Forehand welding is generally considered best for the welding of aluminum since the flame points away from the completed weld and thus preheats the area to be welded. In welding thin aluminum there is little need to impart any motion to the torch other than progressing forward.

On material 3/16 inch thick and over, the torch should be given a uniform lateral motion in order to distribute the weld metal over the entire width of the weld. A slight back and forth motion will assist the flux in oxide removal. The filler rod should be dipped into the weld puddle periodically and withdrawn from the puddle with a forward motion. This method of withdrawal closes the puddle, prevents porosity and assists the flux in removing the oxide film. If multiple passes are required, it is desirable to remove the slag after each pass with the oxyacetylene method. This is not necessary, however, for oxyhydrogen gas welding.

## SHIELDED METAL-ARC WELDING

In the shielded metal-arc welding process, a heavy dip or extruded flux-coated electrode (generally of 1100 or 4043 alloy) is used with DCRP. The flux coating (1) provides a gaseous shield around the arc and molten aluminum puddle (2) chemically combines and removes the aluminum oxide, forming a slag.

When welding aluminum, the process is rather limited due to arc spatter, erratic arc control, limitations on thin material and the corrosive action of the flux if it is not removed properly. Applications for this process are generally

## Shielded Carbon-Arc Welding/57

Table 69.25—Approximate conditions for shielded metal-arc and manual shielded carbon-arc welding of aluminum

| Metal Thick-ness, In. | Electrode or Filler Metal Diameter, In. | Approxi-mate Current, Amp* | Number of Passes || Approximate Filler metal consumption, lbs/100 ft. |||
|---|---|---|---|---|---|---|---|
| | | | Butt | Fillet | Butt | Lap | Fillet |
| 0.081 | 1/8 | 60 | 1 | 1 | 4.7 | 5.3 | 6.3 |
| 0.102 | 1/8 | 70 | 1 | 1 | 5.0 | 5.7 | 6.3 |
| 0.125 | 1/8 | 80 | 1 | 1 | 5.7 | 6.3 | 6.3 |
| 0.156 | 1/8 | 100 | 1 | 1 | 6.3 | 6.5 | 6.5 |
| 0.188 | 5/32 | 125 | 1 | 1 | 8.7 | 9.0 | 9.0 |
| 0.250 | 3/16 | 160 | 1 | 1 | 12 | 12.0 | 12.0 |
| 0.375 | 3/16†, 1/4‡ | 200 | 2 | 3 | 25 | 29.0 | 35.0 |
| 0.500 | 3/16†, 1/4‡ | 300 | 3 | 3 | 35 | 35.0 | 35.0 |
| 1.00 | 5/16 | 450 | 3 | 3 | 130 | 150.0 | 150.0 |
| 2.00 | 5/16 or 3/8 | 550 | 8 | 8 | 400 | 450.0 | 450.0 |

\* Direct current reverse polarity (DCRP) for shielded metal-arc welding. Direct current straight polarity (DCSP) for shielded carbon arc welding.
† For fillet welds.
‡ For butt welds.

limited to minor repair work; plants doing small amounts of welding; and when welding material of 1/8 inch or heavier.

Approximate currents and electrode diameters for welding various thicknesses of aluminum are shown in Table 69.25.

## SHIELDED CARBON-ARC WELDING

The shielded carbon-arc welding process can be used in joining aluminum. It requires flux and produces welds of the same appearance, soundness, and structure as those produced by either oxyacetylene or oxyhydrogen welding. Shielded carbon-arc welding is done both manually and automatically. A carbon arc is used as a source of heat while filler metal is supplied from a separate filler rod. Flux must be removed after welding.

Manual shielded carbon-arc welding is usually limited to a thickness of less than 3/8 inch and is accomplished by the same method used for manual carbon-arc welding of other material. Joint preparation is similar to that used for gas welding. A flux covered rod is used. Filler rod sizes and welding currents shown in Table 69.25 for shielded metal-arc welding are also approximately correct for manual shielded carbon-arc welding.

## ATOMIC HYDROGEN WELDING

This welding process consists of maintaining an arc between two tungsten electrodes in an atmosphere of hydrogen gas. The process can be either manual or automatic with procedures and techniques closely related to those used in oxyacetylene welding. Since the hydrogen envelope or shield surrounding the base metal excludes oxygen, smaller amounts of flux are required to combine or remove aluminum oxide, visibility is very good, there are fewer flux inclusions and a very sound metal is deposited.

More detailed information on the atomic hydrogen welding process and equipment is given in Chapter 26 and 29, Section 2. Table 69.26 indicates approximate conditions for atomic hydrogen welding of aluminum.

**Table 69.26—Approximate conditions for atomic-hydrogen arc welding of aluminum***

| Thickness, In. | Electrode Size In. | Current, Amp | Filler Rod Diameter, In. |
|---|---|---|---|
| 1/16 to 1/8 | 1/16 | 20–25 | 3/32 |
| 1/8 to 3/16 | 1/16 | 25–35 | 1/8 |
| 3/16 to 3/8 | 1/16 or 1/8 | 35–40 | 1/8 or 5/32 |
| 3/8 to 5/8 | 1/8 | 40–50 | 3/16 |
| 5/8 to 3/4 | 1/8 | 60–80 | 3/16 or 1/4 |

\* To obtain maximum welding speeds, sections 3/8 in. or more in thickness may be preheated. Sections lighter than 3/8 in. in thickness are rapidly heated by the welding arc, and preheating is not ordinarily advantageous.

## STUD WELDING

Aluminum stud welding may be accomplished with conventional electric-arc stud welding equipment or using either the capacitor discharge or drawn arc capacitor discharge techniques. Stud welding processes are described in detail in Chapter 51, Section 3.

The conventional electric arc stud welding process may be used to weld aluminum studs 3/16 to 3/4 inch diameter. The necessary equipment consists of a portable or fixed welding gun, a control unit (timing device), aluminum studs, expendable ceramic ferrules or shields, and a d-c power supply capable of supplying a given high current for a short time at a minimum open circuit voltage of 70 to 80 volts; either argon or helium shielding gas may be used.

The aluminum stud welding gun is modified slightly, as compared to the gun used for welding steel studs, by the addition of a special adapter for the control of the high purity shielding gases used during the welding cycle. An added accessory control for controlling the plunging of the stud at the completion of the weld cycle adds materially to the quality of weld and reduces spatter loss. Reverse polarity is used, with the electrode gun positive and the ground work negative. A small cylindrical or cone shaped projection on the end of the aluminum stud initiates the arc and helps establish the longer arc length required for aluminum welding. Alloys 1100, 4043, 5056, 5356 and 6061 are the most commonly used stud alloys. Approximate stud welding factors are listed in Table 69.27 based on the welding gun unit equipped with the plunge control accessory.

The unshielded capacitor discharge or drawn arc capacitor discharge stud welding processes are used with aluminum studs 0.062 to 1/4 inch diameter. Capacitor discharge welding uses a low-voltage electrostatic storage system in which the weld energy is stored at a low voltage in capacitors with high capacitance as a power source.

In the capacitor discharge stud welding process a small tip or projection on the end of the stud is used for arc initiation. The drawn arc capacitor discharge stud welding process uses a stud with a pointed or slightly rounded end and does not require a serrated tip or projection on the end of the stud for arc initiation. In both cases the weld cycle is similar to the conventional stud welding process. However, use of the projection on the base of the stud provides most consistent welding.

The short arcing time of the capacitor discharge process limits the melting so that shallow penetration of the workpiece results. The minimum aluminum work

## Table 69.27—Typical aluminum gas shielded stud welding procedures

| Stud Diameter, in. | Stud Alloy | Time (Cycles) | Current DCRP | Lift, in. | Plunge, in. | Gas Flow† cfh |
|---|---|---|---|---|---|---|
| 3/16 | 4043<br>5356* | 12 | 200 | 3/32 | 1/8–3/16 | 15 |
| 1/4 | 4043<br>5356* | 15 | 250 | 3/32 | 1/8–3/16 | 15 |
| 5/16 | 4043<br>5356* | 20 | 370 | 3/32 | 1/8–3/16 | 15 |
| 3/8 | 4043<br>5356* | 25 | 540 | 3/32 | 1/8–3/16 | 20 |
| 7/16 | 4043<br>5356* | 30 | 570 | 3/32 | 1/8–3/16 | 20 |
| 1/2 | 4043<br>5356* | 43 | 640 | 3/32 | 1/8–3/16 | 20 |

\* 5056 alloy employs the same welding procedures as 5356 alloy.
† Argon or Helium.

thickness considered practical is 0.032 inch. Stud alloys commonly used with these processes are 1100, 4043, 5056, 5356 and 6061.

## ELECTRON-BEAM WELDING

Electron-beam welding is a fusion-joining process in which the workpiece is bombarded with a dense stream of high-velocity electrons, and virtually all of the kinetic energy of the electrons is transformed into heat upon impact (Chapter 54, Section 3).

Electron-beam welding usually takes place in an evacuated chamber. The chamber size is the limiting factor on the weldment size. Conventional arc and gas heating melt little more than the surface. Further penetration comes solely by conduction of heat in all directions from this molten surface spot, thus the fusion zone widens as it deepens. The electron-beam is capable of such intense local heating that it almost instantly vaporizes a hole through the entire joint thickness. The walls of this hole are molten and as the hole is moved along the joint, more metal on the advancing side of the hole is melted. This flows around the bore of the hole and solidifies along the rear side of the hole to make the weld. The intensity of the beam can be diminished to give a partial penetration with the same narrow configuration.

## Table 69.28—Strength of electron-beam welds in some aluminum alloys, transverse weld properties

| Alloy and Temper | Tensile Strength, ksi | Yield Strength .2% Offset 2 in. gage Length, psi x 1000 | Elongation in 2 in., % | Joint Efficiency, % |
|---|---|---|---|---|
| 6061–T4<br>(Postweld Aged to T62) | 40 | .. | .. | 88 |
| 5083–H321<br>(As Welded) | 48 | 36 | .. | 90 |
| 2219–T81<br>(As Welded) | 51 | 39 | 8 | 78 |
| 7075–T6<br>(As Welded) | 51 | 43 | .. | 67 |
| 7075–0<br>(Postweld Heat Treated to T62) | 70 | 60 | .. | 92 |

# 60/Electron-Beam Welding

**Table 69.29—Electron-beam weld settings for several aluminum alloys and thicknesses**

| Material | Thickness, In. | Weld Type | Accelerating Voltage, kv | Beam Current, ma | Welding Speed, ipm | Energy Kilojoules, ............ |
|---|---|---|---|---|---|---|
| 6061-T6 | 0.050 | Sq. Butt | 18.0 | 33 | 100 | 0.36 |
| 2024-T6 | 0.050 | Sq. Butt | 27.0 | 21 | 71 | 0.48 |
| 2014-T6 | 0.120 | Sq. Butt | 29.0 | 54 | 75 | 1.26 |
| 6061-T6 | 0.125 | Sq. Butt | 26.0 | 52 | 80 | 1.03 |
| 7075-T6 | 0.125 | Sq. Butt | 25.0 | 80 | 90 | 1.33 |
| 2219-T81 | 0.500 | Sq. Butt | 30.0 | 200 | 95 | 3.97 |
| 6061-T6 | 0.625 | Sq. Butt | 30.0 | 275 | 75 | 6.60 |
| 5086-H34 | 2.000 | Sq. Butt | 30.0 | 500 | 36 | 25.00 |
| 2219-T87 | 2.375 | Sq. Butt | 30.0 | 1000 | 43 | 41.80 |
| 5456-H343 | 6.000 | Sq. Butt | 30.0 | 1025 | 7 | 263.00 |

Electron-beam welding is generally applicable to edge, butt, fillet, melt-through lap and arc-spot welds. Filler metal is rarely used except for surfacing.

Electron-beam welds are characteristically deep, straight sided, and very narrow. Higher joint efficiencies and reduced distortion may be obtained and shrinkage is reduced (Table 69.28). Figure 54.10 in Section 3 illustrates the weld results, in the same material and thickness, produced by electron beam and by gas tungsten-arc welding.

Most aluminum alloys can be electron-beam welded, but some difficulty may be experienced with cracking in some of the heat treatable alloys such as 6061, 2024 and 7075. The thickness that can be welded with a given heat input varies widely. Thus a given machine may be capable of welding 5 inches of alloy 5083, but only 2 inches of alloy 2219.

## JOINT DESIGN

Square butt joints have been used up to 6 inch thickness. Fit-up of parts may be critical due to the characteristically narrow welds produced by this welding process. In welding thick sections in a single pass it is desirable to maintain the same weld width through the thickness to ensure good root fusion and minimize defects. In some instances this may result in undercutting or a depressed weld face. A second surfacing pass with or without filler may then be utilized to obtain a good bead contour.

## WELDING TECHNIQUE

Initial relative positions of the heat source and the joint must be accurately established as correct initial position is essential to maintain the correct relation between the gun and the work during the welding operation. Typical variables for the electron-beam process are given in Table 69.29.

# ARC CUTTING

## GAS TUNGSTEN ARC CUTTING

All cast or wrought aluminum alloys can be severed using the gas tungsten arc cutting process. This process is described in detail in Section 3, Chapter 48.

Both manual and mechanized cutting torches are available. Aluminum is cut commercially in thicknesses from 1/8 to 5 inches with the gas tungsten arc. The arc cut surfaces are fairly smooth and normally free of contamination. Superior cuts can be made with automatic equipment.

*Arc Cutting*/**61**

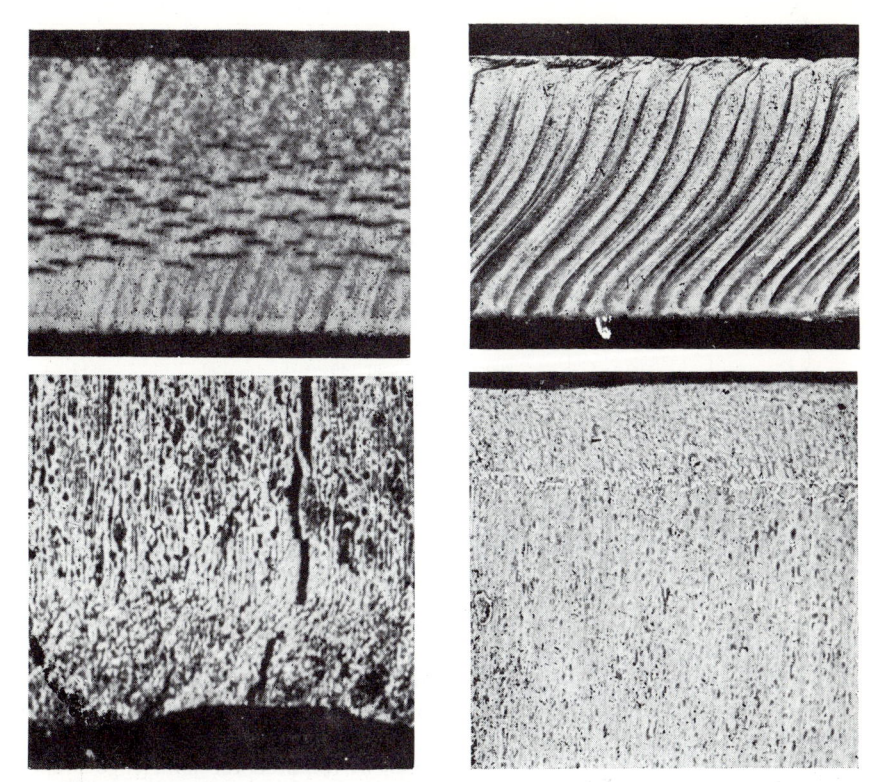

*Fig. 69.30.—(top left) Face of arc-cut heat-treatable aluminum (3X); (lower left) Cross section of arc-cut heat-treatable alloy showing melted zone and heat-affected zone (100X); (top right) Face of arc-cut nonheat-treatable aluminum (3X); (lower right) Cross section of arc cut in nonheat-treatable aluminum (100X)*

The metallurgical effect of arc cutting aluminum varies on the heat-treatable and the nonheat-treatable alloys, as shown in Fig. 69.30. A shallow melted zone forms on the cut surface and partial melting occurs, depending on the alloy.

The tendency for cracking to occur increases with plate thickness and cutting speed. Thicker plates impose a greater restraint on the solidifying metal at the kerf wall and may cause shrinkage cracks. Higher cutting speeds produce a steeper thermal gradient at the face of the cut and therefore generate greater thermal stress.

On the nonheat-treatable alloys the cut surface remains sound and uncracked. Shallow shrinkage cracks may develop when cutting the heat-treatable alloys. An empirical formula has been developed to predict conditions under which cracking might occur in heat-treatable alloys. The formula is $ST=K$, where $S$ is the cutting speed in inches per minute, $T$ is the plate thickness in inches and $K$ is a constant value below which cracking does not occur. The relationship $ST=40$ works well. Thus, a cutting speed for producing a crack-free cut in a 1 in. thick plate of heat-treatable aluminum alloy is determined by dividing the constant (40) by the thickness in inches (1) to obtain 40 inches per minute.

The heat-affected zone next to an arc-cut surface may display reduced

# 62/Arc Cutting

**Table 69.30—Gas tungsten-arc cutting conditions for aluminum**

| Plate Thickness, In. | Travel Speed, In. per min | Current, Amps (DCSP) | Arc Voltage, Volts | Gas Flow,* Cu Ft per Hr | Orifice Diameter, In. |
|---|---|---|---|---|---|
| *Manual Cutting* | | | | | |
| 1/4 | 60 | 200 | 50 | 50 | 1/8 |
| 1/2 | 40 | 280 | 55 | 60 | 5/32 |
| 1 | 20 | 330 | 70 | 70 | 5/32 |
| 2 | 20 | 400 | 85 | 100 | 5/32 |
| *Machine Cutting* | | | | | |
| 1/4 | 300 | 300 | 60/140 | 120 | 1/8 |
| 1/2 | 200 | 300 | 70/140 | 120 | 1/8 |
| 1 | 90 | 375 | 160 | 120 | 5/32 |
| 2 | 20 | 375 | 165 | 120 | 5/32 |
| 3 | 15 | 425 | 170 | 200 | 5/32 |
| 4 | 12 | 450 | 180 | 200 | 3/16 |
| 5 | 10 | 475 | 200 | 200 | 3/16 |

\* Manual Cuts: 80% argon—20% hydrogen gas mixture
Mechanized Cuts: 65% argon—35% hydrogen or
70% nitrogen—30% hydrogen gas mixture

corrosion resistance in the case of high-strength, heat-treatable alloys such as 2014, 2024, and 7075.

Arc cutting of odd-shaped parts or blanks of aluminum can reduce costs as has the use of flame cutting in the fabrication of steel. Stack cutting is also possible.

Not only irregular shapes, but bevels such as required for joint edge preparation, are easily made by arc cutting. Internal holes can also be cut out of sheets, plates or castings. Cuts can be made in the vertical, overhead and flat positions.

Arc cutting does not contaminate the cut edge as do machining methods using a cutting fluid or a lubricant. For higher quality or code quality welding the oxide should be removed from the cut edge prior to welding. Any of the normal ways of oxide removal may be used.

Typical gas tungsten arc cutting conditions are given in Table 69.30.

## GAS METAL-ARC CUTTING

Standard gas metal-arc welding equipment can be used for cutting aluminum. A mild steel wire electrode is generally used, but an aluminum electrode can be used for thickness up to 3/8 inch.

The shielding gas may be pure argon, helium or special mixtures. Argon with 1% oxygen addition usually gives the best quality cut.

During the cutting operation, the electrode extends through the material with its tip just even with the far side. The arc emanates sideways from the electrode, which assumes a tapered shape in the kerf area as it is fed continuously by the gun (Fig. 69.31).

Settings of current, voltage, wire speed and travel speed will affect the rate at which the electrode wire is consumed. These variables should be adjusted

*Arc Cutting*/**63**

*Fig. 69.31.—View of kerf in 1/2 inch thick aluminum plate being cut by the gas metal-arc cutting process using 3/32 inch diameter steel wire. Note that the wire melts in a tapered manner, and is completely consumed at a point level with the lower surface of the plate*

so that the tip of the wire is just flush with the far side of the work during normal operation. Typical cutting conditions are shown in Table 69.31.

The cut usually is started with the wire protruding from the barrel, extending slightly below the lower surface of the plate and about 1/4 inch away from the leading edge of the plate. The travel, wire feed, current, water flow, and gas flow are all started simultaneously. If the cut is to begin in the middle of a piece, the electrode wire can be extended through a drilled hole in the material.

Cut edges are sharp, but drag lines on the face of a cut may be pronounced. Sides of the cut are usually almost parallel. The bottom of the kerf tends to be slightly wider than the top. The cut edges produced by this process are ordinarily not as smooth as those made by the gas tungsten-arc cutting process.

## SHOP PRACTICES

### EDGE PREPARATION

Aluminum materials may be prepared for welding by mechanical or thermal cutting processes. Preweld dressing of surfaces and edges is generally necessary to provide proper weld conditions and to facilitate fit-up. Correct preparation of aluminum for welding is essential in producing quality welds that are uniform and economical. Cleanliness of the weld and proper joint fit-up greatly influence weld quality.

**64**/*Shop Practices*

### Table 69.31—Approximate conditions for gas metal-arc cutting*

| Plate Thickness, Inches | Current, Amps | Gas Flow†, Cu Ft/Hr | Wire Diameter, Inches | Wire Speed, In. Per Min. | Travel Speed, In. per Min. |
|---|---|---|---|---|---|
| \multicolumn{6}{c}{90 Degree Manual Cuts} |
| 1/4 | 830 | 20 | 3/32 | 360 | 75 |
| 3/8 | 850 | 20 | 3/32 | 390 | 68 |
| 1/2 | 850 | 20 | 3/32 | 390 | 56 |
| \multicolumn{6}{c}{90 Degree Machine Cuts} |
| 1/8 | 360 | 10 | 1/16 | 267 | 96 |
| 1/4 | 880 | 20 | 3/32 | 370 | 144 |
| 3/8 | 900 | 20 | 3/32 | 380 | 93 |
| 1/2 | 900 | 20 | 3/32 | 380 | 72 |
| 3/4 | 1200 | 20 | 3/32 | 475 | 47 |
| 1 | 1600 | 20 | 3/32 | 880 | 40 |

* Arc voltage will vary according to the type of power source. Suggested starting points are: 1/4 in.— 21 v; 3/4 in.—29 v.

† Shielding gas: argon plus 1% oxygen for all thicknesses except 1/8 in., where argon only was used.

The thermal cutting processes are fully covered in Chapter 48 Section 3. Most of the standard mechanical processes for metal working may also be used in preparing aluminum for welding.

Aluminum may be easily machined at high speeds. Milling and routing are often used for preparing aluminum edges for welding. The cutting tool can be shaped to the desired edge contour and extremely high speeds up to 25,000 rpm may be employed. Templates or guides may be used to direct the tool, especially when preparing irregularly shaped joints. Portable hand rotary planers of the woodworking type are useful for fitting preparations and weld finishing.

Aluminum sheet and plate may be cut by shearing or sawing. Shearing of aluminum plate up to 1/2 inch thick is possible. Oil or grease embedded in the sheared edges can contaminate the weld deposit and for this reason the shear blades should be kept in good condition. Sawing of aluminum calls for comparatively coarse teeth, free from rough surfaces or sharp corners. Special saw teeth for aluminum will give best results. Saw tooth spacing may vary from 3 to 12 per inch, with the finer tooth spacing being used for thin stock. Guided circular saws, jig saws and band saws may be used, the selection depending upon material thickness and the application. When sawing, the rate of feed and speed should be such as to keep the saw blade cutting at all times, as this reduces the heat generation and increases the life of the blade. As for most mechanical material removing processes, soluble oil solutions may be used as a coolant and lubricant if it is required. Lubricating compounds can cause porosity and should be removed from the joint area prior to welding. Portable electric or air driven circular saws similar to those used on wood are commonly used on aluminum.

Manual methods of edge preparation include chipping with a pneumatic gun, filing and grinding with power tools. Chipping is more often used for removal of defective areas (back-chipping) or for finishing of seams after welding. The chipping tool should have a much greater rake angle than similar tools used on ferrous materials and round-nosed chisels should be spoon-shaped to assist in lifting the metal being removed (see Fig. 69.32). Files for general purpose use on aluminum have deep, curved, single cut, coarse teeth, set about ten to

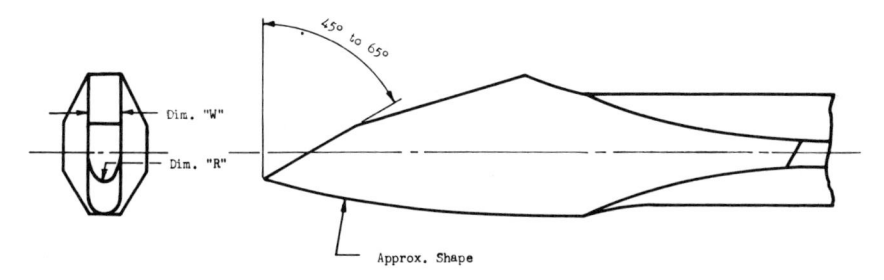

*Fig. 69.32.—Typical chisel configuration for chipping aluminum*

the inch, which furnish chip clearance and side rake for good slicing action and self cleaning. Loaded files can be cleaned by wire-brushing or by dipping in 20% hot caustic soda solution followed by a water rinse. Portable hand grinding may be used for edge preparation of aluminum, but is more generally used to remove weld reinforcements and for removing defective welds. Grinding wheels and discs in general use for aluminum are of coarse grit, open structure and a comparatively soft grade. Special reinforced bonded wheels are now available for safe, high-speed power tool operations. For high quality welding, care should be taken to eliminate all contamination of the prepared joint.

## PREWELD CLEANING AND OXIDE REMOVAL

The cleanliness of weld joint surfaces is very important for all aluminum welding processes. Specialized procedures for specific processes other than fusion welding are covered in the sections on the individual processes.

Moisture, grease, oil films, thick oxides, fume condensates, or other foreign materials on the edges to be joined can cause welds of poor quality. These contaminants release hydrogen and other gases which become entrapped in the weld deposit and cause porosity that may affect weld strength and ductility.

The melting point of the normal oxide film on aluminum is about 3700°F, as contrasted to about 1200°F for pure aluminum. Unless this oxide is properly removed before or broken-up during welding, this temperature differential can allow the aluminum to melt before the oxide film, thus preventing proper coalescence between the deposited filler metal and the base material. The entrapped oxide may reduce weld ductility and form metallurgical notches or cold laps. Surface oxides should be removed to obtain high quality welds. Fusion welding should not be performed on anodically treated aluminum except when the condition is removed from the joint area to be welded.

Degreasing for removal of soils and contaminants may be done with commercial solvents by wiping, spraying, dipping, vapor degreasing, steam cleaning and hot water rinse. Stencil identification marks may be removed with commercial solvents such as paint thinner, acetone or alcohol. The cleaning and welding area must be extremely well ventilated. Harmful gases can be created by the breakdown of some solvents by arc radiation. Due to health hazards, many plants oppose the use of certain materials.*

A simple but effective method of cleaning the weld joint area is to wipe the edges with a clean cloth which contains alcohol or acetone. Caution should be

---

* See AWS Recommended Practices for Inert-Gas Metal-Arc Welding, AWS A6.1-58.

# 66/Shop Practices

**Table 69.32—Chemical treatments\* for oxide removal prior to welding or brazing aluminum**

| Type of Solution | Concentration | Temperature | Type of Container | Procedure | Purpose |
|---|---|---|---|---|---|
| Technical grade Nitric Acid | 50% water<br>50% nitric acid, technical grade | Room | Stainless Steel-347 | Immersion 15 min. Rinse in cold water. Rinse in hot water & dry. | For removing thin oxide film for fusion welding. |
| 1. Sodium Hydroxide (caustic soda) followed by | 1. 5% | 1. 160°F | 1. Mild Steel | 1. Immersion 10–60 seconds. Rinse in cold water. | Removes thick oxide film for all welding and brazing processes. |
| 2. Technical grade Nitric Acid | 2. Concentrated (use as received) | 2. Room | 2. Stainless Steel-347 | 2. Immerse for 30 seconds. Rinse in cold water. Rinse in hot water & dry. | |
| Sulfuric-Chromic | $H_2SO$ —1 gal.<br>$CrO_3$ —45 oz.<br>water —9 gal. | 160–180°F | Antimonal Lead-lined steel tank | Dip for 2-3 min. Rinse in cold water. Rinse in hot water & dry. | For removal of heat-treatment & annealing films and stains & for stripping oxide coatings. |
| Phosphoric-Chromic | $H_3PO_3$(75%) 3.5 gal.<br>$CrO_4$—1.75 lbs.<br>water—10 gal. | 200°F | Stainless Steel-347 | Dip for 5-10 min. Rinse in cold water. Rinse in hot water & dry. | For removing anodic coatings. |

\* There are many proprietary materials and methods available for removing aluminum oxides. Most of these are as efficient as the preparations listed.

used in disposing of used cleaning cloths as they may burn readily. Welding should not be performed after the degreasing operation until the weld joint surfaces are completely free of any residue.

Chemical removal of aluminum oxide may be accomplished through the use of caustic soda, acids and proprietary solutions. A few chemical treatment procedures for aluminum oxide removal in preparation for welding are given in Table 69.32.

Mechanical methods for removing oxide coatings from weld joint surfaces include wire brushing, scraping, filing, rotary planing, sanding, or the use of steel wool. Cleaning by mechanical means, although not as consistent as chemical methods, is usually satisfactory if properly performed. Brushes of stainless steel are recommended because they are easier to keep clean. Motor-driven power brushes are preferred for their faster and more effective action. However, only light pressure should be applied to avoid imbedding foreign particles in the aluminum surface. Brushes are used that have bristles of approximate 0.005 to 0.015 inch diameter, with an overall diameter of 6 inches and a rotation range of 3000 to 3500 rpm. Loose wire from a brush or loose abrasive materials should be prevented from embedment in the weld joint as such foreign items may form inclusions and lead to corrosion or porosity.

Manual wire brushes are also used to good advantage. Manual or power driven wire brushes which have been used on other than aluminum materials should be properly cleaned before being used on aluminum. Periodic cleaning of wire brushes is recommended to lessen contamination. For highest quality multi-pass welds, wire brushing between passes is recommended to remove any films which may have formed. Contamination of weld joint surfaces by hands or gloves should be avoided. Material prepared for welding may be protected by using polyethylene bags or sheets or paper or other clean coverings as a deterrent to dust, fumes or other foreign materials.

## FIT-UP AND TACKING

Proper joint fit-up saves time and materials and aids in the production of high quality welds. Joint design has a great influence on fit-up. Joints designed to be self jigging may facilitate fabrication and can reduce the amount of weld metal to be deposited.

Tack welds may be used to hold the parts to be welded and to attach start and run-off tabs. Tack welds which burn through the joint may cause areas of porosity and incomplete fusion. For highest quality welding it is recommended that tack welds be removed as the welding progresses. If the tack welds are not removed each end of the tack may be chipped to taper the ends gradually to the base metal surface. Tack welds should be small and of sufficient number to maintain proper alignment of the parts. Slightly longer tack welds are usually required for aluminum than for steel. Tack weld craters should be filled and any tack that is cracked should be chipped out before welding is begun if quality welds are to be obtained.

## BACKUP

When aluminum is welded from one side only, some type of backup may be desirable to control penetration. The backup used with aluminum may be permanent, may be incorporated into the joint, may be removable or temporary, or may consist of an inert gas shield. The latter type is generally used with special tooling, although the gas may be fed into the backing groove when using a removable backup.

When permanent backing is to be left in place after welding, strips or extruded sections of aluminum may be used as the backing material. The use of permanent backups may sometimes lead to difficulty as lack of fusion may occur at the root of the weld if the backing material is not properly cleaned or if the fit-up is poor. Permanent backing should not be used in corrosive service unless all edges of the backups are completely welded and all possibilities of crevice corrosion are eliminated.

The removable type of backup is more widely used for aluminum. Backup bars may be made of steel, copper or stainless steel. When using copper care should be used not to contaminate the weld for if the arc burns through to the backup bar spots of aluminum-copper alloy may form which can develop into areas of brittle, corrosive sensitive materials. Grooves may be machined into the backup bar to assist in obtaining adequate root penetration. This groove should be shallow but wide enough so as not to confine the edges of the penetration bead. Grooves range in size from 1/8 to 1/2 inch wide and 0.010 to 3/32 inch deep.

Backup bars may be designed to provide a chilling effect at the root of the weld, thus reducing the heat-affected zone. Water-cooled copper bars give the greatest chill, and stainless steel backup the least. If the chilling effect is too severe thin asbestos paper is sometimes placed between the backup strip and the aluminum part, taking care that the paper does not protrude into the groove of the joint.

## BACK CHIPPING

Full penetration joints which require welding from both sides are generally back chipped to sound metal at the root of the deposited metal before welding the second side. This lessens the possibility of lack of fusion or linear porosity in the weld deposit. Pneumatic chisels are commonly used, although milling cutters, routers and shaping tools are sometimes employed. Chipping offers an advantage over the other methods of material removal as the metal chips removed by the chipping tool give an indication when sound metal has been reached. Care should be used to avoid bridging or covering up areas of incomplete fusion or other types of defects.

## SPECIAL TOOLING FIXTURES

Tooling is an important factor in producing high quality, reproducible welds in aluminum. Adequate jigging and fixturing will save time, reduce tacking requirements and provide better alignment of parts. Jigs should be designed for easy handling and locating of components, uniform clamping pressure for holding dimensions and accessibility for removing the finished weldment. Fixtures may be simple or as elaborate as required, depending upon the item to be welded and the quantity of items to be produced. Accuracy and quality of tooling will be reflected in the finished weldment produced.

## PREHEATING

Preheating of base materials is not generally required for gas metal-arc welding of nonheat treatable aluminum alloys. Preheat of heat treatable alloys may be of some benefit in welding. A preheat of 300°F is usually sufficient and higher preheats should only be used if a postweld heat treatment is to be used. When the use of industrial-type furnaces is not practical, lamps or torches may be used by experienced personnel. Preheating of aluminum castings usually necessitates reheat-treatment after welding to restore strength losses. Pyrometric instruments or temperature-indicating paints or crayons are often used to help control temperature.

If the temperature of the work falls below 32°F, preheating may be desirable. Preheat is commonly used to eliminate moisture from the metal surface in the weld area. When welding thick material by the gas tungsten-arc welding process, particularly material over 1/2 inch thick, some preheat may be beneficial. Preheating may be used to obtain adequate penetration on weld starts, without readjustment of current as welding progresses. Preheating may be necessary to prevent weld cracking in some of the heat-treatable alloys.

Preheat may be used to enhance the quality of the weld obtained by arc welding. Some preheating is always used in gas welding operations. In the lighter gages preheating is obtained from the welding torch while for thicker gages a separate source of heat is generally used.

## CONTROL OF DISTORTION

Because aluminum alloys have relatively high coefficients of thermal expansion as compared to most weldable metals, difficulties may be experienced with distortion whenever unequal expansion or contraction occurs. Distortion may occur during welding or in heat treating operations subsequent to welding. When metal is heated in a localized area, the cooler surrounding metal restrains the heated area, causing it to become distorted. Upon cooling, the restraint of the surrounding metal may result in distortion or buckling. Because of the rapid dissipation of heat by aluminum, the weld metal shrinkage is generally the major contributor to distortion in weldments. Molten aluminum will shrink about three times as much as a similar volume of steel weld metal.

Control of distortion is a matter of proper design, joint preparation and fit-up, choice of joining method and the use of a proper welding sequence. To minimize distortion, parts should be designed to require the least amount of welding. By avoiding excessively wide bevels and over-welding of fillets and by maintaining good fit-up, the amount of deposited weld metal will be reduced. Minimum distortion will result if the weld is located in a stiffened area such as an edge or corner. Welds should be located away from areas which have been severely cold worked, since welding may relieve the locked-in stresses and cause distortion.

Distortion can be minimized by using a welding process with a concentrated heat input, such as gas metal-arc welding, and by depositing an equal amount of weld metal on each side of the joint. Processes such as furnace and dip brazing can sometimes be used to advantage, as total heat input is sufficiently high to anneal the part, the heat is applied uniformly, and low distortion results.

Proper welding sequence is essential to avoid distortion. The following items are suggested for planning a welding sequence.

1. Plan to allow individual pieces and members some freedom of movement for as long as possible to prevent build-up of expansion and contraction forces
2. Joints with greatest contraction should be welded first.
3. Welding on both sides of a structure should progress simultaneously to balance contraction
4. Welds should be made from both sides of a structural member and successive passes should be alternated from one side to the other to equalize stresses
5. Once a weld pass has been started, it should be completed without interruption

The fabrication of aluminum subassemblies in rigid fixtures is common practice and aids in maintaining closer tolerances in the overall assembly. Most aluminum welds possess good ductility and smaller assemblies can be readily straightened. Stress relief of the 5000 series alloy weldments may be effected quite easily with little or no loss in properties by heating to 450° to 550°F for 15 minutes to 4 hours, depending on temperature used. This is usually more convenient on the smaller assemblies and is beneficial to stability during final machining operations.

When butt welding sheets a fixture such as a horn jig with hold-down chill bars clamped rigidly on both sides of the seam, and a stainless steel or water cooled copper back-up with a proper groove for complete penetration, will give a satisfactory, distortion-free weld. Where practical, planishing can be used to remove some locked-in stresses. In sheet metal fabrication, where chill bars cannot be clamped to dissipate heat, dry ice has been employed in isolating the weld zone and minimizing distortion.

## FINISHING AFTER WELDING

The surface of most weld beads usually has a good appearance and consequently does not require additional finishing. Some applications may require specific weld bead surface contour or the removal of all reinforcement to facilitate fit-up. Mechanical finishing may be done in these cases by the various processes previously described for edge preparation.

Chemical finishing such as etching, chemical brightening and various types of chemical conversion coatings may also be applied to weldments. Anodic treatments provide improved corrosion and wear resistance, as well as highly decorative finishes when used in conjunction with polishing or dyeing techniques. Objectionable color changes may result from anodic treatments. These may be minimized by reducing the extent of the weld heat-affected zone by using the most rapid available welding process, such as gas metal-arc or flash welding. Flash welding results in the narrowest heat-affected zone, thus flash-welded joints have good anodizing qualities. The least contrast between the weld heat-affected zone and the base metal after anodic treatment, is obtained with the nonheat treatable alloys, particularly when welded in the annealed condition. Furnace and dip brazing processes do not heat locally and the result is a uniform metal appearance.

Heat treatable alloys such as 6061 and 6063 are frequently used in architectural work, where they are often anodized after welding. The heat of welding causes precipitation of alloying constituents in these alloys. After anodic treatment the heat affected area may appear different from the remainder of the weld. This halo near the weld can be minimized by rapid welding and the use of chilled backup and hold-down bars, or may be avoided by giving the part a solution heat treatment after welding but before the anodic treatment.

Poor color match between the weld metal and the base metal is sometimes encountered in chemically treated weldments. Care must be taken in selecting the filler metal as its composition, particularly when silicon is an alloying constituent, has an effect on color match. Wherever possible it is recommended that welding be done in areas which will not be seen after anodic treatments, thus avoiding color match problems and allowing the use of filler metals with poorer finishing characteristics but better welding characteristics. Other joining processes which do not require heat may also be considered. Lap joints may be difficult to rinse after chemical treatment and should be avoided, since the acid employed can leach out in service. Many adhesive bonds cannot be employed before anodic treatments, but adhesive bonding can be used quite satisfactorily to assemble parts which have previously been treated.

## WELD DEFECTS

### CRACKING

Cracking in the weld metal or in the heat-affected zone is a major structural weld defect which may be found in welding aluminum and its alloys. Weld metal cracks are generally in crater or longitudinal form.

Crater cracks often occur when breaking the arc sharply, leaving a crater. Crater cracks may be detrimental if they are in a highly stressed area, and should be prevented by proper torch manipulation or use of filler metal and back fill technique. In automatic, as in manual welding, a run-off tab may be added at the end of the joint and the weld terminated on this block. Current control devices may be used to facilitate the filling of craters.

Longitudinal cracks in the weld metal are usually the result of incorrect weld metal composition or improper welding procedure. High stresses imposed during welding, particularly in restrained joints, may also cause a longitudinal crack by exceeding the strength of the weld metal if the weld bead is too small or too shallow or if the filler metal is of insufficient strength.

# Weld Defects/71

Cracking in the heat affected zone of the base material occurs primarily with the heat-treatable alloys. It is usually associated with eutectic melting or precipitation of brittle constituents at the grain boundaries. To overcome this condition use high welding speeds, processes minimizing heat input to the metal, and filler alloys with a lower melting point than the base metal.

To minimize heat-affected zone cracking, care should be taken to reduce the restraint imposed during welding and in cooling after welding. High welding speeds are beneficial and selection of filler alloy can be critical. Preheat is sometimes used. Heat-treatable alloys welded in the solution-treated condition are slightly less sensitive to this cracking when in the fully heat treated and aged condition.

## POROSITY

Gas pockets or voids in the weld metal are frequently observed in cross sections of fusion welded joints in aluminum. A small amount of porosity scattered uniformly throughout the weld has little or no influence on the strength of joints in aluminum. If clusters, or gross porosity are present this can adversely affect the weld joint. Various welding codes limit the amount and distribution of porosity acceptable.

Hydrogen is a major cause of porosity as it is very soluble in molten aluminum but has low solubility in solid aluminum. Thus hydrogen can be picked up by the molten weld pool during welding and released upon solidification. The presence of foreign materials such as moisture, oil, grease or heavy oxides in the weld area during welding can cause excessive porosity. In the heat-affected zone porosity generally arises from gas in base materials such as castings, but may also diffuse into the base material from the weld pool.

Other contributing factors that can cause gross porosity are improper voltage or arc length and improper or erratic wire feed in gas metal-arc welding causing a variable arc. Filler wire, contaminated either in its manufacture or shop handling, a leaky torch, moist or contaminated inert shielding gas or insufficient shielding gas when employed are all sources of porosity.

Since welding speeds in conjunction with good arc transfer are also associated with metal soundness, it may necessitate selecting a welding process with a proper solidification rate to aid in the reduction of porosity.

## INCOMPLETE FUSION

Incomplete fusion is defined as a failure to fuse adjacent layers of weld metal or weld metal to base metal. It may be detected by radiographic or ultrasonic inspection. If not oriented in a plane parallel to the X-ray beam however, it can be difficult to observe by radiography.

The major cause of incomplete fusion in aluminum welds is incomplete removal of the oxide film before welding or unsatisfactory cleaning between passes. The applied weld bead will usually have a dirty gray appearance when pre-weld or inter-pass weld cleaning is inadequate. Insufficient joint bevel or back-chipping, or improper amperage or voltage often contribute to incomplete fusion.

## INADEQUATE PENETRATION

Inadequate penetration occurs when the weld does not penetrate the full depth of a prepared joint or does not penetrate to indicated requirements in a tee joint. In both the butt and the tee joint inadequate penetration is generally caused by low welding current, improper filler metal size, improper joint preparation or excessive welding speeds for the current employed.

## INCLUSIONS

Inclusions in aluminum welds may be of two types: metallic and nonmetallic. In gas tungsten-arc welding the use of excessive current for a given electrode size will cause melting and deposition of tungsten in the weld. Improperly adjusted high frequency and rectification of the alternating current may also cause this defect. Tungsten inclusions can be attributed to weld starting with a cold electrode, by dipping the electrode into the molten pool, or by touching the filler rod to the electrode. Fine widely scattered particles of tungsten have little effect on the properties of a gas tungsten-arc weld; however, many codes require that welds be essentially free of this defect. Copper inclusions can occur in gas metal-arc welds as a result of a burn-back of the electrode to the contact tube. Copper inclusions cause a brittle weld and can be a serious corrosion hazard and should be removed from the weld deposit. Tungsten and copper inclusions may be detected visually and by radiographic examination since the high density of the tungsten causes it to appear as white spots on the X-ray film.

Improper use of wire brushes in cleaning the weld groove or cleaning between passes may also result in metallic inclusions if bristles from the wire brush become entrapped in the weld.

Nonmetallic inclusions are often the result of poor base metal cleaning when utilizing soldering or brazing procedures or when flux shielded metal-arc welding is improperly employed.

## REPAIR WELDING

Repair of defective welds is readily accomplished in all weldable wrought aluminum alloys. Weld defects often may be repaired with little or no effect in the weld structure in most cases. In the higher strength aluminum alloys such as the 2000 and 7000 series, the proper filler metal, welding process, and repair procedure must be employed.

The defective portion of a weld must be entirely removed for satisfactory repair. The pneumatic chipping hammer is usually the most expedient and economical device for removing defects. However, the accessibility of the area to be repaired is a governing factor. Disk sanding, manual grinding or machining is often used. The repair cavity must have smooth contours and be free of foreign matter. The ends of the repair cavity should be tapered gradually from the bottom of the groove to the outside surface.

The welding processes and filler metals used for repair welding are generally the same as those used for the original welding. Usually the welding current and voltage settings would also be similar to those originally used, however, somewhat higher currents may be used to assure proper penetration into the repaired area, with reduced currents during the final joint filling operation. Penetrant or X-ray inspection may be employed to assure the effectiveness of the repair.

## PROPERTIES AND PERFORMANCE OF WELDMENTS

Development of the gas shielded-arc welding processes has brought significant improvements in the performance of aluminum welds. These processes, which include gas tungsten-arc and gas metal-arc welding, have made welding a principal fabricating tool in the aluminum industry. They have made practical the use of higher strength filler metals and have permitted the welding of alloys not joinable by other fusion processes. Welds of increased strength and ductility have resulted.

The properties and performance of weldments may be influenced by many factors, including the composition, form and temper of the base material, the filler alloy used, the welding process, travel speed, rate of cooling, joint design and service environment. The effect of these and other variables should be considered. In many instances weldments are designed so that the welds are in noncritical areas and in case of an overload the assembly will fail at some other location. Most of the information given here applies to situations where the weld and adjacent metal are critical from the standpoint of strength and performance (Table 69.32A).

## METALLURGICAL EFFECTS OF WELDING

The properties and performance of aluminum parts are greatly influenced by microstructural changes that take place during the welding operation. An understanding of these changes is essential in predicting the properties and ultimate performance of the weldment.

When a fusion weld is made in aluminum two basic types of material must be considered. They are the weld metal which has a cast structure, and the base metal which may be wrought or cast. The properties of the cast aluminum in the weld zone are influenced by composition and rate of solidification. The rate of solidification of the weld metal depends upon the welding process and technique plus all the factors affecting heat input and transfer away from the molten pool. A higher rate of solidification generally produces a finer microstructure and greater strength.

The effects of welding upon aluminum-base metals vary with the distance from the weld and may be divided roughly into areas which reflect the temperature attained by the metal. The widths of these areas and their distance from the weld varies with the welding process, thickness or geometry of the part, and the speed of welding. Within each area or zone, certain microstructural changes take place upon welding which largely determine the as-welded properties of the alloy. The heat-affected zone in joints made by the gas shielded-arc welding processes rarely extends beyond two inches from the center line of the weld. From the standpoint of tensile properties the weakest point would be immediately adjacent to the weld. Gas welding usually affects a wider area. In the nonheat-treatable alloys there are usually three zones, as shown in Table 69.33.

An illustration of these zones in a cross section of a gas metal-arc weld in 5456-H321 aluminum is shown in Fig. 69.33. Very little change in microstructure can be noted in the base material.

The heat-treatable aluminum alloys contain alloying elements which exhibit a marked change in solubility with temperature change. These elements are very soluble in the aluminum at elevated temperature but have low solubility at room temperature. They tend to separate out as various microconstituents in the base metal structure. The high strengths of the heat-treatable alloys are due to the controlled solution and precipitation of some of these microconstituents. Conversely, most of the difficulties in welding these alloys are due to uncontrolled melting, solution and precipitation of some constituents.

**74**/*Properties and Performance*

Table 69.32A—Relative areas and weights of aluminum and steel structural members having equal strengths (steel—1.0)

| Alloy & Temper of Aluminum Sheet & Plate[3] | Thickness, In. | Minimum Mechanical Properties, Psi ||| | Tension Members Having Equal Tensile Yield Strengths[1] || Beams Having Equal Bending Strengths[1,2] || Plates Having Equal Bending Strengths[1,2] ||
| | | Base Metal || Across Butt Welds || | | | | | |
| | | Tensile Strength | Tensile Yield Strength[4] | Tensile Strength | Tensile Yield Strength[5] | Area of Aluminum vs Steel | Weight of Aluminum vs Steel | Area of Aluminum vs Steel | Weight of Aluminum vs Steel | Area of Aluminum vs Steel | Weight of Aluminum vs Steel |
|---|---|---|---|---|---|---|---|---|---|---|---|
| 3003–H14 | 0.009–1.000 | 20,000 | 17,000 | 14,000 | 7,000 | 1.9–4.7 | 0.70–1.65 | 1.6–2.8 | 0.55–1.00 | 1.4–2.2 | 0.50–0.75 |
| 5052–H34 | 0.009–1.000 | 34,000 | 26,000 | 25,000 | 13,000 | 1.3–2.5 | 0.45–0.85 | 1.2–1.9 | 0.40–0.65 | 1.1–1.6 | 0.40–0.55 |
| 5454–H34 | 0.020–1.000 | 39,000 | 29,000 | 31,000 | 16,000 | 1.1–2.1 | 0.40–0.70 | 1.1–1.6 | 0.40–0.55 | 1.1–1.4 | 0.35–0.50 |
| 5083–H113 | 0.188–1.500 | 44,000 | 31,000 | 40,000 | 24,000 | 1.0–1.4 | 0.35–0.48 | 1.0–1.2 | 0.35–0.44 | 1.0–1.2 | 0.35–0.41 |
| 5086–H34 | 0.020–1.000 | 44,000 | 34,000 | 35,000 | 19,000 | 1.0–1.7 | 0.35–0.60 | 1.0–1.4 | 0.35–0.50 | 1.0–1.3 | 0.35–0.45 |
| 5456–H321 | 0.126–1.250 | 46,000 | 33,000 | 42,000 | 26,000 | 1.0–1.3 | 0.35–0.45 | 1.0–1.2 | 0.35–0.40 | 1.0–1.1 | 0.35–0.40 |
| 6061–T6[6] | 0.010–5.000 | 42,000 | 35,000 | 24,000 | 17,000 | 0.9–1.6 | 0.35–0.58 | 1.0–1.4 | 0.35–0.49 | 1.0–1.3 | 0.35–0.45 |
| 6061–T6[7] | 0.010–5.000 | 42,000 | 35,000 | 42,000 | 35,000 | 0.9 | 0.35 | 1.0 | 0.35 | 1.0 | 0.35 |

[1] Lower figure in each column is based on yield strength of base metal. Higher figure in each column is based on yield strength across butt welds. Yield strength of steel is considered to be 33,000 psi.
[2] The aluminum and steel beams are considered to be of different sizes but to have similar cross sections, so that area is proportional to yield strength raised to the two-thirds power.
[3] The aluminum and steel plates are considered to have the same width but different thickness, so that area is proportional to the square root of the yield strength.
[4] Yield strength of base metal is measured at 0.2% offset in 2 inches or 4 diameters.
[5] Yield strength across butt welds corresponds to 0.2% offset in 10-in. gage length. These are approximate minimum values based on limited test data.
[6] Welded with 5356 or 5556 filler wire. Not heat treated after welding.
[7] Welded with 4043 filler wire, heat treated and aged after welding.

*Properties and Performance/* **75**

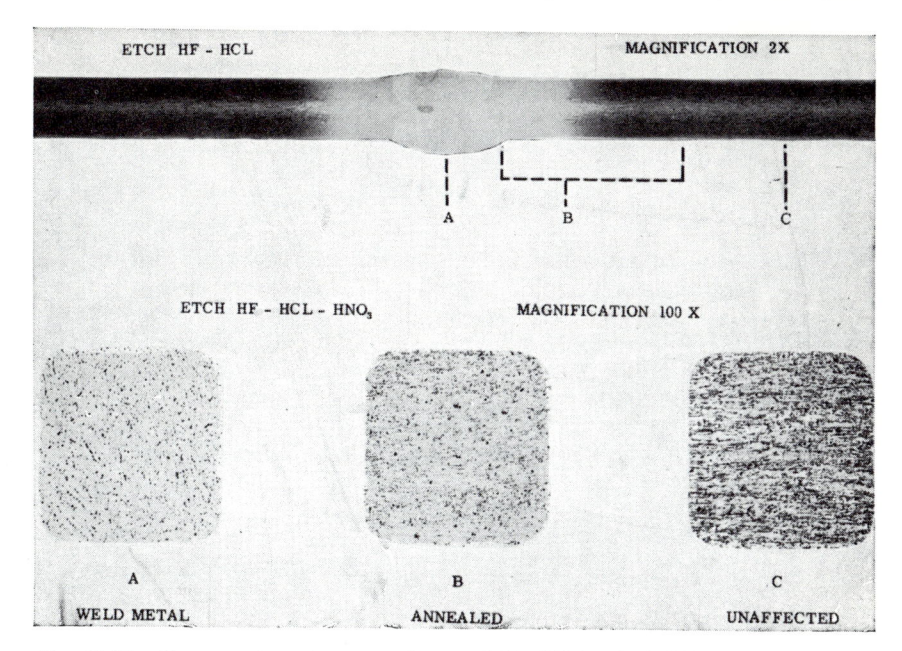

*Fig. 69.33.—Cross section of gas metal-arc weld in 3/8 in. thick 5456-H321 aluminum plate. Microstructures are shown in various zones*

The alloying elements in heat-treatable aluminum alloys are dissolved in the aluminum at high temperature by a process commonly known as solution heat treatment. They are maintained in solid solution by rapidly quenching from this temperature. The solution of specific elements or compounds in aluminum governs the strengths of these alloys in the as-quenched temper. Additional increases in strength are effected by precipitation of a portion of the soluble elements in finely divided form. Precipitation may take place at room temperature following quenching, or may be accelerated by a thermal treatment at a moderately elevated temperature, usually in the range of 210° to 350°F. Alloys susceptible to either of these precipitation treatments are designated as age-hardenable.

The influence that the heat of welding has on the microstructure of heat-treatable alloys is shown in Fig. 69.34. Many of the factors that affect the weldability of these alloys do so by changing the rate of heating or cooling, thereby directly influencing the microstructure.

Welds in the heat-treatable alloys generally exhibit five microstructural zones (Table 69.34).

The five zones noted are generally quite evident in welds made in the heat-treatable alloys in which copper or zinc are the major alloying constituents. An

**Table 69.33—Effect of welding on nonheat-treatable aluminum alloys**

| Zone | Description |
|---|---|
| Weld metal | Weld bead with as-cast structure where base metal is alloyed with weld metal. |
| Annealed zone | Region where heat from welding has caused recrystallization or annealing. |
| Unaffected | Region where heating has not affected the structure. |

**76**/*Properties and Performance*

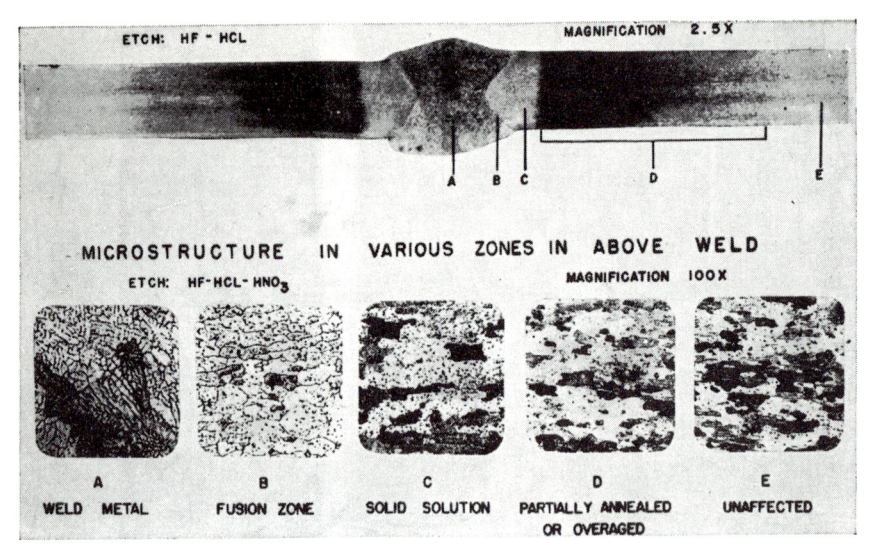

*Fig. 69.34.—Cross section of gas metal-arc weld in 3/8 in. thick 2014-T6 aluminum*

illustration of these zones in a cross-section of a gas tungsten-arc weld in 2219-T87 aluminum is shown in Fig. 69.35.

Alloys of the magnesium-silicon type such as 6061 exhibit microstructural changes in the heat-affected zone that are somewhat different from those observed with the above alloys. A cross section of a weld made in 6061-T4 and aged to T6 is shown in Fig. 69.36. The principal heat effect in 6061-T6 is generally overaging.

## STRENGTH AND DUCTILITY OF BUTT WELDS

The heat of welding decreases the strength of both heat-treatable and nonheat-treatable aluminum alloys, except in the annealed or as-cast condition. High welding speed and rapid weld cooling result in stronger joints with a narrower heat-affected zone particularly when welding the heat-treatable aluminum alloys. Weld strengths given in this section are with the weld bead reinforcement machined flush to the base material. Strength with the bead on may be somewhat higher.

## NONHEAT-TREATABLE ALLOYS

The nonheat-treatable alloys require a relatively short time at the annealing temperature to lose the effects of strain hardening. The heat of welding exceeds this temperature and the base material in the heat-affected zone adjacent to the weld generally reaches the annealed condition characterized by lowered strength and increased ductility. For this reason, in design calculations based on ultimate tensile strength, the minimum annealed tensile strength of the base metal is generally considered as the minimum strength of butt welds for the nonheat-treatable alloys.

The popularity of some of the aluminum-magnesium-manganese alloys such as 5083 and 5456, for use in welded construction is due to their high annealed strengths, as may be seen in Table 69.35. This table lists the average transverse weld strength, the minimum annealed strength used in design, and the average elongations for butt welds in the commonly welded nonheat-treatable alloys.

It may be noted that no temper designations are given for the nonheat-treatable alloys in Table 69.35. In general the weld properties of these alloys are much less affected by the base metal temper than the heat-treatable alloys. The same is generally true for the effect of metal thickness.

The excellent ductility exhibited by welds in the nonheat-treatable alloys is indicated by the high values of elongation. Weldments in these alloys are capable of developing extensive deformation prior to failure due to a favorable distribution of strain in the weld, heat-affected zone and base plate. The higher strength solid solution hardening alloys of the aluminum-magnesium or aluminum-magnesium-manganese types (5000 series) are particularly favorable because of the closer matching of strength and ductility in the various zones across the weld joint.

Table 69.34—Effect of welding on heat-treatable aluminum alloys

| Zone | Description |
| --- | --- |
| Weld metal | Weld bead with as cast structure where base metal is alloyed with weld metal. |
| Fusion zone | Region where partial melting of the base metal occurs, primarily at the grain boundaries. |
| Solid solution zone | Region where the heat from welding is high enough to dissolve soluble constituents which are partially retained in solid solution if cooling is sufficiently rapid. |
| Partially annealed or overaged zone | Region where the heat from welding has caused precipitation and/or coalescence of particles of soluble constituents. |
| Unaffected | Region where heating has not affected the structure. |

## HEAT-TREATABLE ALLOYS

The strengths of the heat-treatable aluminum alloys are also decreased by the heat of welding. However, they require a substantial time at the annealing temperature to fully soften the metal. As a result, only partially annealed properties are observed in the heat-affected zone in the as-welded condition. These properties may vary considerably, according to the rate of heat dissipation in the assembly. However, they are almost always lower than the strengths and elongations observed in welds in many of the alloys in the 5000 series of nonheat-treatable aluminum alloys. The one major exception is some of the newer 7000 series alloys which naturally age quite rapidly after welding to provide increased tensile and yield strength.

Properties of groove welds in some of the heat-treatable alloys are given in Table 69.36. The values given are average and cover a wide range of material thicknesses, welded with either the gas tungsten-arc or gas metal-arc welding process, using many different joint designs and welding procedures.

The speed of welding has a marked effect upon the properties of welds in the heat-treatable alloys. High welding rates not only decrease the width of the heat-affected zone, but they minimize the deleterious effects of microstructural changes such as eutectic melting, grain boundary precipitation, overaging and grain growth. To achieve maximum benefits of increased welding speed, it is usually necessary to go to machine welding, and to employ the more rapid gas shielded-arc welding processes. The gas metal-arc welding process using d-c reverse polarity current and the gas tungsten-arc process with d-c straight polarity are noted for high heat input and fast travel speed.

**Table 69.35—Tensile strength & elongation of gas-shielded arc welded butt joints in nonheat-treated aluminum alloys‡**

| Base Alloy | | | Average Ultimate Tensile Strength (psi x 10³) | Minimum Annealed Ultimate Tensile Strength (psi x 10³) | Average Yield Strength (psi x 10³) 0.2% Offset in 2 in. | Minimum Yield Strength (psi x 10³) 0.2% Offset in 2 in. | Free Bend elongation (%) | Tensile Elongation in 2 in. (%) |
|---|---|---|---|---|---|---|---|---|
| Aluminum Association Designation | Former ASTM Designation | Filler Alloy | | | | | | |
| EC | 996A | ER1260 | 10 | 9 | 4 | 4 | 63 | 29 |
| 1060 | 990A | ER1260 | 10 | 9 | 5 | 5 | 63 | 29 |
| 1100 | M1A | ER1100 | 13 | 11 | 6 | 6 | 54 | 29 |
| 3003 | G1B | ER1100 | 16 | 14 | 7 | 7 | 58 | 24 |
| 5005 | G1A | ER5356 | 16 | 14 | 9 | 8 | 32 | 15 |
| 5050 | GR20A | ER5356 | 23 | 16 | 12 | 10 | 36 | 18 |
| 5052 | GM41A | ER5356 | 28 | 25 | 14 | 13 | 39 | 19 |
| 5083 | GM40A | ER5183 | 43 | 40 | 22 | 18 | 34 | 16 |
| 5086 | GR40A | ER5356 | 39 | 35 | 19 | 17 | 38 | 16 |
| 5154 | GM31A | ER5254 | 33 | 30 | 18 | 16 | 39 | 17 |
| 5454 | GM51A | ER5554 | 35 | 31 | 16 | 14 | 40 | 17 |
| 5456 | GS11A | ER5556 | 46 | 42 | 23 | 20 | 28 | 14 |
| *6061-T6 | GS11A | ER4043 | 27 | 24 | 17 | 17 | 16 | 8 |
| *6061-T6 | | ER5356 | 30 | 24 | 17 | 18 | 25 | 10 |

* Heat Treated Alloy—as welded condition.
‡ Reduced section tensile.

Properties and Performance/**79**

Table 69.36—Typical strength and elongation of butt joints in heat-treatable aluminum alloys*

| Alloy and Temper | Base Alloy Properties ||| Filler Alloy | As Welded |||| Postweld Heat Treated and Aged ||||  |
|---|---|---|---|---|---|---|---|---|---|---|---|---|---|
| | Tensile Strength Psi x 1000 | Yield Strength 0.2% Offset 2 in. gauge Psi x 1000 | Elonga- tion % in 2 inch** | | Tensile Strength Psi x 1000 | Yield Strength 2% Offset Psi x 1000 | Elongation || Tensile Strength Psi x 1000 | Yield Strength** Psi x 1000 | Elongation || |
| | | | | | | | % in 2 inch gauge | Free Bend % | | | % in 2 inch | Free Bend % | |
| 2014–T6 | 70 | 60 | 11 | 4043 | 34 | 28 | 4 | 9 | 50 | 46 | 2 | 5 | Sol HT; aged to T62 |
| 2014–T6 | 70 | 60 | 11 | 2014 | 32 | 28 | 2 |  | 50 | 37 | 4 |  | Aged to T62 |
| 2219 T81 & T87 | 66 | 50 | 10 | 2319 | 35 | 26 | 3 | 20 | 43 |  | 2 |  |  |
| 2219 T81, T87 |  |  |  |  |  |  |  |  |  |  |  |  |  |
| 2219 O, T31, T81, T87 | 60 | 42 | 10 | 2319 | 35 | 26 | 3 | 20 | 50 | 38 | 7 |  | Sol HT; aged to T62 |
| 6061–T4 | 35 | 21 | 22 | 4043 | 27 | 18 | 8 | 16 | 35 | 40 | 8 | 11 | Aged to T62 |
| 6061–T6 | 45 | 40 | 12 | 4043 | 27 | 18 | 8 | 16 | 44 |  | 5 |  | Sol HT; aged to T62 |
| 6061–T6 | 45 | 40 | 12 | 5356 | 30 | 19 | 11 | 25 |  |  |  |  | Sol HT; aged to T62 |
| 6063–T4 | 25 | 13 | 22 | 4043 | 20 | 10 | 12 | 16 | 30 |  | 13 |  | Sol HT; aged to T62 |
| 6063–T6 | 35 | 31 | 12 | 4043 | 20 | 12 | 8 | 16 |  |  |  |  |  |
| 6063–T6 | 35 | 31 | 12 | 5356 | 20 | 12 | 12 | 16 |  |  |  |  |  |
| 6070–T6 | 55 | 51 | 10 | 4643 | 30 | 30 | 10 |  | 50 |  |  |  |  |
| 6071–T6 | 54 | 51 | 10 | 5356 | 30 | 30 | 12 |  | 54 | 45 | 8 |  | Sol HT; aged to T62 |
| 6071–T6 | 54 | 51 | 10 | 4643 | 30 | 30 | 12 |  | 54 | 45 | 8 |  | Sol HT; aged to T62 |
| 7039–T61 | 58 | 48 | 13 | 5039 | 48 | 26 | 12 | 21 |  |  |  |  |  |
| 7039–T64 | 65 | 55 | 13 | 5039 | 50 | 25 | 13 | 19 |  |  |  |  |  |
| 7039–T64 | 65 | 55 | 13 | 5183 | 45 | 25 | 13 | 5 |  |  |  |  |  |
| 7039–T64 | 65 | 55 | 13 | 5356 | 44 | 25 | 2 |  |  |  |  |  |  |
| 7075–T6 | 83 | 73 | 11 | 5356 | 37 | 30 | 2 |  | 70 | 63 | 2 |  | Sol HT; aged to T62 |

\* Reduced section tensile
\*\* 0.2% offset in 2" gauge

## 80/Properties and Performance

**Table 69.37—Effect of welding conditions on strength of butt joints in alloy 6061 with filler alloy 4043**

| Key* | Base Alloy and Temper | Thickness (in.) | Welding Process and Conditions | As Welded Tensile Strength, psi x 1000 | As Welded Yield Strength 0.2% Offset in 2 in. Gauge psi x 1000 | As Welded % Elongation in 2 in. Gauge | Aged After Welding Tensile Strength, psi x 1000 | Aged After Welding Yield Strength 0.2% Offset in 2 in. Gauge psi x 1000 | Aged After Welding % Elongation in 2 in. Gauge | Solution Heat Treated and Aged After Welding Tensile Strength, psi x 1000 | Solution Heat Treated and Aged After Welding Yield Strength 0.2% Offset in 2 in. Gauge psi x 1000 | Solution Heat Treated and Aged After Welding % Elongation in 2 in. Gauge |
|---|---|---|---|---|---|---|---|---|---|---|---|---|
| A | 6061-T4 | ½ | AC-GTA 96 ipm | 33 | 21 | 6 | | | | | | |
| B | 6061-T6 | ½ | AC-GTA 96 ipm | 33 | 26 | 2 | | | | | | |
| C | 6061-T4 | ⅛ | DCSP-GTA 20 ipm | 34 | 21 | 8 | 41 | 26 | 3 | 44 | 40 | 5 |
| D | 6061-T6 | ⅛ | DCSP-GTA 35 ipm Single Pass | 36 | 24 | 6 | | | | 44 | 40 | 5 |
| E | 6061-T6 | ¼ | Auto-GMA One Pass Each Side 40 ipm | 37 | 20 | 6 | | | | 43 | 40 | 5 |
| F | 6061-T4 | 3 | Auto-GMA Multipass V Groove | 25 | 13 | 10 | | | | 34 | 40 | 4 |
| G | 6061-T6‡ | 3 | Auto-GMA Multipass V-grove | 27 | 14 | 13 | | | | 45 | 40 | 4 |

* Letters in this column refer to lines in text.
‡ 4643 filler was used

The thickness of the material being welded has an influence on the weld properties of the heat-treatable alloys. Welds made in thin sheets will have higher weld properties than welds in plate of the same alloy because of higher welding speeds and more rapid heat dissipation. Other factors that affect weld strength are size of weld, joint design (which influences dilution and weld metal composition), and the reinforcing effect of the base metal on the weld zone. This effect is greater in thin material than in thick material.

## POSTWELD HEAT-TREATMENT

The heat-treatable aluminum alloys may be reheat-treated after welding to bring the base metal in the heat-affected zone back to nearly its original strength. The joint will then usually fail in the weld metal except when the weld bead reinforcement is left intact. In this case, failure normally occurs in the fusion zone at the edge of the weld. The strengths obtained in the weld metal after reheat treatment will depend on the filler metal used. In cases where filler metal of other than base metal composition is employed, strength will depend upon the percent dilution of filler metal with base metal. For highest strength, it is essential that the weld metal respond to the heat treatment used. Although reheat treatment increases strength, some loss in weld ductility may occur.

Weldments in some of the heat-treatable alloys exhibit very poor ductility due to grain boundary melting or precipitation in the fusion zone just adjacent to the weld bead. If the condition is not too severe, postweld heat treatment may redissolve most of the soluble constituents, giving a more homogeneous structure with a slight improvement in ductility and a much greater increase in weld strength.

In cases where complete reheat treatment of a weldment is not practical parts can be welded in the solution heat-treated condition and then artificially aged after welding. A substantial increase in properties over the normal as-welded strengths can sometimes be obtained in this manner when high welding rates are employed. For example, if alloy 6061 is welded in the -T4 temper and then aged to -T6, the strength of the joint may approach 40,000 psi, a great improvement over the 27,000 psi as-welded strength (Table 69.37). However, the properties rarely attain those of a weldment fully reheat treated (solution heat treatment plus aging).

Preheat markedly reduces the strength of welds in the heat-treatable alloys and may also impair corrosion resistance. It is rarely recommended, except when postweld solution heat treatment is to be given to the part. Then it may help to minimize the incidence of cracking during welding and to aid in the control of bead contour.

Abnormal microstructure in aluminum, as in other materials, may sometimes lead to difficulties in welding. Areas of segregation such as stringers of low melting constituents in extrusions can lead to porosity and cracking. Grain size and orientation may have a marked effect on weldability. An example of a fracture in a 2014-T6 plate to forging weldment is shown in Fig. 69.37. The adverse grain size and orientation in the forging contributed to the brittle behavior when the weldment was subjected to a burst test.

Welding of heat-treatable alloys in the solution heat-treated -T4 condition rather than in the -T6 condition often aids in minimizing cracking due to a more uniform microstructure in the solution heat-treated material, and the lower strength -T4 material imposes less restraint during weld solidification.

**82**/*Properties and Performance*

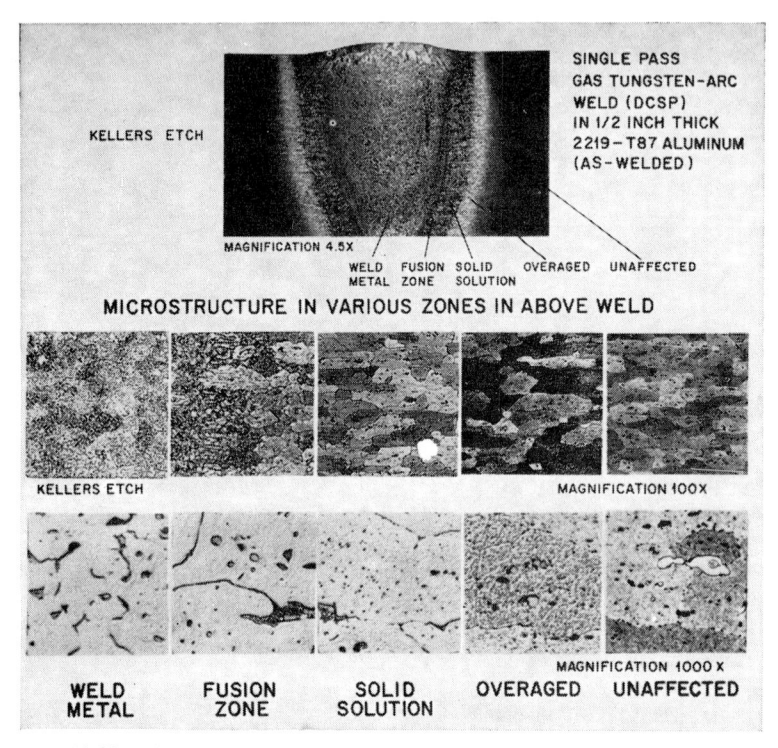

*Fig. 69.35.—Cross section of gas tungsten-arc weld in 2219-T87 aluminum*

Repair welding is usually more difficult with the heat-treatable alloys, due to microstructural changes caused by the heat of the original weld. Restraint is usually greater in repair welds, and cracking may occur in the heat-affected zone of the base metal or in the previously deposited weld metal. Joint strength may also be lowered when repairs are made.

## ALUMINUM-MAGNESIUM-SILICON ALLOYS (6000 SERIES)

Alloys of this series have been used to a much greater extent in welded structures than any of the other heat-treatable alloys. Alloy 6061 is commonly welded in both sheet and plate thicknesses, and may be used in the as-welded condition or given a postweld heat treatment when weld strength is an important consideration. Alloy 6063 is a lower strength alloy used mainly in the as-welded condition. The newer alloys 6070 and 6071 have higher strengths and good weldability.

Properties of typical groove welds in 6061 alloy are given in Table 69.37. It may be seen that the strength and elongation vary widely with the thickness, temper and heat treatment.

Higher as-welded strength may be achieved by rapid welding. This is particularly true in sheet gages (lines A through D, Table 69.37). A further increase in strength may be achieved by welding the material in the solution heat-treated -T4 condition and then postweld aging (line C, Table 69.37). In heavier ma-

*Properties and Performance*/ **83**

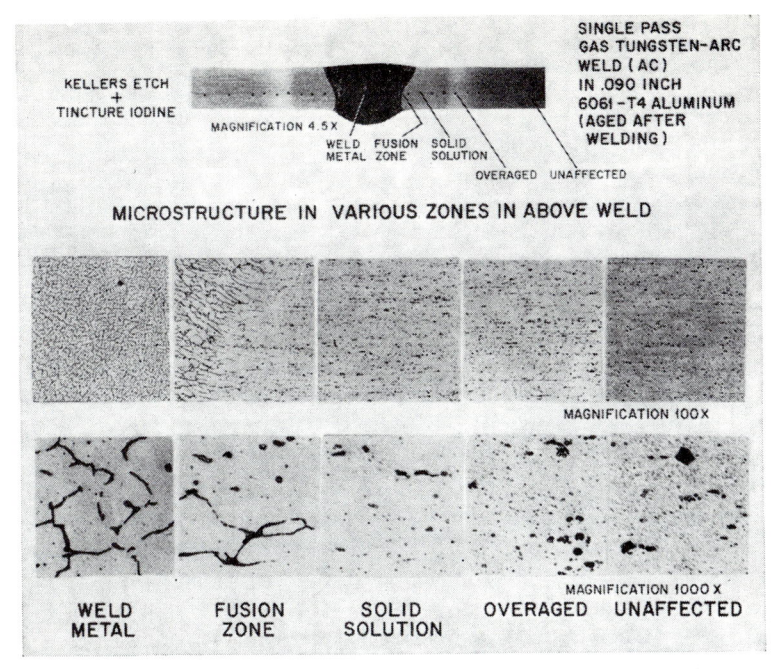

*Fig. 69.36.—Cross section of weld in 6061-T4 and aged T-6*

terial the improvement in strength may not be as marked. In very heavy gages, the properties of a fully reheat-treated weldment may be lower because the filler used is not heat treatable and must rely on dilution from the base material to achieve a heat-treatable composition. This effect is shown in line F for a single V-groove weld in 3 in. thick 6061 plate. When the joint design provides insufficient dilution and the weldment is to be postweld heat treated, consideration should be given to the use of filler alloy 4643 in place of filler alloy 4043 (line G, Table 69.37).

*Fig. 69.37.—Fracture in a 2014-T6 plate-to-forging weldment illustrating the effect of grain size and orientation on weldability. (left) forging, (center) weld metal, (right) plate*

## ALUMINUM-COPPER ALLOYS (2000 SERIES)

Until quite recently only a limited amount of commercial welding (other than resistance welding) had been done with the 2000 series alloys, most of this on alloys 2014 and 2024 in sheet gages. A newer alloy, 2219 which is basically a binary Al-6Cu alloy, is readily weldable and has extensive use in large welded missile tankage.

Weld cracking is a problem in most of the Al-Cu alloys, other than 2219, particularly in heavier thicknesses or when welded under restraint. Welds in 2014 and 2024 generally exhibit low ductility. Properties of groove welds in 2014 and 2219 are given in Table 69.36. In general, high welding speed in conjunction with a high quench rate and maximum transfer of heat into the base metal is necessary to achieve the best as-welded properties. Post weld heat treatment may be used to obtain a further improvement in strength, particularly yield strength, as shown in Table 69.36. Caution should be used to avoid treatments which could decrease stress corrosion resistance.

## ALUMINUM-ZINC ALLOYS (7000 SERIES)

The 7000 series includes some of the highest strength heat-treatable aluminum alloys, 7075 being an example. They are widely used in air-frame structures and for highly stressed parts. One of the major drawbacks of many of the 7000 series is their poor weldability (other than resistance welding).

Several recently introduced Al-Zn-Mg alloys of the 7000 series such as 7039 combine good weldability with high as-welded strength. By naturally aging after welding, without solution heat treatment, the yield strength as well as the tensile strength is increased and high joint efficiency is obtained. Even higher strengths are attainable by artificially aging or by full postweld heat treatment.

These new 7000 series alloys offer decided property advantages over the Al-Cu 2219 alloy in applications where in-process solution heat treatment must be employed, such as spun-hemispheres for missile tankage. Maximum base-metal properties can be obtained by conventional heat treatment whereas the competitive base metal properties of 2219-T87 depend on in-process cold working which may be difficult with most structural configurations.

Gas tungsten-arc welding is readily accomplished on the Al-Zn-Mg alloys with procedures and machine settings similar to those used for the 5000 series alloys. For gas metal-arc welding, high current and travel speed together with a short arc length are desirable to assure good fusion with the side wall of the joint. Helium shielding is often preferred.

Individual alloys vary in mechanical properties with alloy content, heat treatment, and in their ability to be welded. Properties of groove welds are given in Table 69.36.

## SHEAR STRENGTH OF FILLET WELDS

Fillet welds do not have the symmetry of groove welds, and loading is usually a combination of shear with various magnitudes of tension and bending. Tests of fillet welds loaded in both the longitudinal and transverse directions have shown strength to be a function of the filler metal alloy. Results of these tests are shown in Figs. 69.38 and 69.39. Symmetrical specimens were used and bending was avoided in testing. The high magnesium content filler metals produce the highest strength fillet welds in the as-welded condition. The pure aluminum filler exhibits the lowest fillet weld strength.

*Fig. 69.38.—Typical curves indicating shear strength vs longitudinal fillet weld size for 6 aluminum alloys*

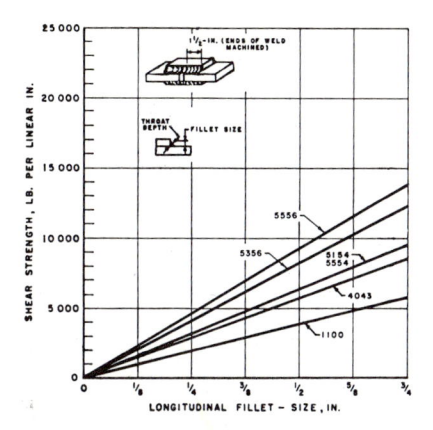

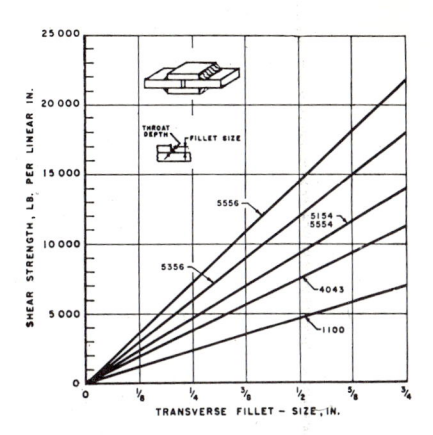

*Fig. 69.39.—Typical curves indicating shear strength vs transverse fillet weld size for 6 aluminum alloys*

## IMPACT STRENGTH

Aluminum weldments hold up quite well under impact loadings, particularly in the nonheat-treatable alloys.

Aluminum and aluminum alloys do not exhibit a brittle transition range at low temperatures as do many ferrous materials, but maintain their ductility and resistance to shock loading at extremely low temperatures. Their tensile and yield strengths actually improve as temperature decreases.

A considerable amount of impact testing of ferrous materials and weldments at room and subzero temperature has been done with the Charpy V-Notch or Izod tests, and some data has also been obtained on aluminum. However, with some aluminum alloys and tempers the specimens do not fracture but merely bend, giving high impact values. This bending invalidates the test. In general, Charpy V-Notch and Izod test values obtained for aluminum should only be used for comparison purposes.

## FATIGUE STRENGTH

The fatigue strength of welded structures follow the same general rules that apply to other kinds of fabricated assemblies. Fatigue strength is governed by the peak stresses at points of stress concentration, rather than by nominal stresses. Anything that can be done to reduce the peak stresses by eliminating stress raisers will tend to increase the life of the assembly under repeated loads.

Curves representing the average fatigue strengths for transverse welded butt joints in three aluminum alloys are shown in Fig. 69.40. For the shorter cyclic lives the fatigue strengths reflect differences in static strength. However, for very large numbers of cycles the difference between the alloys is small. The fatigue strength of a groove weld may be significantly increased by such means as removing weld bead reinforcement or by peening the weldment. If such procedures are not practical it is desirable that the reinforcement fair into the base plate gradually to avoid any abrupt changes in thickness. For welding processes that produce relatively smooth weld beads, there is little or no increase in strength with further smoothening. The benefit of smooth weld beads can be nullified by excessive spatter during welding. Spatter marks sometimes develop severe stress raisers in the base metal adjacent to the weld.

Investigations have been made on the effect of stress concentrations. For long life the allowable stress for plate joined by transverse fillet welds is less than half that of plate joined with transverse groove welds.

Welds in aluminum alloys usually perform very well under repeated load conditions. Tests have shown that properly designed and fabricated welded joints will generally perform as well under repeated load conditions as riveted joints designed for the same static loading.

## EFFECT OF TEMPERATURE

The minimum tensile strength of aluminum welds at other than room temperature is listed in Table 69.38. Actually the performance of welds follows closely that of the annealed base metal in the nonheat-treatable alloys. At temperatures as low as −320°F the strength of aluminum increases without loss of ductility; it is therefore a particularly useful metal for low temperature or cryogenic applications.

As the temperature rises above room temperature, aluminum alloys lose strength. The 2000 series alloys exhibit highest strength at elevated temperatures. Alloys in the aluminum-magnesium group possessing 3.5% magnesium or more are not recommended for sustained temperatures exceeding 150°F because of a susceptibility to stress corrosion.

## CORROSION RESISTANCE

Many of the aluminum alloys can be welded without reducing the resistance of the assembly to corrosion. In general, the welding method does not influence corrosion resistance. However, if a flux is used the residue must be removed after welding.

The excellent corrosion resistance of the nonheat-treatable alloys is not changed appreciably by welding. Combinations of these alloys have good resistance to corrosion. For installations involving prolonged elevated temperature service (above 150°F), however, limitations are placed on the amount of cold work that is permissible for some of the 5000 series alloys, particularly those with higher magnesium content, as they may show susceptibility to stress corrosion.

The aluminum-magnesium-silicon alloys such as 6061 and 6063 have high resistance to corrosion in the unwelded and welded conditions, and are not noticeably affected by such factors as temper, operating temperature and nature and magnitude of stress and environment.

Some of the heat-treatable alloys, particularly those containing substantial amounts of copper and zinc, may have their resistance to corrosion lowered by the heat of welding. These alloys exhibit grain boundary precipitation in the heat-affected zone, and the electrical potential of this zone is normally anodic to the remainder of the weldment. In a corrosive environment selective corrosion on the grain boundaries may take place. In the presence of stress this corrosion can proceed more rapidly. Postweld heat treatment provides a more homogeneous structure and improves the corrosion resistance of these alloys. If the assembly can not be reheat-treated and aged after welding, better resistance to corrosion is observed if the original material is welded in the -T6 temper, rather than in the -T4 temper.

**Table 69.38—Minimum tensile strengths at various temperatures across arc-welded butt joints in aluminum alloys**

| Base Alloy Aluminum Association Designation | Filler Alloy Metal | Ultimate Tensile Strength (Psi)* |||||| 
|---|---|---|---|---|---|---|---|
| | | −300° F | −200° F | −100° F | 100° F | 300° F | 500° F |
| 2219–T37† | 2319 | 48,500 | 40,000 | 36,000 | 35,000 | 31,000 | 19,000 |
| 2219–T62‡ | 2319 | 64,500 | 59,500 | 55,000 | 50,000 | 38,000 | 22,000 |
| 3003 | ER 1100 | 27,500 | 21,500 | 17,500 | 14,000 | 9,500 | 5,000 |
| 5052 | ER 5356 | 38,000 | 31,000 | 26,500 | 25,000 | 21,000 | 10,500 |
| 5083 | ER 5183 | 54,500 | 46,000 | 40,500 | 40,000 | ...... | ...... |
| 5086 | ER 5356 | 48,000 | 40,500 | 35,500 | 35,000 | ...... | ...... |
| 5454 | ER 5554 | 44,000 | 37,000 | 32,000 | 31,000 | 26,000 | 15,000 |
| 5456 | ER 5556 | 56,000 | 47,500 | 42,500 | 42,000 | ...... | ...... |
| 6061–T6 | ER 4043 | 34,500 | 30,000 | 26,500 | 24,000 | 20,000 | 6,000 |
| 6061–T6 | ER 4043 | 55,000 | 49,500 | 46,000 | 42,000 | 31,500 | 7,000 |
| 7039–T61# | 5039 | 62,000 | ...... | 52,000 | 48,000 | ...... | ...... |

\* Alloys not listed at 300° F and 500° F are not recommended for use at sustained operating temperatures of over 150° F.
† As welded.
‡ Heat treated and aged after welding.
# Naturally aged 30 days.

The corrosion resistance of welded assemblies fabricated of clad material is superior to that of welded assemblies in nonclad material. Paint protection is recommended when welded joints of the unclad 2000 or 7000 series alloys are employed in outdoor environments.

## FRACTURE CHARACTERISTICS

The fracture characteristics of weldments may be described in terms of their resistance to rapid crack propagation at elastic stresses, or their ability to deform plastically in the presence of stress raisers and avoid the low-energy initiation and propagation of cracks. Resistance to rapid crack propagation may be measured in terms of tear resistance.

A fracture toughness test is also useful for this purpose, but only for relatively low ductility material. Most aluminum alloy weldments are too ductile for this test to be of any significance. The ability of weldments to deform plastically and redistribute load to adjacent regions may be expressed in terms of notch toughness. The relationship of the tensile strength of notched specimens to the joint yield strength provides alternate but generally coarser measures of these characteristics.

Regardless of the criterion used to measure fracture characteristics, depending on the filler metal used, aluminum alloy weldments are usually at least as tough as the base aluminum alloy. In nonheat-treatable alloys, where welding anneals a narrow zone on each side of the weld, the weld has the same high resistance to rapid crack propagation as annealed material and much more than the cold worked base metal. The elongation of specimens taken across a weld in cold worked base metal may be low, suggesting that this is not the case. This low value is actually the result of the nonuniform strengths of regions within the

**88**/*Properties and Performance*

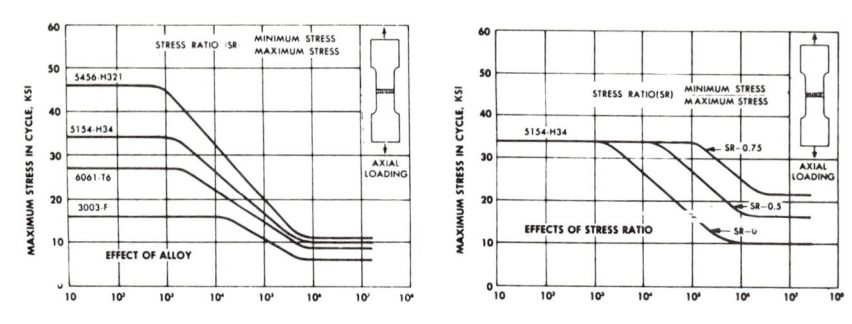

*Fig. 69.40.—Direct stress fatigue test results for welded aluminum butt joints for inert gas arc welds*

gage length and the resultant strain concentration at the weld. The same situation exists for heat-treated alloys in the as-welded condition where tear resistance or notch toughness is much greater than that of the heat-treated base metal. Heat treatment or aging after welding increases the strength of the weldment and brings its fracture characteristics more in line with those of the base material, particularly when base and filler metal alloys are of essentially the same composition. Where composition of a heat treatable filler alloy differs from the base metal such as 4043 filler metal, 6061 base metal, the weldment may be less tough than the base metal after the assembly is reheat-treated.

A relative merit rating of aluminum alloy weldments in order of increasing tear resistancee and notch toughneess is shown in Fig. 69.41.

## WELDING OF ALUMINUM ALLOY CASTINGS

In general, the welding techniques employed on aluminum alloy castings are similar to those used for wrought products. Sound welds of good quality can be obtained. A gas shielded-arc welding process is generally preferred for welding castings. The choice of filler metal is made on much the same basis as with wrought alloys. Castings containing dross, gas porosity, shrinkage or inclusions will have poor weldability and low weld properties, and this should be considered when procuring castings for welding. Edges to be joined should be prepared and free of contamination. Preheating may be required to overcome cracking or distortion and facilitate welding unless the welding process requires a flux. Sand or permanent-mold castings can be welded to themselves or to a wrought product with equal ease.

The nominal compositions, properties and relative weldability ratings of the various casting alloys are given in Tables 69.6 and 69.7. The weldability ratings are based on sound castings and sound welds free of discontinuities.

Many castings depend upon heat treatment for their strength. These alloys cannot be welded without a partial loss of mechanical properties and in some cases the resistance to stress corrosion in the weld area may be reduced. After welding they can be reheat-treated to restore their original properties. The selection of the proper filler metal is essential if the joint is expected to respond to heat treatment. Refer to filler metal chart for casting welding (Tables 69.11 and 69.12).

The strength of a butt joint made between a casting and a wrought product is dependent on the strength of the casting provided the strength of the heat-

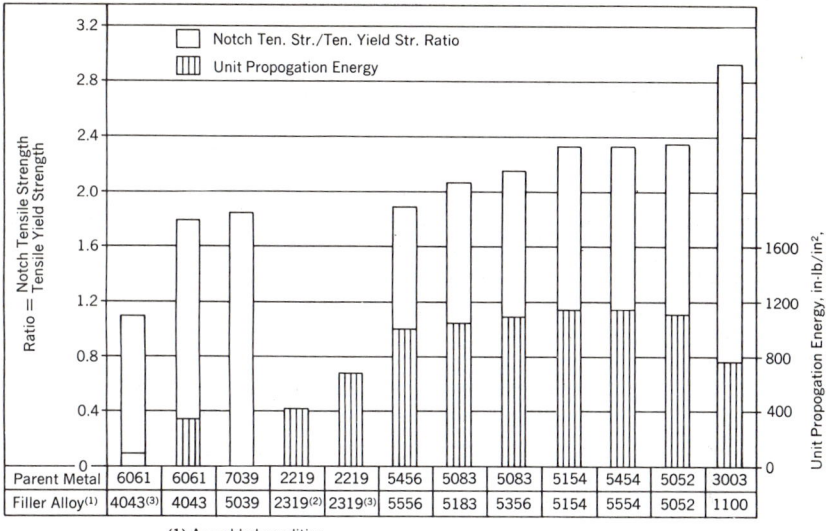

*Fig. 69.41.—Relative ratings of aluminum alloy weldments in order of increasing tear resistance. Tear resistance (unit propagation energy) is at right and notch toughness (ratio of notch-tensile strength to tensile yield strength) is on left*

affected zone of the wrought product is greater than that of the casting. For highest strengths and greatest ductility, castings with silicon as the alloying constituent should be welded with filler metal containing silicon and filler metal containing magnesium should be used on magnesium alloy castings (Table 69.38A).

## FOUNDRY WELDING

Sand castings and permanent mold castings are commonly welded in the foundry. Small defects are corrected, metal is provided for machining and minor design variations are accomplished.

In foundry welding the filler metal alloy is usually identical to that of the casting material. Preparation for welding generally starts with the removal of all dross and unsound metal. Where an as-cast surface is to be welded the joint is vigorously wire brushed to remove any sand or foreign material. In some castings it is recommended that the surface be scarfed to a depth of 1/8 inch in the weld area.

After flaws have been repaired and necessary welds made, any flux must be cleaned off. Any required heat treatment of cast parts must be done after welding.

## RESISTANCE WELDING

The resistance welding processes (spot, seam and flash welding) are important in fabricating aluminum alloys. These processes are especially useful in joining the high strength heat-treatable alloys, which are difficult to join by fusion welding, but which can be joined by the resistance welding processes with practically no loss in strength.

The plastic range of aluminum is narrower than that of steel, but it softens rapidly as the temperature is increased. This results in a slight movement of the welding electrode into the material being welded. While this movement is small, it must take place during a very short interval of about 0.002 to 0.005 of a second. As a result considerable acceleration of the moving electrode assembly is necessary if contact is to be maintained between the welding electrodes and the material being welded. For this reason the moving electrode system should possess low inertia and should be guided so as to minimize friction.

Aluminum exhibits considerable shrinkage upon cooling from the liquid to the solid state (about 6-7%). This property is most pronounced in the high strength heat treatable alloys such as 2024 and 7075 and can lead to cracking. The nonheat-treatable alloys and the 6000 series alloys are less prone to cracking during welding as a result of this shrinkage.

The natural oxide coating on aluminum has a rather high and erratic electrical resistance. To obtain spot or seam welds of the highest strength and consistency it is usually necessary, therefore, to reduce this oxide coating prior to welding.

## WELDABILITY RATINGS OF ALUMINUM ALLOYS

Although all aluminum alloys can be spot and seam welded some alloys or combination of alloys are more weldable than others. The relative weldability of the various wrought and cast aluminum alloys is given in Tables 69.2,5,6 and 7.

In general, the high strength alloys 2024 and 7075 are easier to weld, since they have less tendency for sheet separation and better weld strength consistency. However, they have a greater tendency toward cracking and porosity than the lower strength alloys. In fact shrinkage cracks in weld metal are confined almost entirely to the copper and zinc-bearing alloys such as 2024 and 7075.

The temper of the alloy also influences weldability. With a given alloy, the annealed −0 temper material is more difficult to weld than the harder tempers. In general, the softer tempers are much more susceptible to excessive indentation and sheet separation, and show wider variations in weld strength. This is attributed to greater deformation under the welding force, causing uneven current and pressure distribution when making the weld.

## CORROSION RESISTANCE

In the melted and heat-affected zones created by resistance welding metallurgical changes take place which can affect corrosion resistance. Spot and seam welds in the nonheat-treatable alloys such as 1100, 3003 and 5052 are not selectively attacked by corrosion. Spot welded structures of these materials will have the same corrosion resistance as the unwelded material. Welds in the heat treatable magnesium-silicon alloys such as 6061 and 6063 have good corrosion resistance.

Spot and seam welds in clad heat-treatable alloys are protected from corrosive attack by the cladding, and therefore have good corrosion resistance. Welds in bare 2000 and 7000 series alloys may be attacked preferentially under severely corrosive conditions, and should not be used in a corrosive environment unless properly protected.

## RESISTANCE SPOT WELDING
### Equipment

While conventional machines may be used optimum results are obtained only if certain refinements are incorporated into these machines. Some of these desirable features are:

1. Ability to handle high current for short weld times
2. Precise electronic control of current and length of time it is applied
3. Rapid follow-up of the electrode force by employing anti-friction bearings and lightweight low inertia heads
4. High structural rigidity of the welding machine arms, holders and platens in order to minimize deflection under the high electrode forces used for aluminum, and to reduce magnetic deflections
5. A variable or dual force cycle to permit forging the weld nugget
6. Slope control to permit a gradual buildup and tapering off of the welding current
7. Postheat current to allow slower cooling of the weld nugget
8. Good cooling of the Class I electrodes to prevent tip pickup or sticking. Refrigerated cooling is often helpful.

Based on electrical characteristics spot welding equipment can be classified as (1) direct energy equipment, taking power only during welding and (2) stored energy equipment storing energy continuously or during the interval between welds and releasing the energy during welding. Direct energy spot welding machines for aluminum may be further classified as single phase a-c, single phase a-c with slope control, three-phase frequency converter type, or three-phase dry disk rectifier type. Stored energy machines can be of three types: electrostatic, electromagnetic, or electrochemical (storage battery) type. Very few of the latter two varieties are in use today, however.

*Single Phase A-C Welding Equipment*—Conventional single phase a-c machines will produce good spot welds in all aluminum alloys. It is not usually necessary to purchase a special machine for welding aluminum to meet most commercial standards. However, to meet the quality requirements of some specifications a welding machine designed for welding aluminum may be required.

One of the chief objections to a-c spot welding machines is that the high currents for welding aluminum place a very high electrical demand on the system supplying the machine. This current demand is of intermittent nature, single phase, has a very low power factor, and may disturb other electrical equipment. Also, the wide variation in line voltage caused by one spot welding machine may affect other spot welding machines on the same line, causing nonuniformity in welding or occasional dud welds. One method of alleviating this condition is to use special substations reserved for a single welding machine. Another method is to install static capacitors in series in the primary winding of the welding transformer. The manufacturer of the welding equipment should be consulted with regard to the proper size and number of condensers required.

*Single Phase A-C Slope Control Equipment*—This modification of single phase a-c spot welding, whereby a control is adapted to the a-c machine to regulate up and down slope time and current, is highly recommended for aluminum welding. With up slope control the welding current starts at a fraction of the weld current setting being used and gradually increases until it reaches the desired maximum current. Down slope is the gradual decrease in the current from the welding current setting to the final or postweld current.

The advantage of a-c slope control equipment over the conventional a-c spot welding equipment is essentially as follows: By gradually building up the welding current the up slope portion of the cycle permits the electrodes to come into uniform contact with the material prior to the higher welding current, and permits the use of lower welding forces. This results in less indentation and better appearance of weld surfaces, minimizes the tendency toward expulsion either at the interface between the electrode and the work or between the parts being welded, and may result in a substantial increase in tip life.

The down slope portion of the cycle, by allowing the current to taper off and prevent rapid chilling of the weld nugget, permits better forging which results in finer grain structure and eliminates cracks and voids in the weld nugget, and wider variation in amount and time of application of forging force.

A current wave form diagram for a slope control spot weld is shown in Fig. 69.42.

*Three-Phase Equipment*—Three-phase, direct energy a-c spot welding machines have been developed to reduce the unbalanced demand on the power supply inherent in single-phase a-c machines. The high power factor of these machines reduces the kva load on the power source. Moreover, these machines produce excellent quality welds in aluminum. One reason for this is their partial control over the shape of the welding current wave. The gradual increase of the welding current with these machines is similar to the slope control used with single phase a-c machines. Another advantage of these three-phase welding machines is that they are not affected by varying amounts of magnetic material in the throat of the machine. This is of greater importance, however, in welding steel or other magnetic material than in welding aluminum.

Three-phase, direct energy a-c spot welding machines may be of the frequency converter or dry disk rectifier types. The three-phase frequency converter type of welding machine uses a special transformer with a three-phase primary winding and a single-phase secondary.

The three-phase dry disk rectifier type machine has a three-phase transformer supplying low voltage, high current, three-phase power to dry disk rectifiers which deliver direct current to the weld.

## *Electrostatic Stored Energy Welding Machines*

In electrostatic stored energy (condenser discharge) machines energy is stored in capacitors or condensers. A three-phase full wave rectifier is used to charge the capacitor bank to a predetermined voltage. To make a weld the bank of condensers is discharged through a suitable welding transformer. A major advantage of this type of machine is the balanced line load and high power factor which reduce the peak kva demand and minimize power line disturbances.

## *Electrode Force*

Since aluminum exhibits considerable shrinkage upon solidification, porosity and cracking may result unless the electrodes can maintain pressure on the solidifying weld nugget. In addition to low inertia heads, machines for welding

# Resistance Welding/93

aluminum generally have a means of increasing the electrode force as the weld nugget solidifies. This permits forging of the nugget and an improvement in soundness.

Variable force cycles usually consist of three stages. In the first stage a high precompression force is exerted to seat the electrodes firmly on the aluminum and establish good electrical contact. The force is then reduced while the weld is being made. After the weld nugget has formed the force is again increased to forge the nugget. Some force systems omit the precompression stage. Others use the same value of force for both the precompression and forge stages of the cycle.

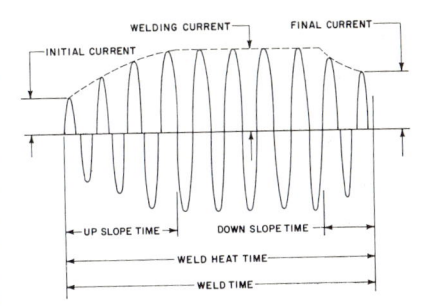

*Fig. 69.42.—Current wave diagram for a single-phase a-c slope controlled resistance spot welding machine*

Low force during welding permits the use of lower currents and minimizes sheet separation while a high forging force reduces the tendency toward cracking. Some equipment uses a fixed ratio of approximately 1 to 2 between weld and forge forces; other machines permit independent adjustment of the two forces. The use of variable force cycles makes the machine settings less critical and increases the range in which good quality welds can be produced. When the correct cycle has been determined welds of a given size can usually be produced with lower welding current than required in single force systems. However, to be effective the application of forge force must be properly timed in relation to the welding current.

## *Electrodes and Electrode Holders*

The proper choice of electrode shape and the maintenance of this shape in production are essential in obtaining consistent spot welds on aluminum. The welding electrode serves as a means of conducting the welding current into the parts being welded, exerts sufficient pressure on the material to hold it in place while the weld is made, and conducts the heat out of the parts to prevent the weld zone from reaching the outside surfaces of the material. At least one electrode must be shaped so that a high concentration of current will be obtained in the weld. Electrodes machined to a spherical radius on one or both sides of the work are used for most welding operations. Consistent strength and size of the weld can be obtained by refinishing the electrodes periodically with a contoured tool faced with a fine abrasive cloth (Fig. 69.43).

It is essential that electrodes be made from materials of high hardness and electrical and thermal conductivity. A number of copper alloys with hardnesses above Rockwell B-65 and electrical conductivities greater than 75% of that of pure copper are used (RWMA Class 1 or Class 2, Group A). Hard drawn copper electrodes of conical or dome shape will not maintain their shape in high production welding operations and their use is to be avoided.

Electrodes must be of sufficient diameter to carry the welding currents used without undue heating. A 5/8 inch diameter electrode is suitable for currents up to 65,000 amperes, and a welding time of 15 cycles when the rate of welding is not more than 40 welds per minute. Where higher welding currents, longer welding times or greater welding speeds are used, 7/8 or 1-1/4 inch diameter elec-

# 94/Resistance Welding

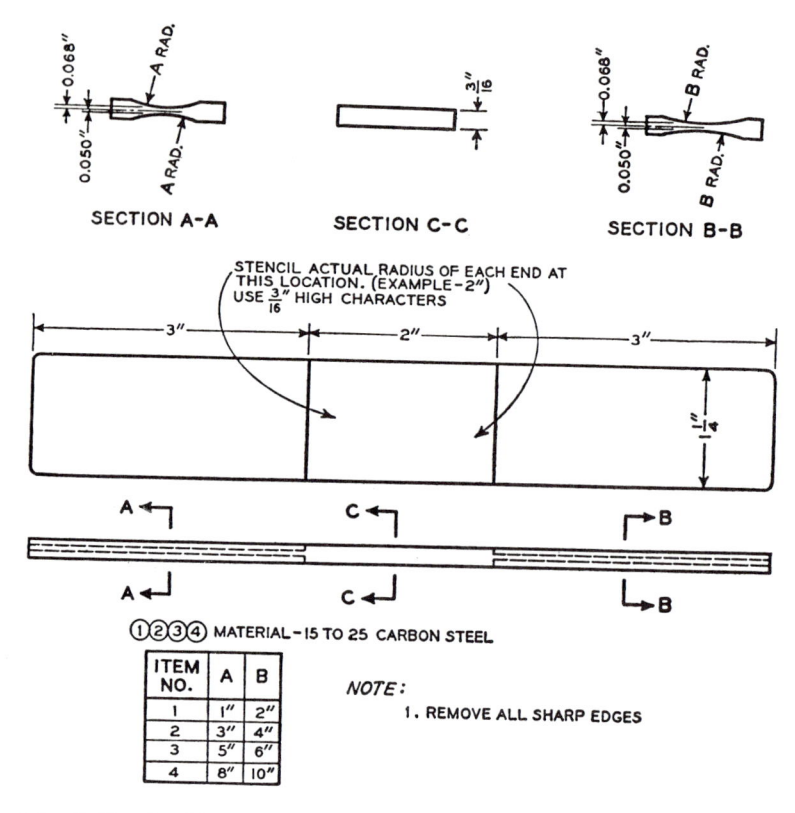

*Fig. 69.43.—Double ended dressing tool for cleaning spot welding electrode tips*

trodes should be used. For welding currents less than 20,000 amp and welding times less than 8 cycles, 1/2 inch diameter electrodes are satisfactory.

The electrodes must be water cooled by a stream directed to the end of the electrode. Cooling should extend to within 3/8 inch of the welding face. Electrodes with fluted water holes to provide more cooling surface and to help direct the flow are available. A water flow of one or more gpm should be maintained through the electrode. Cooling water temperature should be below 60°F and should not vary more than 10°F. If the water temperature varies widely, refrigeration may be helpful in improving electrode tip life and weld consistency.

With continued welding a coating of aluminum alloy tends to form over the face of each electrode. The condition is commonly called tip pickup. The copper-aluminum alloy formed is of low electrical conductivity and if welding is continued the electrodes will tend to stick to the work and the surface of the material being welded will tend to melt. The pickup or coating may be removed by dressing the electrode with a fine grade of abrasive cloth. With dome-shaped electrodes, care should be taken to maintain the original electrode shape. Special contoured tools are made for this purpose. With stored energy welding machines electrode pickup may be minimized by reversing the direction of current flow through the electrodes on successive welds. Excessive electrode pickup is gen-

## Resistance Welding/95

**Table 69.38A—Typical tensile properties of butt welds in a few cast aluminum alloys**

| Alloy | Filler | Tensile Strength (psi) As Welded | Heat Treated and Aged after Welding |
|---|---|---|---|
| **Sand Cast** | | | |
| 355–F | 4043 | 23,000 | 40,000 |
| 356–F | 356 | 22,500 | |
| 356–T6 | 4043 | 27,000 | |
| A356–T7 | 4043 | 26,000 | |
| **Permanent Mold** | | | |
| 214–F | 5356 | 25,000 | [a] |
| 220–T4 | 5356 | 27,000 | 42,500 |
| 355–T6 | 355 | | 35,000 |
| C355–T7 | 4043 | 32,000 | |
| 356–T6 | 356 | 22,000 | 33,500 |
| 356–T6 | 4043 | 28,000 | 32,000 |
| 356–T6 | 5154 | 23,300 | |
| A356–T6 | 4043 | 28,000 | |

[a] Nonheat-treatable alloy.

erally the result of improper surface preparation of the material prior to welding, insufficient electrode force, or excessive welding current.

Both straight and offset electrodes are suitable for spot welding aluminum. However, it is good practice to use straight electrodes whenever possible as greater deflection and skidding may be experienced with offset electrodes under similar operating conditions. When offset electrodes are necessary, the amount of offset should be held to the minimum permitted by the shape of the assembly being welded. Only offset electrodes which have cooling to within 3/8 inch of the tip surface should be used. Ell-type electrode holders are preferred to offset tips as less skidding is encountered.

Conventional electrode holders are suitable for welding aluminum. To facilitate changing of electrodes the ejector type electrode holder may be used. Removal of an electrode from this type of holder is accomplished by striking an ejector plug on the end of the holder with a rawhide mallet. This type of holder is a great convenience in many production operations. Offset type holders may sometimes be required to weld assemblies not accessible to straight holders.

## SURFACE PREPARATION

Welds of uniformly high strength and good appearance depend upon a consistently low surface resistance between the workpieces. For many products, such as cooking utensils made from 3003 or 1100 aluminum alloys, the stock as received for welding is clean enough to afford welds of adequate strength and consistency. On the other hand, aircraft construction, governed by military specifications such as MIL-W-6858, demands the utmost in cleaning and deoxidation and requires continual checking of surface resistance.

For most applications some cleaning operations are necessary before spot or seam welding aluminum. Surface preparation for welding generally consists of removal of grease, oil, dirt or identification markings, and reduction and improvement of consistency of the oxide film on the aluminum surface. Typical methods of surface preparation are given in Table 69.39.

*Cleaning*—The first step in surface preparation may utilize commercial sol-

**Table 69.39—Typical cleaning methods for aluminum prior to resistance spot and seam welding**

| Method | Application | Procedure |
|---|---|---|
| 1<br>Precleaner<br>(Degreaser) | Applicable to all alloys and products to be resistance welded. | Remove identification marks by hand rubbing with paint thinner or alcohol. Degrease with solvent by vapor, dip or wash method. |
| 2<br>Hot alkaline cleaner<br>(Degreaser) | All alloys and products prior to one of the deoxidizing treatments (4-8). If heavy soil or grease is present use method 1 first. | Immerse or spray with hot (160-200° F) inhibited alkaline cleaner* (such as sodium carbonate or trisodium phosphate with added inhibitor such as sodium silicate). 5-10 minute immersion. Rinse and dry. Should give water break free surface. |
| 3<br>Heavy oxide remover | Heat treated alloys, extrusions, forgings or badly stained parts may require removal of very heavy oxide film prior to one of the following treatments. | Immerse in 5% sodium hydroxide solution at 160° F for 20 to 50 sec. Rinse in cold water. Rinse in room temperature concentrated technical grade nitric acid. Rinse in cold water. Quick rinse in hot water and dry rapidly. |
| 4<br>Mechanical oxide removal | Applicable to all alloys for cleaning small areas or very large parts that cannot be immersed. | Wire brush at surface speed of 4000 ft. per min. with rotary brush, stainless steel bristles 0.003 or 0.004 in. dia., or hand rub where required with steel wool or abrasive. |
| 5<br>General purpose deoxidizer | Used on all alloys when necessary to obtain uniform surface resistance. | Immerse in following solution at 75° F for 2 to 6 min.:<br>(12%) technical grade nitric acid)<br>(0.4%) technical grade hydrofluoric acid)<br>(0.2%) wetting agent)<br>Rinse one min. in cold water. Quick rinse in hot water and dry rapidly. |
| 6<br>Clad alloy deoxidizer | Applicable to clad alloys and 1060, 1100 and 3003. | Immerse in following solution at 190° F for 1½ to 3 min.:<br>(10% technical grade nitric acid)<br>(6 oz. sodium sulfate per gallon)<br>(0.1% wetting agent)<br>Rinse vigorously 5 min. in cold running water. Dry rapidly. |
| 7<br>Bare alloy deoxidizer | Applicable to bare heat treated alloys such as 6061. | Immerse in solution at 185° F for 1½ to 3 min.:<br>(15% technical grade nitric acid)<br>(13 oz. sodium sulfate per gallon)<br>(0.1% wetting agent)<br>Rinse vigorously 5 min. in cold running water. Dry rapidly. |
| 8<br>Proprietary cleaners | As recommended by supplier. | Immerse in solution or proprietary product as recommended by the supplier. |

\* Many proprietary inhibited hot alkaline cleaners are available.

vents to remove materials such as grease, oil, dirt or identification markings. Parts may be degreased by wiping, vapor degreasing or spraying, depending upon the size and quantity.

Since degreasing does not produce a chemically clean surface, it may be followed by cleaning with a solution specially formulated to produce low, consistent surface resistance on aluminum. After cleaning operations the parts should be capable of supporting a water film without a break.

*Oxide Removal*—While welding may sometimes be performed without altering the aluminum oxide coating, better quality welds will usually result if both surfaces of the material are degreased and chemically cleaned prior to welding. Oxides may be removed either by mechanical or chemical means.

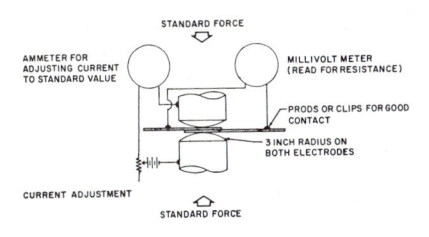

*Fig. 69.44.—Schematic of equipment for measuring surface contact resistance*

Mechanical methods are employed where the volume of production is small or where the size of the assemblies does not permit the handling necessary for chemical methods of oxide reduction. Mechanical oxide removal may be performed with a fine grade of abrasive cloth, fine stainless steel wool or a fine motor driven stainless steel wire brush. Glass brushes or aluminum wool have also been used. Mechanical oxide removal is primarily a hand operation which may be slow and costly. Its effectiveness depends upon the skill of the operator. While the contact resistance of surfaces cleaned by this method may sometimes be lower than that of parts cleaned by the chemical method, uniformity is not as good.

Rinsing in boiling water after cleaning is not recommended, since this generally reduces the consistency of the surface resistance. A number of chemical cleaning solutions are commercially available which are especially designed to prepare aluminum for resistance spot welding. These should be used in accordance with the recommendations of the manufacturer.

The maintenance of chemical treating solutions at the proper strength is necessary to insure satisfactory preparation of the surfaces for spot welding. Measurement of the surface resistance after treatment of small coupons of the alloy being welded is recommended as a control procedure. Additions can be made to the solution as required to maintain the surface resistance of the control samples at a desired value.

## MEASUREMENT OF SURFACE CONTACT RESISTANCE

As no visual inspection method can determine whether the proper cleaning and deoxidizing procedure has been employed, it is necessary to make actual measurements of surface resistance to insure properly prepared surfaces. Equipment for measuring surface resistance is available commercially or may be made by using a press and suitable measuring instruments. A diagram of this type of equipment is shown in Fig. 69.44.

The material to be measured is placed between two 5/8 inch diameter spot welding electrodes with 3 inch spherical radius contours, and standardized current and tip force are applied (50 ma d-c and a force of 600 pounds are frequently used). The surface resistance may be established by measuring the potential drop between the two pieces of material with a millivolt meter or by using a Kelvin or Wheatstone bridge. It is important that the test be carried out under identical conditions of force, applied current, electrode size and contour. The test is sensitive to small changes in procedure. Values of surface resistance are usually obtained by averaging at least 10 readings on each specimen. Movement of the specimen as the electrode force is applied may break the oxide coating and cause false low readings. The presence of burrs on the specimens may also affect the accuracy of the test by giving low readings.

Using the above-mentioned test conditions, the contact resistance of properly cleaned aluminum alloys will range from 10 up to about 100 microhms, while that of unclean stock may run up to 1000 microhms or higher. Best welding results are usually obtained when the cleaning practices are established to obtain

### Table 69.40—Minimum strength and nugget diameter for resistance spot welds in aluminum alloys

| Nominal Thickness of Thinnest Sheet, Inches | Nugget Diameter, Inches Minimum | Nugget Diameter, Inches Average* | Below 19,500 psi Load/Spot, Lbs Min. | Below 19,500 psi Load/Spot, Lbs Min. Avg.* | 19,500 to 28,000 psi Load/Spot, Lbs Min. | 19,500 to 28,000 psi Load/Spot, Lbs Min. Avg.* | 28,000 to 56,000 psi Load/Spot, Lbs. Min. | 28,000 to 56,000 psi Load/Spot, Lbs. Min. Avg.* | 56,000 psi and above Load/Spot, Lbs. Min. | 56,000 psi and above Load/Spot, Lbs. Min. Avg.* |
|---|---|---|---|---|---|---|---|---|---|---|
| 0.016 | 0.10 | 0.12 | 50  | 65  | 70   | 90   | 100  | 125  | 110  | 140  |
| 0.020 | 0.11 | 0.13 | 80  | 100 | 100  | 125  | 135  | 170  | 140  | 175  |
| 0.025 | 0.13 | 0.15 | 110 | 140 | 145  | 185  | 175  | 200  | 185  | 235  |
| 0.032 | 0.14 | 0.17 | 165 | 210 | 210  | 265  | 235  | 295  | 260  | 325  |
| 0.040 | 0.16 | 0.19 | 225 | 285 | 300  | 375  | 310  | 390  | 345  | 435  |
| 0.050 | 0.18 | 0.21 | 295 | 370 | 400  | 500  | 430  | 540  | 465  | 585  |
| 0.063 | 0.20 | 0.24 | 395 | 495 | 570  | 715  | 610  | 765  | 670  | 840  |
| 0.071 | 0.22 | 0.26 | 450 | 565 | 645  | 810  | 720  | 900  | 825  | 1035 |
| 0.080 | 0.23 | 0.27 | 525 | 660 | 765  | 960  | 855  | 1070 | 1025 | 1285 |
| 0.090 | 0.24 | 0.29 | 595 | 745 | 870  | 1090 | 1000 | 1250 | 1255 | 1570 |
| 0.100 | 0.26 | 0.30 | 675 | 845 | 940  | 1175 | 1170 | 1465 | 1490 | 1865 |
| 0.125 | 0.28 | 0.34 | 785 | 985 | 1050 | 1315 | 1625 | 2035 | 2120 | 2650 |

\* Average of three or more specimens, depending upon quality level desired.

surface resistances of 50 microhms. However, a narrow spread in readings is generally preferable to very low average values with an occasional high reading.

The use of surface resistance measuring equipment is often required by welding specifications such as MIL-W-6858.

## DESIGN FOR RESISTANCE SPOT WELDING

Satisfactory performance of spot welds in service depends to a great extent upon joint design. Spot welds should always be designed to carry shear loads. However, when tension or combined loadings may be expected special tests

### Table 69.41—Recommended dimensions for aluminum tension-shear test specimens

| Nominal Sheet Thickness, In. | Specimen Width (W), In. Recommended | Specimen Width (W), In. Minimum | Recommended Length (L), In. |
|---|---|---|---|
| 0.030 and under | ¾ | ⅝ | 3 |
| 0.031–0.050 | 1 | ¾ | 4 |
| 0.051–0.100 | 1¼ | 1 | 5 |
| 0.101–0.130 | 1½ | 1¼ | 6 |
| 0.131 and over | 2 | 1½ | 8 |

*Resistance Welding*/**99**

should be conducted to determine the actual strength of the joint under service loading, as the strength of spot welds in direct tension may vary from 20 to 90% of the shear strength.

The shear strength of spot welds can vary to a considerable extent with the alloy welded, thickness of the material welded, machine settings, weld spacing and edge distance or overlap. In a spot welded joint strength may also depend upon not only the individual spot strength but also on the number and pattern of the spots. The minimum required strength per weld and the minimum average strength are given in Table 69.40 for spot welds made to Specification MIL-W-6858. For industrial applications where a lesser degree of quality control is used, somewhat lower values may be specified. The strengths given in Table 69.40 are based upon spot welds of a given diameter. Welds of greater diameter will sometimes have higher strength. Welds of smaller diameter than those shown in the table should be avoided as weld schedules that produce small diameter spot welds in aluminum are likely to result in a substantial number of dud welds under production conditions. Tensile-shear specimens should conform to Table 69.41. Tip radius and welding current affect weld diameter and penetration directly.

Recommended spot weld spacing, edge distance, overlap, and clearance for spot welding aluminum are shown in Table 69.42.

**Table 69.42—Recommended minimum resistance spot weld spacing, edge distance, overlap and clearance for spot welding aluminum**

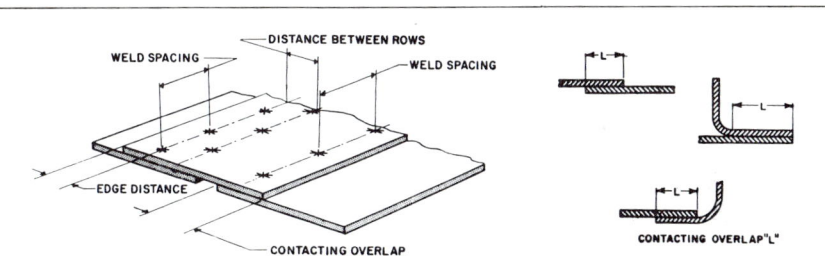

| Material thickness*, Inches | .016 | .020 | .025 | .032 | .040 | .050 | .063 | .071 | .080 | .090 | .100 | .125 |
|---|---|---|---|---|---|---|---|---|---|---|---|---|
| Minimum weld spacing.† (center to center) Inches | 3/8 | 3/8 | 3/8 | 1/2 | 1/2 | 5/8 | 5/8 | 3/4 | 3/4 | 7/8 | 1 | 1 1/4 |
| Minimum distance between rows of staggered welds, Inches | 1/4 | 1/4 | 5/16 | 5/16 | 3/8 | 3/8 | 3/8 | 7/16 | 1/2 | 1/2 | 1/2 | 5/8 |
| Minimum edge distance (center of weld to nearest edge of sheet) Inches | 5/32 | 3/16 | 7/32 | 1/4 | 1/4 | 5/16 | 3/8 | 3/8 | 3/8 | 7/16 | 7/16 | 1/2 |
| Minimum contacting overlap, flange width or "flat" required. Inches | 5/16 | 3/8 | 7/16 | 1/2 | 9/16 | 5/8 | 3/4 | 13/16 | 7/8 | 15/16 | 1 | 1 1/8 |
| Minimum unobstructed area required to place a weld, diameter, Inches | 9/16‡ | 9/16‡ | 9/16‡ | 11/16 | 11/16 | 11/16 | 11/16 | 11/16 | 11/16 | 15/16 | 15/16 | 15/16 |

\* For combinations of unequal thickness, use the thickness one lower than the heaviest gage to be joined as the thickness controlling dimensions indicated.

† Minimum weld spacing is that spacing for which no special precautions need be taken to compensate for shunted current effects of adjacent welds. It is measured from weld center to center.

‡ Using 1/2-in. dia. electrodes.

Spot weld spacing is an important consideration in design, as very close spacings may partially short circuit the current due to the high conductivity of aluminum when an adjoining spot weld is made. Closer spacing than that given in Table 69.42 will require special techniques and higher welding currents.

A spot placed too close to the edge of a sheet may force-out or bulge the metal between the spot and the edge of the sheet. In extreme cases, the metal may split, causing a crack from the spot to the edge of the sheet.

A certain minimum unobstructed area must be present around a spot weld in order to make the joint accessible. A guide to the diameter of the unobstructed area required to accommodate a normal straight electrode is given in Table 69.42. Offset electrodes generally need the same or greater area, depending on the degree of offset and the size of the members being joined.

Jigging of the pieces to be joined by means of clamps, spring fasteners or tack welds is recommended. If this is not done some electrode force may be spent in bringing the components into contact, thus affecting the quality of the weld. Mating parts assembled for welding should fit so that the surfaces to be joined by the weld are in contact with each other or can be made to contact each other by manual pressure at the area where the weld is to be placed.

In welding large assemblies it is often difficult to keep the surfaces being welded normal to the electrodes. If this is not done, oval or odd-shaped welds of doubtful quality may result. It is recommended that for large assemblies, slings or roller tables at the proper height be provided to support the part being welded. All tooling that will pass through the magnetic field during the welding

**Table 69.43—Resistance spot welding schedule for standard single phase A-C type equipment**

| Material Thickness,*† Inches | Electrode Dimensions Diameter,· Inches | Electrode Dimensions Radius,‡ Inches Top-Bottom | Net Electrode Force (Weld), Lbs. | Welding Current Approximate Amps | Welding Time Approximate (Cycles) |
|---|---|---|---|---|---|
| 0.016 | 5/8 | 1–Flat | 320 | 15,000 | 4 |
| 0.020 | 5/8 | 1–Flat | 340 | 18,000 | 5 |
| 0.025 | 5/8 | 2–Flat | 390 | 21,800 | 6 |
| 0.032 | 5/8 | 2–Flat | 500 | 26,000 | 7 |
| 0.040 | 5/8 | 3–Flat | 600 | 30,700 | 8 |
| 0.050 | 5/8 | 3–Flat | 660 | 33,000 | 8 |
| 0.063 | 5/8 | 3–Flat | 750 | 35,900 | 10 |
| 0.071 | 5/8 | 4–4 | 800 | 38,000 | 10 |
| 0.080 | 7/8 | 4–4 | 860 | 41,800 | 10 |
| 0.090 | 7/8 | 6–6 | 950 | 46,000 | 12 |
| 0.100 | 7/8 | 6–6 | 1050 | 56,000 | 15 |
| 0.125 | 7/8 | 6–6 | 1300 | 76,000 | 15 |

\* Thickness is the thickness of one sheet of a two-sheet combination.

† Types of aluminum alloy—1100-H12-H18, 3003-H12-H18, 3004-H32-H38, 5050-H32-H38, 5052-H32-H38, 5154-H32-H38, 6061-T4-T6, and 6063-T4-T6.

‡ A spherical radius to a flat or almost spherical radius is recommended unless the contour of the part is such that unlike radii are necessary to effect a heat balance.

Resistance Welding/**101**

Table 69.44—Resistance spot welding schedule for single phase A-C slope control type machines

| Alloy | Material Thickness* Inches | Electrode Dimensions, Inches Diameter | Tip Radius† | Net Electrode Force, lbs. Weld | Forge | Time,‡ Cycles (60 per second) Up Slope | Weld Heat | Down Slope | Weld Time | Weld Current, Approximate Amps (RMS x 10³) Initial | Weld | Final Post Heat |
|---|---|---|---|---|---|---|---|---|---|---|---|---|
| 2024 and 7075 | 0.025 | 5/8 | 3 | 500 | 1100 | 2 | 4 | 4 | 8 | 7.0 | 22.0 | 11.0 |
|  | 0.032 | 5/8 | 3 | 600 | 1275 | 2 | 5 | 4 | 9 | 8.0 | 24.0 | 13.0 |
|  | 0.040 | 5/8 | 3 | 700 | 1400 | 2 | 6 | 5 | 11 | 9.0 | 27.0 | 15.0 |
|  | 0.050 | 5/8 | 3 | 800 | 1700 | 3 | 8 | 5 | 13 | 10.0 | 30.0 | 17.0 |
|  | 0.063 | 5/8 | 6 | 950 | 2000 | 3 | 10 | 6 | 16 | 11.0 | 34.0 | 20.0 |
|  | 0.071 | 5/8 | 6 | 1100 | 2200 | 3 | 12 | 6 | 18 | 12.0 | 37.0 | 22.0 |
|  | 0.080 | 5/8 | 6 | 1200 | 2500 | 3 | 13 | 7 | 20 | 13.0 | 40.0 | 25.0 |
|  | 0.090 | 7/8 | 6 | 1400 | 3000 | 4 | 15 | 8 | 23 | 14.0 | 43.0 | 28.0 |
|  | 0.100 | 7/8 | 6 | 1700 | 3700 | 4 | 16 | 9 | 25 | 15.0 | 47.0 | 31.0 |
|  | 0.125 | 7/8 | 6 | 2600 | 5500 | 5 | 20 | 10 | 30 | 16.5 | 55.0 | 33.0 |
| 5052 and 6061 | 0.025 | 5/8 | 3 | 450 | 1000 | 2 | 4 | 4 | 8 | 6.5 | 21.0 | 11.0 |
|  | 0.032 | 5/8 | 3 | 550 | 1150 | 2 | 5 | 4 | 9 | 7.5 | 23.0 | 13.0 |
|  | 0.040 | 5/8 | 3 | 600 | 1300 | 2 | 6 | 5 | 11 | 8.0 | 25.0 | 14.0 |
|  | 0.050 | 5/8 | 3 | 700 | 1500 | 3 | 8 | 5 | 13 | 9.0 | 28.0 | 16.0 |
|  | 0.063 | 5/8 | 6 | 825 | 1750 | 3 | 10 | 6 | 16 | 10.0 | 31.0 | 18.0 |
|  | 0.071 | 5/8 | 6 | 900 | 2000 | 3 | 12 | 6 | 18 | 11.0 | 33.0 | 20.0 |
|  | 0.080 | 5/8 | 6 | 1000 | 2200 | 3 | 13 | 7 | 20 | 12.0 | 36.0 | 22.0 |
|  | 0.090 | 7/8 | 6 | 1200 | 2500 | 4 | 15 | 8 | 23 | 13.0 | 40.0 | 25.0 |
|  | 0.100 | 7/8 | 6 | 1400 | 2900 | 4 | 16 | 9 | 25 | 14.0 | 44.0 | 28.0 |
|  | 0.125 | 7/8 | 6 | 2000 | 4000 | 5 | 20 | 10 | 30 | 18.0 | 53.0 | 37.0 |

\* Thickness is the thickness of one sheet of a two-sheet combination.
† A spherical radius to a flat or similar spherical radius is recommended unless the contour of the part is such that unlike radii are necessary to effect a heat balance.
‡ See current wave form for definition of time.

# 102/Resistance Welding

**Table 69.45—Resistance spot welding schedule for three phase frequency converter type equipment**

| Material Thickness* Inches | Electrode Dimensions, Inches | | Net Electrode Force,‡ Lbs. | | Welding Current, Approximate,‡ Amps (RMS x 10³) | | Welding Time, (Approximate) Cycles (60/Second) | |
|---|---|---|---|---|---|---|---|---|
| | Diameter | Tip Radius† | Weld | Forge | Weld | Post Heat | Cycles Weld | Post Heat |
| 0.020 | ⅝ | 3 | 500 | .... | 26.0 | None | ½ | None |
| 0.025 | ⅝ | 3 | 500 | 1500 | 34.0 | 8.5 | 1 | 3 |
| 0.032 | ⅝ | 4 | 700 | 1800 | 36.0 | 9.0 | 1 | 4 |
| 0.040 | ⅝ | 4 | 800 | 2000 | 42.0 | 12.6 | 1 | 4 |
| 0.050 | ⅝ | 4 | 900 | 2300 | 46.0 | 13.8 | 1 | 5 |
| 0.063 | ⅝ | 6 | 1300 | 3000 | 54.0 | 18.9 | 2 | 5 |
| 0.071 | ⅝ | 6 | 1600 | 3600 | 61.0 | 21.4 | 2 | 6 |
| 0.080 | ⅞ | 6 | 2000 | 4300 | 65.0 | 22.8 | 3 | 6 |
| 0.090 | ⅞ | 6 | 2400 | 5300 | 75.0 | 30.0 | 3 | 8 |
| 0.100 | ⅞ | 8 | 2800 | 6800 | 85.0 | 34.0 | 3 | 8 |
| 0.125 | ⅞ | 8 | 4000 | 9000 | 100.0 | 45.0 | 4 | 10 |

\* Thickness is the thickness of one sheet of a two-sheet combination.
† A spherical radius to a flat or similar spherical radius is recommended unless the contour of the part is such that unlike radii are necessary to effect a heat balance.
‡ Values for alloys 2014-T3-T4-T6, 2024-T3-T4 and 7075-T6. Somewhat lower values may be used for 5052, 6061, etc.

**Table 69.46—Resistance spot welding schedule for three-phase rectifier-type equipment**

| Material Thickness* Inches | Electrode Dimensions, Inches Diameter | Electrode Dimensions, Inches Tip Radius* | Net Electrode Force,‡ Lbs. Weld | Net Electrode Force,‡ Lbs. Forge | Welding Current,‡ Approximate, Amps (RMS x 10³) Weld | Welding Current,‡ Approximate, Amps (RMS x 10³) Post Heat | Welding Time, (Approximate) Cycles (60/Second) Weld | Welding Time, (Approximate) Cycles (60/Second) Post Heat |
|---|---|---|---|---|---|---|---|---|
| 0.016 | 5/8 | 3 | 440 | 1000 | 19.0 | None | 1 | None |
| 0.020 | 5/8 | 3 | 520 | 1150 | 22.0 | None | 1 | None |
| 0.032 | 5/8 | 3 | 670 | 1540 | 28.0 | None | 2 | None |
| 0.040 | 5/8 | 3 | 730 | 1800 | 32.0 | None | 3 | None |
| 0.050 | 5/8 | 8 | 900 | 2250 | 37.0 | 30.0 | 4 | 4 |
| 0.063 | 5/8 | 8 | 1100 | 2900 | 43.0 | 36.0 | 5 | 5 |
| 0.071 | 5/8 | 8 | 1190 | 3240 | 48.0 | 38.0 | 6 | 7 |
| 0.080 | 7/8 | 8 | 1460 | 3800 | 52.0 | 42.0 | 7 | 9 |
| 0.090 | 7/8 | 8 | 1700 | 4300 | 56.0 | 45.0 | 8 | 11 |
| 0.100 | 7/8 | 8 | 1900 | 5000 | 61.0 | 49.0 | 9 | 14 |
| 0.125 | 7/8 | 8 | 2500 | 6500 | 69.0 | 54.0 | 10 | 22 |

\* Thickness is the thickness of one sheet of a two-sheet combination.
† A spherical radius to a flat or similar spherical radius is recommended unless the contour of the part is such that unlike radii are necessary to effect a heat balance.
‡ Values for alloys 2014-T3-T4-T6, 2024-T3-T4 and 7075-T6. Somewhat lower values may be used for alloys such as 5052 and 6061.

Resistance Welding/**103**

**104**/*Resistance Welding*

**Table 69.47—Resistance spot welding schedule for electrostatic (condenser discharge) type equipment**

| Material Thickness*† Inches | Electrode Dimensions‡ Diameter Inches | Electrode Dimensions‡ Tip Radius Inches | Net Electrode Force, Lbs. Weld | Net Electrode Force, Lbs. Forge | Capacity Mfd. | Charging Voltage Kilo. Volts | Transf. Turns Radio | Total Energy Watt Seconds |
|---|---|---|---|---|---|---|---|---|
| 0.020 | 5/8 | 3 | 376 | 692 | 240 | 2.15 | 300:1 | 555 |
| 0.032 | 5/8 | 3 | 580 | 1300 | 240 | 2.7 | 300:1 | 875 |
| 0.040 | 5/8 | 3 | 680 | 1580 | 360 | 2.55 | 300:1 | 1172 |
| 0.050 | 5/8 | 3 | 890 | 2100 | 600 | 2.56 | 300:1 | 1952 |
| 0.063 | 5/8 | 3 | 1080 | 2680 | 720 | 2.7 | 300:1 | 2622 |
| 0.071 | 5/8 | 3 | 1230 | 3150 | 960 | 2.75 | 450:1 | 3630 |
| 0.080 | 7/8 | 3 | 1550 | 4000 | 1440 | 2.7 | 450:1 | 5250 |
| 0.090 | 7/8 | 3 | 1830 | 4660 | 1920 | 2.65 | 450:1 | 6750 |
| 0.100 | 7/8 | 3 | 2025 | 5100 | 2520 | 2.7 | 450:1 | 9180 |

\* Thickness is the thickness of one sheet of a two sheet combination.
† Types of Aluminum alloy—2014-T3-T4-T6, 2024-T3-T4, and Clad 7075-T6.
‡ Where practical a spherical radius is recommended. This radius should be the same on top and bottom electrodes for like gage and material combinations unless the contour of the part is such that unlike radii are necessary to effect a heat balance.

operation should be made of nonmagnetic materials. Aluminum, fiberglass and other types of plastic materials are often used in spot welding fixtures.

## RESISTANCE SPOT WELDING SCHEDULES

Spot welds made on any of the equipment previously discussed will have the same shear strength, provided the welds are of equal size and are of good quality. Typical welding schedules for the various types of equipment are given in Tables 69.43 through 69.48. These schedules may be used as a starting point for developing the proper welding schedule for the part in question. Modifications will undoubtedly be required for material of a different alloy, temper or type of cleaning. The schedules given in Tables 69.44 through 69.48 should produce welds that qualify under government specifications such as MIL-W-6858. Table 69.43 gives machine settings for commercial quality spot welds made on single phase equipment. In general, single phase equipment without slope control does not produce welds of a consistency to meet military specifications.

The standards and specifications to which welds are produced vary widely according to service requirements. Some specifications are very specific as to the procedures for qualification of the welding equipment and certification of welding schedules, as well as the quality control and inspection to be applied. If welding is to be done to one of these specifications, the practices specified should be followed closely, with the above schedules used as a guide in establishing the machine settings.

## SHOP PRACTICES

To set up a spot welding machine to produce satisfactory spot welds the production of sample welds is necessary. A series of welds should be made on stock of the same gage, alloy, surface condition and spot spacing as the job to be welded. The schedules given in Tables 69.43 through 69.48 may be used as a starting point. Weld specimens may be torn apart by driving a chisel between the sheets at a point between the welds or by a peel test of a sample weld (Fig. 10.73, Section 1). Each spot weld should pull a button of diameter equal to twice the thickness of the material plus 1/16 inch or more. In general, buttons of this size will meet commercial standards but will not necessarily meet aircraft standards such as MIL-W-6858A. If the spot diameter is small it may be enlarged by varying the current or tip radius. If expulsion of metal from the weld between the sheets is occurring, the welding force should be increased or the current reduced. If the outside surfaces of the sheets exhibit evidence of excessive darkening, surface melting or sticking to the electrodes after only one or two welds have been made, either the force should be increased or the current decreased, assuming the sheets have been properly cleaned.

Spot welds in aluminum alloys 2014, 2024, 6061 and 7075 in either bare or clad form will not always pull buttons completely through the sheet when the thickness of material is greater than about 0.080 inch. In these materials the weld is tested as previously described and the diameter of the fractured area determined.

When the peel test indicates that welds of the proper size are being produced, some test welds can be made to determine the shear strength. The shear test

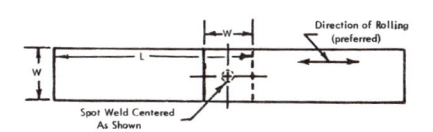

*Fig. 69.45.—Recommended dimensions for aluminum tension-shear test specimens*

# 106/Resistance Welding

specimen shown in Fig. 69.45 is recommended. Welds also can be sectioned for metallographic examination to determine nugget diameter and penetration. Radiographic examination is often used to determine weld soundness.

When welding unequal thicknesses of materials the thickness of the thinner material governs the machine settings and the diameter of the weld. Where more than two thicknesses are welded the settings are governed by the outside sheets using values of welding current and welding force slightly higher than normal.

## RESISTANCE SPOT WELD DEFECTS AND CAUSES

The four major factors affecting weld quality are: surface cleanliness and uniformity of the material, contour and cleanliness of the electrodes, welding force, and welding current.

Electrode pickup can occur with all types of spot welding equipment. It is usually the result of excessive heating at the interface between the tips and the work. In severe cases there is actual melting or burning of the surface of the parts. Pickup may be caused by improper cleaning of the parts, poorly cleaned electrodes, use of the wrong electrode material, inadequate cooling of the electrodes or skidding. Other causes may be inadequate welding force or excessive welding current or time.

Cracks and porosity may be closely allied with tip force. The factors which tend to produce cracks or porosity may be: excessive thermal rise inside the weld, an excessively high cooling rate or inadequate or improper application of welding force. Spot welds in some high strength alloys such as 2024 and 7075 are subject to cracking if welding current is too high or welding force too low. Cracking may also result from too rapid quenching after the welding current cuts off. Changes in the down slope or use of postheat may eliminate cracking. On dual force equipment adjustment of the forge delay time may also eliminate cracking by applying the forging action at the proper time in the weld cycle.

Expulsion of molten metal from the weld nugget is usually caused by exces-

Table 69.48—Resistance spot welding schedule for electromagnetic type equipment

| Material Thickness*, Inches | Electrode Dimensions, Inches || Net Electrode Force, Lbs.‡ || Welding Current, Approx. (Amps)‡ |
|---|---|---|---|---|---|
| | Diameter | Radius† | Weld | Forge | |
| 0.016 | ⅝ | 4 | 332 | 1000 | 21,000 |
| 0.020 | ⅝ | 4 | 350 | 1050 | 23,000 |
| 0.025 | ⅝ | 4 | 383 | 1150 | 25,000 |
| 0.032 | ⅝ | 4 | 450 | 1350 | 28,000 |
| 0.040 | ⅝ | 4 | 475 | 1425 | 31,000 |
| 0.050 | ⅝ | 4 | 515 | 1550 | 36,000 |
| 0.063 | ⅝ | 6 | 700 | 2100 | 41,000 |

\* Thickness is the thickness of one sheet of a two-sheet combination.
† A spherical radius to a flat or similar spherical radius is recommended unless the contour of the part is such that unlike radii are necessary to effect a heat balance.
‡ Types of aluminum alloy—2014-T3-T4-T6, 2024-T3-T4 and 7075-T6.

sive heat or improper force. It is often due to improper cleaning. Reducing the welding current slightly or increasing the welding force slightly will generally eliminate expulsion. If expulsion of metal between the sheets cannot be entirely eliminated by changing the machine settings, a more thorough method of cleaning the material should be adopted. A light rubbing with fine steel wood just before welding is often beneficial.

Weld penetration of between 20 and 80% of the thickness of the joint is usually satisfactory. Weld penetration depends upon current and electrode contour. An increase of current will increase penetration while a greater radius on the electrode tip will decrease penetration.

Excessive indentation and sheet separation tend to go together. One of the major causes of these defects is the use of material of too soft a temper. These defects may sometimes be minimized by the use of less force, increasing the radius of the welding tip, or reducing the current. In general, sheet separation less than 10% of sheet thickness is considered satisfactory.

Irregularly shaped welds are undesirable and may be traced to improper fit-up of parts, improper electrode alignment, skidding, inadequate surface preparation, or an irregular electrode contour.

Inadequately fused welds in clad sheet may have unwelded cladding in the weld nugget. This defect is undesirable and can usually be avoided by a moderate increase in current.

## INSPECTION AND TESTING

Uniform spot weld quality can be obtained only by the use of proper equipment, rigid adherence to established welding procedures, close control of machine settings, and the use of qualified personnel. To ensure spot weld quality a correct welding procedure and schedule should be developed and maintained during production by a regular program of inspection.

Machine settings should be checked periodically and verified by frequent tests on materials of the same alloy and gage as the work being done. This may be done by peel testing, by conducting periodic tensile shear tests, and by sectioning a weld, etching and examining to determine penetration and nugget diameter.

Visual examination is the chief means of inspection. It may be used to detect electrode pickup or surface burning, cracks, skidding and excessive indentation. Radiography may be used with some alloys to detect internal defects such as cracks, porosity, cladding inclusions, and segregation, and to evaluate the size and shape of the nugget and the weld structure. Radiography will also detect external defects such as expulsion, pits and tip pickup. In general, radiographic examination is used principally in the establishment of welding schedules and not as a production testing method.

Destructive tests, such as the peel test previously described, are used mainly in the shop for set up and checking. The tensile-shear test is used to get a quantitative value of the strength of the weld. Dimensions of shear test specimens are given in Fig. 69.45. These sample strips are overlapped a distance equal to their width and a spot weld is made in the center of the overlap. The weld is then tested in tension in a suitable machine until failure occurs. An evaluation of the consistency of welding may be made by welding a panel containing a series of spot welds using the overlaps given in Fig. 69.46 and a spacing equal to the minimum width. This panel may then be sheared or sawed into individual shear test specimens. Testing of a series of welds such as this can provide infor-

## 108/Resistance Welding

mation as to average strength, minimum strength obtained from the series and variation.

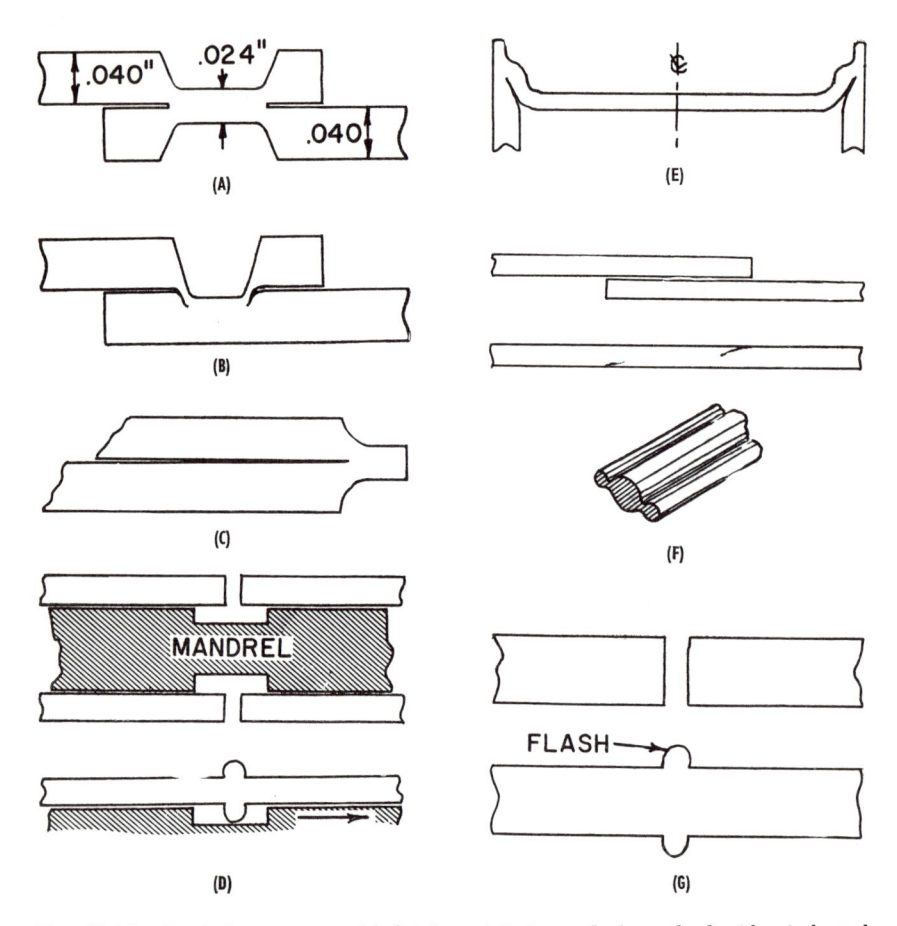

Fig. 69.46.—*Typical pressure welded joints. (A) Lapped sheet; both sides indented; (B) Lapped sheet; one side indented; (C) Edge of lapped sheet; both sides indented; (D) Butt weld, tube; (E) Draw weld; (F) Lapped wire; (G) Butt weld, solid stock*

Examination of a weld cross section is used to reveal the size, shape, structure and penetration of spot welds. Spot welds should be very carefully sectioned to the exact center of the weld zone. The sample is then polished, etched and examined. Macro-examination at less than 10 magnifications may be used to determine the diameter and penetration of the weld, but it is not reliable for detecting internal cracks, porosity, or weld structure. These require suitable metallographic polishing, etching and examination at higher magnifications, an evaluation of the weld structure to determine amount of cracking, porosity, and inclusions.

Indentation of spot welds may be determined either with ball tip micrometers or surface indicators. Sheet separation may be determined with feeler gages.

## RESISTANCE SEAM WELDING

Seam welding of aluminum and its alloys is very similar to spot welding except that the electrodes are replaced by wheels. The spots made by a seam welding machine can be overlapped to form a gas or liquid-tight joint. By adjusting the timing the seam welding machine can produce uniformly spaced spot welds equal in quality to those produced on a regular spot welding machine and at a faster rate. This procedure is called roll spot or intermittent seam welding.

Equipment used for seam welding aluminum should have the same features as that employed for spot welding aluminum. However, somewhat higher welding currents and forces may be required for seam welding because of the greater shunting effect of the current. For this reason it may be necessary to use a seam welding machine of greater capacity than would be used for spot welding a given gage of material.

Welding may be done either with the seam welding electrodes in motion or while they are stopped for an instant. Applying the welding current when the electrodes are motionless results in a better surface appearance and better weld quality in aluminum.

Seam welding electrodes or wheels may be from 3/8 to 1 inch thick and are usually from 6 to 9 inch diameter. A smaller diameter may sometimes be required, depending on the configuration or accessibility of the parts being welded.

One or both of these wheels are dressed to a 1 to 10 inch radius. The wheels are cooled internally or the wheels and the work are cooled by a generous flow of water directed against the periphery of the wheel near the weld. One of the wheels is usually driven at a speed which is adjustable from 1 to 5 fpm.

It is essential for a-c seam welding that the weld timer initiate and cut off the current in a predetermined sequence with the supply voltage. Electronically controlled timing equipment is the only satisfactory means available for doing this with sufficient accuracy to produce uniform welds in aluminum.

When producing a series of overlapping spot welds, one weld is made at each application of current. The speed of the rolls, together with the on-off time, is adjusted to get the number of spots per inch shown in Table 69.49. Various combinations of cycles may be used, although the ratio of on time to off time should be from 1:5 to 1:3.

Excessive welding speed will result in the work sticking to the welding wheel. This can be corrected by increasing the cycle time, and decreasing the roll speed to give the desired number of welds per inch. Where a continuous pressure-tight weld is not required the seam welding machine may be used to place spot welds at any uniform spacing from about 3/8 to 6 inch or greater. In this case, the speed of welding will be from 60 to 180 welds per minute.

In spot welding, aluminum may stick to the electrodes; in seam welding it can adhere to the electrode rollers or wheels. It may be removed by dressing with a suitable grade of abrasive cloth. A moderately coarse grade of cloth is used to produce a rough surface on the wheel which prevents slipping between the wheel and the work. On continuous seam welding, the wheels must be cleaned after three to five revolutions, and on intermittent welding after 10 to 20 revolutions. Continuous dressing of the electrodes may be performed by using a medium fine grade of commutator stone held against each wheel under 5 to 10 lbs pressure.

Typical settings for seam welding aluminum alloy 5052-H34 using a single

Table 69.49—Machine settings for producing continuous gas-tight resistance seam welds on standard single phase a-c type equipment

| Thickness of One Sheet, Inches | Spots per Inch | On-Plus Off-Time, Cycles, 60/Sec.[a] | Electrode Travel Speed, Ft./Min.[b] | On Time Cycles, 60/Sec. Min. | On Time Cycles, 60/Sec. Max.[c] | Welding Force, Lbs.[d] | Welding Current, Amp. (RMS x $10^3$) | Width of Weld (Approximate), Inches[e] |
|---|---|---|---|---|---|---|---|---|
| 0.010 | 25 | 3½ | 3.4 | ½ | 1 | 420 | 19.5 | 0.080 |
| 0.016 | 21 | 3½ | 4.1 | ½ | 1 | 500 | 22.0 | 0.095 |
| 0.020 | 20 | 4½ | 3.3 | ½ | 1½ | 540 | 24.0 | 0.100 |
| 0.025 | 18 | 5½ | 3.0 | 1 | 1½ | 600 | 26.0 | 0.110 |
| 0.032 | 16 | 5½ | 3.4 | 1 | 1½ | 690 | 29.0 | 0.130 |
| 0.040 | 14 | 7½ | 2.9 | 1½ | 2½ | 760 | 32.0 | 0.140 |
| 0.050 | 12 | 9½ | 2.6 | 1½ | 3 | 860 | 36.0 | 0.160 |
| 0.063 | 10 | 11½ | 2.6 | 2 | 3½ | 960 | 38.5 | 0.190 |
| 0.080 | 9 | 15½ | 2.1 | 3 | 5 | 1090 | 41.0 | 0.220 |
| 0.100 | 8 | 20½ | 1.8 | 4 | 6½ | 1230 | 43.0 | 0.260 |
| 0.125 | 7 | 28½ | 1.5 | 5½ | 9½ | 1350 | 45.0 | 0.320 |

[a] Use next higher full cycle setting if timer is not equipped to give antipole starting of current.
[b] Should be adjusted to give desired spots per inch.
[c] On-time must be set at full cycle setting if on plus off time is set at full cycle setting.
[d] Welding force and welding current are adjusted to give desired width of weld. Values are for 5052-H34 aluminum alloy. Use lower force for softer tempers or alloys and higher force for harder tempers or alloys.
[e] These values will not meet MIL-W-6858A.

phase a-c seam welding machine are given in Table 69.49. This table may also be used as a basis for developing welding schedules for other alloys or tempers.

Quality control for seam welding is the same as was described for spot welding except that an additional test for gas or liquid tightness may be used called the pillow test (Fig. 10.74, Section 1). By pressurizing the specimen the pressure tightness of a seam weld may be determined.

## FLASH WELDING

All aluminum alloys may be joined by the flash welding process. This process is particularly adapted to making butt or miter joints between two parts of similar cross section. It has also been adapted to joining aluminum to copper in the form of bars and tubing. The joints so produced fail in tension outside of the weld area. The equipment used for flash welding is usually highly specialized and expensive. Consequently the process is used primarily for mass production. The flash welding process is described in more detail in Chapters 31 and 32, Section 2.

Flash-welding machines of the alternating current and storage battery types are presently used on aluminum alloys. On machines of 75 kva or lower capacity, platen motion may be produced by direct mechanical drive. On machines of higher capacity platen motion is generally produced by a hydraulic system. A machine for flash welding aluminum should have a secondary current capacity of approximately 100,000 amp per square inch of material being welded. Secondary voltages from 2 to 18 volts have been used. The amount of material upset varies from 1/4 to 1/2 inch. The flashing time varies from 30 cycles for welds in small sections, such as 1/4 to 5/16 inch outside diameter aluminum tubing, to 70 cycles for 1/4 x 2 inch solid bars, and longer time as cross sectional area increases.

The welding current is cut off or decreased at the beginning of upset. The hot upsetting period ranges from 5 to 25 cycles in duration, depending upon the alloy and the area of section being welded. Upset current duration may vary from 1 to 10 cycles. High, uniform upset velocity is an important factor in making a high quality flash weld. Upset force is a function of alloy and temper. It may vary from 15,000 to 45,000 psi on the cross sectional area at the weld.

The parts to be flash welded are clamped by hard drawn copper or copper alloy dies which have been accurately shaped to fit each part. These workholding clamps must be substantial to withstand the upset forging forces without deflection. They must hold the work firmly during upset without marking or crushing the aluminum parts. Water cooling helps dissipate the heat developed during welding.

Flash welding of aluminum requires perfect alignment of the joint members. This is reflected in the high accuracy required of the dies and platens which guide the dies through the welding cycle. Ferrous metals can be flash welded with comparatively wide platen openings. Aluminum requires relatively narrow platen or die openings.

Pinch off dies have been developed for use with aluminum which permit as little as 0.005 inch final die spacing. These dies are sharpened and trim off upset metal or flash at the end of the upset stroke. These pnch-off dies also improve weld quality.

## STRENGTH OF FLASH WELDS

The mechanical strength of flash welded joints is good both in the heat-treatable and the nonheat-treatable alloys. Joint efficiencies of at least 80% of base material in any temper may be expected. Efficiencies of 100% in the annealed temper are readily obtained. However, joints of highest quality are normally obtained by welding a given alloy in a harder temper. Elongations measured across the weld on the nonheat-treatable alloys are about half of the elongation of the base material. In the heat treated tempers of alloys such as 2024, 6061 and 7075, weld strength is at least 80% of the strength of the base material but the elongation at the weld may be reduced to about one-fifth of that of the base metal. Postweld heat treatment of flash welds in the heat-treatable alloys usually results in a slight increase in strength and joint efficiency and a much greater increase in elongation.

Flash weld corrosion resistance is generally excellent. The finishing characteristics of flash welded joints are excellent and anodic finishes on flash welded joints generally show less color contrast at the joint than are obtained on welds made by any other method.

## FLASH WELDING SCHEDULES

The schedules for flash welding aluminum and its alloys will vary greatly with the equipment used and the size and shape of the parts. The schedules are usually the result of a considerable amount of trial and error. When flash welding is being considered for an application the welding machine manufacturer should be consulted for details on the spacings and machine settings most suitable for the job. A description of the various types of flash welding machines and some of their mechanical and electrical features is given in Chapter 32, Section 2. Details of the flash welding process itself, including design, inspection and recommended practices, are covered in Chapter 31, Section 2.

## HIGH FREQUENCY RESISTANCE WELDING

Resistance welding with high frequency current has been developed for high-speed production of welded tubing.

In this application squeeze rolls forge the moving edges together while the metal is heated to welding temperature by high frequency current.

The welding current enters the metal through contact shoes placed near the joint. The current flows in the paths of low inductance on and slightly below the surface of the edges, heating the edges of the joint to the plastic range. The hot metal is then squeezed together, forming a forged weld joint.

Very high welding speeds can be achieved with this process. Aluminum tubing of 0.030 inch wall thickness has been welded at rates of 350 feet per minute.

This process is not limited to straight tubing; strip to strip, strip to tube and tapered tubes have also been successfully welded. High frequency induction welding is also used for similar applications.

A further description of the two processes is given in Chapter 35, Section 2.

## SOLID STATE BONDING

The absence of a liquid metal phase is characteristic of solid state bonding where the parts being joined are relatively free from heat-affected zones and dilution. Clean surfaces are brought together under selected pressure conditions causing plastic flow and a metallurgical bond is formed between the parts, in some cases augmented by the application of heat.

## PRESSURE WELDING

Solid state bonding by pressure deformation without heat application produces a weld zone harder, stronger and less ductile than the base metal and in some joints, a reduction in section. Diffusion is minimized while cast structure and heat effect are eliminated. This permits the welding of dissimilar metals and aids in the retention of corrosion resistance (Chapter 50, Section 3).

Butt and lap type joints are used. Since intimate contact between joint surfaces is essential to good bonds they must be free from oxide and any form of contamination. Surface preparation includes degreasing and abrading or machining just prior to welding. Stiff bristle wire brushing is preferred just before lap welding. (See Shop Practices.)

Techniques for pressure welding vary greatly in the method of obtaining deformation, upset or flow. Typical joints are shown in Fig. 69.46. These joints indicate the end results obtained by using pressure dies, rolling or upsetting. Trimming can be combined by die design.

Pressures 60,000 to 100,000 psi will be required for suitable joints, depending on alloy and temper. Welding at elevated temperatures up to 450°F reduces the pressure required and permits lap welding additional alloys and metal formations. Heated dies may assist welding. Die alignment must be maintained as the dies are forced together causing the metal to flow plastically and weld.

Lap welds have been made at room temperature in thin foil up through 1/4 inch. Anodically treated aluminum foil can be lap welded without brushing since the oxide breaks up under deformation to provide the desired surface condition. In this weld, thickness reduction of 60 to 75% is required for satisfactory welding. Lap welds show good strength in shear and tension, but are poor in bending.

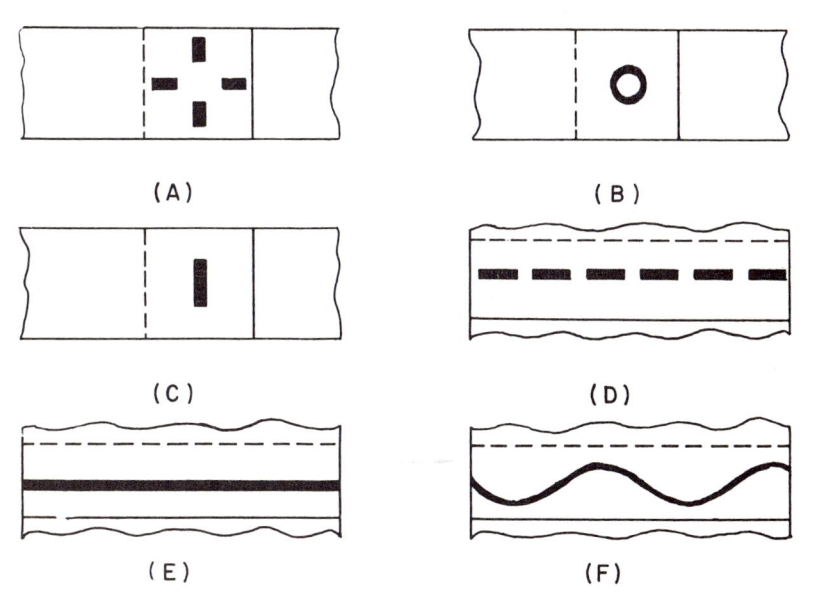

*Fig. 69.47.—Typical indentor configurations employed in pressure welding. (A) and (C) bar type; (B) ring type; (D), (E) and (F) intermittent and continuous seam type*

## 114/Solid State Bonding

The configuration of lap weld indentors can vary widely from short bars to a continuous line. Typical variations are illustrated in Fig. 69.47. Draw welding is a form of lap welding where the lapped joint is drawn through a die and reduced in thickness.

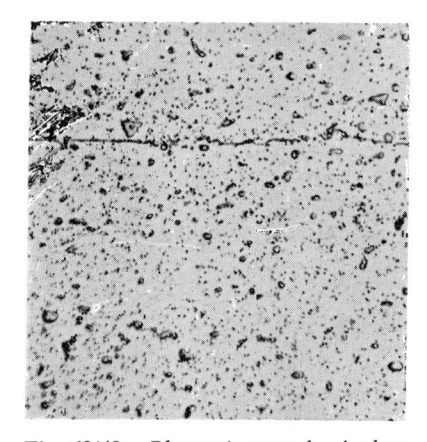

*Fig. 69.48.—Photomicrograph of ultrasonic spot weld in 3003-H14 aluminum alloy (X500)*

*Fig. 69.49.—Photomicrograph of ultrasonic spot weld in 2024-T3 aluminum alloy*

When the part being welded is at an elevated temperature the pressure required to effect plastic flow is less than when the part is at room temperature. Surface pretreatment requirements may be reduced. Work hardening by deformation is reduced and as temperatures increase annealing may be achieved. Better plastic flow may be achieved with softer weld metal but joint strength may be lower. See Chapter 33, Forge Welding.

Excellent lap welds are obtained with the lower strength nonheat-treatable alloys such as EC, 1100 and 3003. Greater deformation is required for the harder alloys, especially harder tempers. Alloys containing more than 3% magnesium, those of 2000 and 7000 series, and castings are not readily lap welded.

Butt pressure welds can be made in most aluminum alloys. The weld is usually stronger than the original material due to work hardening during welding, but the welds do not develop the severe notch effect encountered in lap welds. Butt welds normally develop 100% joint efficiency and are excellent in tension, bending and fatigue life. Butt welds can be made in wire rod, tube and simple extruded shapes. Commercial equipment is available for butt welding wire as small as 0.15 inch and up to and including 3/8 inch rod. Wire brushing is not required for butt pressure welding.

### FRICTION WELDING

Friction welding has been developed to produce pressure welds at elevated temperatures and has been highly successful for joining aluminum to a wide variety of other metals (Chapter 52, Section 3).

### ULTRASONIC WELDING

Ultrasonic welding is a relatively new method of joining foil and sheet gage

Solid State Bonding/**115**

aluminum alloys. In this process (Chapter 49, Section 3), high frequency mechanical energy produces solid state metallurgical bonding. While all aluminum alloys can be ultrasonically welded, the degree of weldability varies with alloy and temper.

Ultrasonic welds in aluminum alloys look much like resistance spot or seam welds and are often characterized by a roughened spot or seam on the surface of the welded materials.

Photomicrographs of ultrasonic welds in 3003-H14 and 2024-T3 aluminum alloys are shown in Figs. 69.48 and 69.49 respectively. Solid state bonding is evident over a significant portion of the weld area. No significant melting, annealing or other heat effects are visible. Slight recrystallization is evident at the weld interface in the 2024-T3 alloy weld.

For relatively low-strength aluminum alloys ultrasonic spot welds exhibit approximately the same strength as resistance spot or seam welds. In the higher strength alloys, however, the strength of ultrasonic welds can exceed the strength of resistance welds. The primary reasons for this increase in strength are that ultrasonic welding produces no melted or heat-affected zones in the material being welded and the size of the weld is generally greater. As there is no fusion of the base materials aluminum may be readily joined to a wide variety of dissimilar metals and alloys.

Ultrasonic welding equipment is commercially available in a variety of sizes from 100 w to 4 kw spot and seam welding machines. Aluminum in thicknesses from 0.00017 to 0.092 inch can be spot welded with available equipment. However, there appears to be no basic reason why larger equipment cannot be developed to weld heavier gages or increase welding speed. Ring welds can also be made with special equipment.

Ultrasonic welding generally requires less surface preparation than any other welding method. Many aluminum alloys can be welded in mill-finished condition.

Table 69.50—Base metal-brazing alloy combinations for brazing aluminum

| Base Alloy | Brazing Alloy Aluminum Association Designation | Brazing Alloy AWS–ASTM Classification Number | Optimum Brazing Range, °F |
|---|---|---|---|
| EC, 1100, 3003, Cast 406 | 4343<br>4047 | BA1Si–2<br>BA1Si–4 | 1110–1140<br>1090–1120 |
| 3004, 5005, 5050, 6063, 6951 | 4343<br>4047<br>4045 | BA1Si–2<br>BA1Si–4<br>BA1Si–5 | 1110–1140<br>1080–1120<br>1090–1120 |
| Cast C612 | 4145<br>4047<br>4045 | BA1Si–3<br>BA1Si–4<br>BA1Si–5 | 1080–1120<br>1080–1120<br>1090–1120 |
| 6053, 6061, Cast A612 | 4145<br>4047<br>4045 | BA1Si–3<br>BA1Si–4<br>BA1Si–5 | 1080–1100<br>1080–1100<br>1090–1100 |
| Cast 43, Cast 356 | 4245 | ....... | 1040–1060 |

# 116/Solid State Bonding

**Table 69.51—Brazing alloys for aluminum**

| Brazing Alloy Designation ASA | AWS-ASTM Classification Number | Nominal Composition % Si | Cu | Zn | Melting Range °F | Normal Brazing Range, °F | Available as: Rod | Sheet | Clad* | Powder | Brazing Process Torch | Furnace | Dip | Remarks |
|---|---|---|---|---|---|---|---|---|---|---|---|---|---|---|
| 4343 | BAlSi-2 | 7.5 | .. | .. | 1070–1135 | 1110–1150 |  | X | X |  |  | X | X |  |
| 4145 | BAlSi-3 | 10 | 4 | .. | 970–1085 | 1060–1120 | X | X |  |  | X | X | X | Desirable where control of fluidity is necessary. |
| 4047 | BAlSi-4 | 12 | .. | .. | 1070–1080 | 1080–1120 | X | X |  | X | X |  | X | Fluid in entire brazing range. |
| 4045 | BAlSi-5 | 10 | .. | .. | 1070–1095 | 1090–1120 |  | X | X |  |  | X | X |  |
| 4245 | ...... | 10 | 4 | 10 | 960–1040 | 1040–1060 | X |  |  |  | X | X | X | Particularly useful for brazing castings. |

* As a cladding on aluminum brazing sheet (Table 69.52).

Alloys containing high percentages of magnesium or the complex heat-treated alloys may have thick oxide films which must be removed before satisfactory ultrasonic welds can be produced. An advantage of ultrasonic welding over spot welding in this respect is that surface preparation is simpler, and once accomplished, is longer lasting. While ultrasonic welds can generally be made through thin anodic coatings, heavy anodic films such as those used on decorative and reflective applications are difficult to weld through. It is generally recommended that the coating be removed from the area to be welded.

In general, the same joint designs employed for resistance welding are suitable for ultrasonic welds although optimum welding patterns have not as yet been developed. However, minimum edge distance, spot spacing and ratio of part thicknesses are not as critical. When compared to other solid state bonding methods, less allowance may be made for overall deformation of the weld area, since ultrasonic welds exhibit overall deformation of less than 5%.

The main variables in ultrasonic welding are: welding power, welding time and clamping force. As a general rule, all three of these variables increase with the gage of material being welded. For example, aluminum foil 0.001 inch thick can be welded with approximately 100 w of power for 0.05 second welding time with approximately 50 to 75 pounds of clamping force. Aluminum alloys such as 2024 inch thicknesses of 0.080 inch require 4 kw of power for approximately one second, and a clamping force of approximately 700 pounds.

## BRAZING

Many aluminum alloys can be brazed. Aluminum brazing alloys are used which provide an all aluminum structure with excellent corrosion resistance, good strength and appearance, and which permit any aluminum finishing method. The melting point of the brazing filler metal is relatively close to that of the material being joined. As a result close temperature control is necessary.

Relative brazability of aluminum alloys is given in Tables 69.2,5,6 and 7. Most commonly brazed alloys, brazing material, and brazing temperatures are listed in Table 69.50. Most 2000 and 7000 series wrought alloys and many cast alloys cannot be brazed because their melting temperatures are below that of the commercial brazing filler metals. Alloys with a high Mg content, such as 5154, 5086 and 5456, are difficult to braze because of poor wetting characteristics. The brazing temperature required for aluminum assemblies is determined by the melting points of the base metal and the brazing filler metal. Actual brazing temperatures for specific assemblies should be determined experimentally.

### BRAZING FILLER METAL

Tables 69.51 and 52 describe the brazing filler metals available for aluminum. Brazing filler metal may be applied in wire form or as shim stock. Brazing sheet consisting of either heat-treatable or nonheat-treatable core alloy and clad on one or both sides with brazing alloy is also available. This material is widely used for furnace and dip brazed assemblies. A third method of supplying brazing filler metal is as a powder mixed with flux in the form of a paste. Alloy BAlSi-4 is most commonly used for manual torch brazing.

### BRAZING FLUX

Flux is required in all aluminum brazing operations. Aluminum brazing fluxes consist of various combinations of fluorides and chlorides and are supplied as a

**Table 69.52—Clad aluminum brazing sheet**

| Commercial Brazing Sheet Designation | Number of Sides Coated | Core Alloy | Cladding Composition | Thickness Sheet, Inches | % Cladding on Each Side | Optimum Brazing Range, °F |
|---|---|---|---|---|---|---|
| No. 11 | 1 | 3003 | BA1Si–2 (4343) | 0.063 and less | 10 | 1110–1150 |
| No. 12 | 2 | | | 0.064 and over | 5 | |
| No. 21 | 1 | 6951 | BA1Si–2 (4343) | 0.090 and less | 10 | 1110–1140 |
| No. 22 | 2 | | | 0.091 and over | 5 | |
| No. 23 | 1 | 6951 | BA1Si–5 (4045) | 0.090 and less | 10 | 1090–1120 |
| No. 24 | 2 | | | 0.091 and over | 5 | |
| No. 100 | 1* | 3003 | BA1Si–2 (4343) | 0.063 and less | 10 | 1100–1140 |
| | | | | 0.064 and over | 5 | |

* This product consists of a core clad on one side with brazing alloy, and on the other side with an alclad surface for maximum resistance to corrosion.

dry powder. For torch and furnace brazing the flux is mixed with water to make a paste which is brushed, sprayed, dipped, or flowed onto the entire area of the joint and brazing filler metal. Torch and furnace brazing fluxes are quite active, may severely attack thin aluminum, and must be used with care. In dip brazing the bath consists of molten flux. Less active fluxes can be used in this application and thin components can be safely brazed.

### DESIGN OF BRAZED JOINTS

Brazed joints should be of lap, flange, lock seam, or tee type. Butt or scarf joints are not generally recommended. Tee and line contact joints allow excellent capillary flow and the formation of reinforcing fillets on both sides of the joint.

For maximum efficiency lap joints should have an overlap of at least twice the thickness of the thinnest joint member. An overlap greater than 1/4 inch may lead to voids or flux inclusions. In this case, the use of straight grooves or knurls in the direction of brazing filler metal flow is beneficial.

Joint clearance will vary depending upon the process and lap length. For dip brazing 0.003 inch to 0.006 inch clearance is generally suitable. For other methods clearances from 0.005 to 0.010 inch are used for laps less than 1/4 inch long. Longer laps may require clearances up to 0.025 inch for adequate brazing filler metal penetration.

Closed assemblies should allow easy escape of gases and in dip brazing, easy entry as well as drainage of flux. Good design for long laps requires that brazing filler metal flows in one direction only for maximum joint soundness. The joint design must also permit complete postbraze flux removal.

### FIXTURES FOR BRAZING

Whenever possible parts should be designed to be self-jigging. When using fixtures differential expansion can occur between the assembly and the fixture to distort the parts. Stainless steel or inconel springs are often used with fixtures to accommodate differences in expansion. Fixture material can be mild steel or stainless steel. However, for repetitive furnace brazing operations and for dip brazing to avoid flux bath contamination, fixtures of nickel, inconel or aluminum-coated steel are preferred.

## PRECLEANING

Precleaning is essential for the production of strong leak-tight brazed joints. Vapor or solvent cleaning will usually be adequate for the nonheat-treatable alloys. For heat-treatable alloys, however, chemical cleaning is necessary to remove the thicker oxide film (Table 69.32).

## FURNACE BRAZING

Furnace brazing is performed in gas, oil, or electrically heated furnaces. Temperature regulation within $\pm 5°F$ is generally necessary to secure consistent results. Continuous circulation of the furnace atmosphere is desirable since it reduces brazing time and results in more uniform heating. Products of combustion in the furnace can be detrimental to brazing and ultimate serviceability of brazed assemblies in the heat-treatable alloys.

## TORCH BRAZING

Torch brazing differs from furnace brazing in that the heat is localized. Heat is applied to the part until the flux and brazing filler metal melt and wet the surfaces of the base metal. The process resembles gas welding except that the brazing filler metal is more fluid and flows by capillary action. Torch brazing is often used for the attachment of fittings to previously welded or furnace brazed assemblies, joining of return bends and similar applications.

## DIP BRAZING

In dip brazing operations a large amount of molten flux is held in a ceramic pot at the dip brazing temperature. Dip brazing pots are heated internally by direct resistance heating. Low voltage, high current transformers supply alternating current to pure nickel, nickel alloy or carbon electrodes immersed in the bath. Such pots are generally lined with high alumina content fire brick and a refractory mortar. Externally gas-fired or resistance-heated metal pots made of nickel have been used but have very short life. An aluminum automotive radiator fabricated by dip brazing is shown in Figure 69.50.

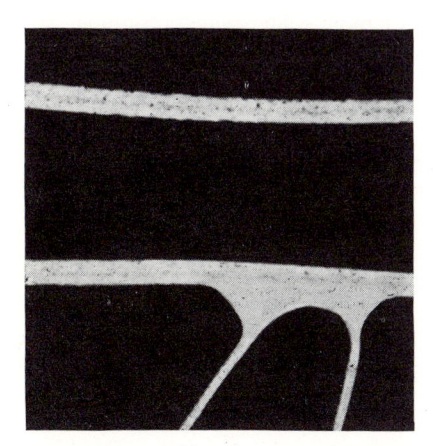

*Fig. 69.50.—(X50) Aluminum automotive radiator fabricated by dip brazing, using No. 12 brazing sheet except for 3003 fins and tube connections. Detail of fin-to-tube joint is shown on the right*

## POSTBRAZE CLEANING

It is always necessary to clean the brazed assemblies, since brazing fluxes accelerate corrosion if left on the parts. The most satisfactory way of removing the major portion of the flux is to immerse the hot parts in boiling water as soon as possible after the brazing alloy has solidified. The steam formed removes a major amount of residual flux. If distortion from quenching is a problem the part should be allowed to cool in air before being immersed in boiling water.

The remaining flux may be removed by a dip in concentrated nitric acid for 5 to 15 minutes depending upon the design of the part. The acid is removed with a water rinse, preferably in boiling water in order to accelerate drying. An alternate cleaning method is to dip the parts for 5 to 10 minutes in a 10% nitric plus 1/4% hydrofluoric acid solution at room temperature. This treatment is also followed by a water rinse. Other methods may also be used.

For brazed assemblies consisting of sections thinner than .010 inch and parts where maximum resistance to corrosion is important, a common treatment is to immerse in hot water, followed by a dip in a solution of 10% nitric acid and 10% sodium dichromate for 5 to 10 minutes. This is followed by a hot water rinse. When the parts emerge from the hot water rinse they are immediately dried by forced hot air, as from a unit heater, to prevent staining (Table 69.24).

# SOLDERING

Aluminum and many aluminum base alloys can be soldered by techniques similar to those used for other metals (Chapter 47, Section 3). In addition, abrasion and reaction soldering are more commonly used with aluminum than with other metals. Aluminum, however, requires special fluxes. Rosin fluxes are not satisfactory.

## SOLDERABILITY OF ALUMINUM ALLOYS

The most readily soldered aluminum alloys contain no more than 1% magnesium or 5% silicon. Alloys containing greater amounts of these constituents possess poor flux wetting characteristics. High copper and zinc-containing alloys have poor soldering characteristics because of rapid solder penetration and loss of properties. General solderability of the aluminum alloys is given in Tables 69.2, 69.5, 69.6 and 69.7.

Aluminum castings generally have poor solderability because of their composition. In addition, the surface condition of castings often makes them more difficult to solder than wrought alloys. The surface can be more difficult to clean and any surface porosity can hamper complete flux removal.

Residual stresses from quenching or cold working may interfere with making a satisfactory soldered joint. Stress accelerates penetration of solder along the grain boundaries and can cause cracking or loss in properties. Intergranular penetration can be minimized through stress relieving by heating to about 700°F prior to soldering. This occurs naturally when high-temperature zinc soldering aluminum.

Clad alloys often possess improved soldering characteristics over the bare alloy. The cladding of Alclad alloys can improve solder and flux wetting characteristics and reduce diffusion of the solder into the alloy. This is particularly useful when low-temperature soldering the 2000 to 7000 series aluminum alloys.

In addition to aluminum alloy claddings, another metal, such as copper or zinc, can be applied to the aluminum surface to facilitate soldering. Copper can be electroplated or rolled onto the aluminum and permits low-temperature soldering with solders and fluxes normally used to solder copper. Zinc-clad assemblies can be joined by merely fluxing and heating to about 800°F, at which point the cladding melts to form the joints. These joints have high mechanical strength and good corrosion resistance. Zinc-clad aluminum can also be soft soldered, employing either zinc chloride or rosin-alcohol fluxes and tin-lead solders. The soldering time and temperature must be controlled so that alloying between the cladding and soft solder does not progress to the point where the soft solder is in direct contact with the underlying aluminum surface (Fig. 69.51).

## JOINT DESIGN

The designs used for soldering aluminum assemblies are similar to those used with other metals. The most commonly used design are forms of simple

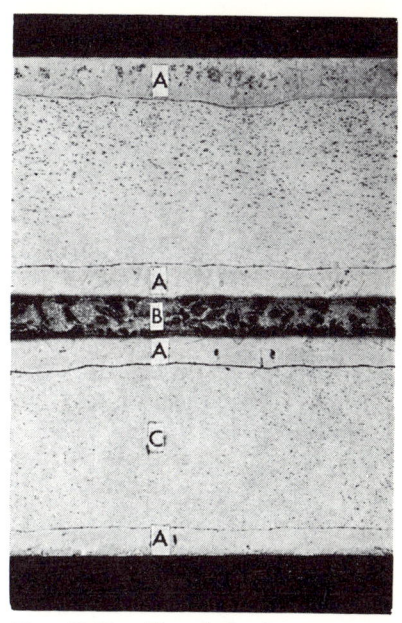

*Fig. 69.51.—Zinc-clad aluminum soldered with 50% Sn-50% Pb solder. The layer of zinc (A) effectively separates the solder (B) from the aluminum (C)*

lap, crimp and T-type joints. Joint clearance varies with the specific soldering method, base alloy combination, solder composition, joint design and flux composition employed. However, as a guide, joint clearance ranging from 0.005 to 0.020 inch is required when chemical fluxes are used, and 0.002 to 0.010 inch spacing is employed when a reaction type flux is used.

## SOLDERS

The commercial solders for aluminum can be classified into three general groups according to their melting points. Table 69.53 shows this classification and presents the characteristics of each group.

## LOW TEMPERATURE SOLDERS

Low temperature solders usually have melting points in the range of 300° to 500°F. This group consists of solders that contain tin and lead plus zinc and/or cadmium. The best of the group have the highest percentages of tin and zinc. Solders in this group produce joints with the least corrosion resistance, but they are the easiest to use in soldering operations. The mechanical strength of joints made with low temperature solders approach that of soldered joints in copper, which exhibit a shear strength of about 6000 psi.

## INTERMEDIATE TEMPERATURE SOLDERS

The intermediate temperature solders have melting points in the range of 500-700°F. Solders in this group contain tin or cadmium in various combinations with zinc, plus small amounts of aluminum, copper, lead, nickel or silver.

**122**/Soldering

Table 69.53—Summary of major processes for joining aluminum to other metals or materials

| Joining Process | Ferrous Alloys | Copper Alloys | Nickel Alloys | Magnesium Alloys | Titanium Alloys | Silver Alloys | Zinc Alloys | Lead Alloys | Tin Alloys | Precious Alloys | Refractory Metals, Molybdenum, Tantalum, Tungsten | Electro-Plates or Hot Dip Coatings | Ceramics, Glass, Etc. | Plastics, Rubber, Wood, Etc. |
|---|---|---|---|---|---|---|---|---|---|---|---|---|---|---|
| Gas Welding | C | C | C | X | | | X | X | X | | | | | X |
| Arc Welding | B | B | C | X | | | X | X | X | | C | C | X | X |
| Resistance spot or seam | B | X | | X | | | | | | C | | | X | X |
| Flash Welding | X | A | X | X | | | | | | | | | | |
| Torch and furnace brazing | B | C | B | X | B | | X | X | X | | | C | C | X |
| Dip Brazing | A | X | C | X | | | X | X | X | | C | C | | X |
| Soldering | A | A | A | C | C | C | C | X | X | A | | A | B | X |
| Zinc solder | B | B | C | B | B | A | A | A | A | C | B | A | B | |
| Tin-lead solder | A | A | A | | | C | | C | C | C | C | C | | |
| Diffusion Bonding | A | A | A | A | A | A | A | A | A | A | | A | A | |
| Pressure Welding | A | A | A | A | | C | C | A | A | C | C | C | B | A |
| Ultrasonic Welding | C | C | C | | C | | | | | | | | | |
| Adhesive Bonding | | | | | | | | | | | | | | |
| Use of transition joints | | | | | | | | | | | | | | |

A—Easily joined. No special technique, such as precoating the aluminum or other metal, is required.
B—Readily joined, but may require special techniques.
C—Possible, but limited experience.
X—Impractical or not recommended.
(Combinations of process and metal on which no information is available are left blank.)

Some of the more common of these solders are the 70 tin-30 zinc and 60 zinc-40 cadmium base solders. As a result of their higher zinc content, these intermediate temperature solders generally wet aluminum more readily, form larger fillets, and produce stronger and more corrosion-resistant joints than the low temperature solders.

## HIGH TEMPERATURE SOLDERS

The high temperature solders usually have melting points in the range of 700° to 800°F. These zinc-base solders contain 3 to 10% aluminum and small amounts of other metals such as copper, silver, nickel, and iron to modify their melting and wetting characteristics. The high zinc solders have the highest strength of the aluminum solders, with shear strengths in excess of 15,000 psi. They are also the least expensive and form the most corrosion-resistant soldered assemblies.

## PREPARATION FOR SOLDERING

Grease, dirt and other foreign material must be removed from the surface of aluminum before soldering. In most instances only solvent degreasing is required. If the surface is heavily oxidized, however, wire brushing or chemical cleaning may be required.

## OXIDE REMOVAL

To solder aluminum successfully, the oxide layer must be removed by mechanical abrasion, ultrasonic dispersion, or fluxing.

*Abrasion.*—Rubbing the surface of aluminum under a molten solder layer permits soldering. Fiberglass brushes, stainless steel brushes, stainless steel wool, or the solder rod can be used for the surface abrasion to break up the oxide and allow the molten solder to contact and bond to the underlying metal surface.

*Ultrasonic Dispersion.*—The second means of removing the aluminum oxide film is to erode it from the aluminum surface by using ultrasonic energy. When the ultrasonically vibrating tip is brought into contact with molten solder numerous voids form within the molten metal. This phenomenon is known as cavitation. The collapse of these voids creates an abrasive affect that removes the oxide film from aluminum and permits the molten solder to bond (Fig. 69.52).

*Fluxes.*—The third method of removing aluminum oxide films is by employing a flux. The two general types of commercially available fluxes are the chemical type and the reaction type.

Most chemical flux residues are mildly corrosive and should be removed from aluminum parts thinner than 0.005 inch. Some fluxes contain activating agents such as zinc chloride and ammonia compounds. The residue left by these modified fluxes significantly accelerates corrosion. It is therefore recommended that flux residue be removed, if possible. Since flux residues are electrical conductors, they should be removed from soldered electrical apparatus.

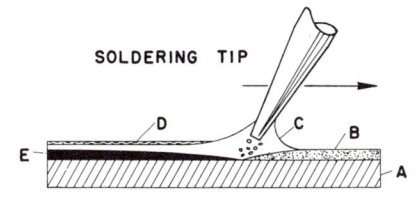

Fig. 69.52.—*Diagram representing soldering with ultrasonic abrasion. (A) base metal (B) oxide surface (C) molten solder (bubbles represent oxide cavitation) (D) oxide on surface of molten solder (E) solidified solder*

The major constituent of reaction fluxes is zinc chloride. Fluxes for furnace or automatic flame soldering, where the filler has been preplaced, possess a high percentage of zinc chloride and completely expend themselves upon reaching the reaction temperature. Fluxes for manual torch soldering contain a high proportion of other halides in addition to zinc chloride to provide an effective flux cover during the manual filler addition. Upon reaching a specific temperature these fluxes penetrate the aluminum oxide, react with the underlying aluminum to deposit metallic zinc, and evolve gaseous aluminum chloride which appears as a white smoke. The deposit of molten zinc is sometimes sufficient to produce soldered joints without additional solder. This type of flux is used at temperatures above 650°F and is suitable for soldering the aluminum alloys containing magnesium. The flux residue accelerates corrosion and should be removed by thorough washing.

## ALUMINUM SOLDERING TECHNIQUES

The higher melting point solders normally used to join aluminum assemblies plus the excellent thermal conductivity of aluminum normally dictate that a large capacity heat source must be used to bring the joint area to proper soldering temperature. Uniform, well controlled heating should be provided.

## TORCH SOLDERING

Air-fuel gas torches are commonly used to solder aluminum assemblies. The operation is usually manual but may be automatic. Abrasion or ultrasonic techniques can be used or a flux can be painted on the joint, and solder can either be preplaced or manually fed. The best torch soldering technique is to heat the assembly on both sides of the joint area until solder flow can be initiated in the joint. The flame is then moved directly over the joint, slightly behind the front of the solder flow. In this way, the flame does not come into direct contact with the flux.

## SOLDERING IRONS

Aluminum sheet thicker than 0.064 inch is difficult to heat with a soldering iron, even though the area of the assembly is small. An auxiliary heat source, such as a hot plate, is often used. Flux may be applied to the joint and solder wire is manually fed into the joint. The soldering iron is then brought into direct contact with the soldered joint immediately behind the front of solder flow. When chemical fluxes are used, the iron should not be brought into direct contact with the flux, or it will be charred and its fluxing efficiency reduced or destroyed. When removing the chemical flux residue, the part should be washed in alcohol. Water, when used for flux removal, can trigger corrosive attack of low-temperature soldered joints.

## FURNACE SOLDERING

Furnace soldering can be used with all types of solders for aluminum, but it is most commonly used for high-temperature soldering. Distortion of parts due to differential thermal expansion is low. The solder is preplaced at the joints and the flux is applied by spraying, brushing, or immersion.

## REACTION FLUX SOLDERING

This process is unique to aluminum and is found in heat exchanger fabrication. The flux contains a high percentage of zinc chloride and upon reaching the reaction temperature (650° to 720°F), the zinc chloride reacts chemically with the aluminum oxide to deposit zinc at the joints. Sufficient zinc is usually deposited from the flux alone for line contact joints, such as when joining fins to heat exchanger passages. If additional zinc deposition is required, zinc particles can be mixed with the flux or preplaced zinc or zinc-aluminum solder can be employed. Heating can be supplied by furnace, gas flame, or resistance.

The reaction fluxes are usually very hygroscopic and thus normal propyl or normal butyl alcohol is used as a vehicle rather than water. Water will cause the formation of oxychlorides which hamper satisfactory fluxing action and flow.

When soldering in a furnace, good exhaust of the work areas is required to exhaust the alcohol vehicle as well as the copious fumes of the flux reaction.

## DIP SOLDERING

Dip soldering is well suited to joining aluminum, because the solder pot is an excellent large capacity heat source. The method is ideal for joining assemblies at a high production rate. The same techniques and production schedules normally used to solder other metals can often be retained with aluminum. Any of the conventional solders and fluxes recommended for use with aluminum can be used when dip soldering is employed.

## RESISTANCE SOLDERING

Resistance soldering may be applied to joining aluminum to itself or to other metals. It is also suitable for spot or tack soldering.

Flux is usually applied to the joint area by painting and the solder is either preplaced in the joint or fed manually. A metal or carbon electrode is then brought into contact with the joint area and maintained in position while current passes through the joint until solder flow occurs. Since the heat is generated in the aluminum, there is little danger of damaging the flux by excessive heating. After soldering, the flux residue should be removed.

## CHARACTERISTICS OF SOLDERED ALUMINUM JOINTS

### Mechanical Strength

While it is often of secondary importance, the mechanical strength developed by soldered aluminum assemblies ranges from a minimum approximately equal to the strength of soft solders (about 6000 psi) to a maximum greater than 40,000 psi shear stress. The intermediate and high temperature solders retain considerable strength at temperature levels where soft solders melt (about 360°F). High-temperature solders can develop usable strengths at temperatures as high as 600°F; however, creep can be experienced under conditions of stress at temperatures above 250°F.

### Corrosion Resistance

The corrosion resistance of soldered aluminum joints may be excellent to poor, depending upon the choice of solders and the degree of removal of residual soldering fluxes. When aluminum is soldered, a thin interfacial alloy layer is formed between the solder and the aluminum. In most instances, the rate of corrosion is greater in this interfacial area.

The rate of corrosion of soldered aluminum assemblies is greatest in the presence of good electrolytes, such as salt solutions. It is considerably less in the presence of poor electrolytes, such as condensed moisture, and insignificant in dry atmospheres. Painting or coating the joint area minimizes corrosion.

Generally solder systems with high zinc solders are highly resistant to corrosive attack. Assemblies prepared with pure zinc or zinc-aluminum solders have withstood outdoor corrosive attack for many years and are considered satisfactory for most applications requiring long outdoor service life. Corrosion resistance of assemblies joined with presently available intermediate and low temperature solders is usually satisfactory for interior or protected applications.

At present, a truly noncorrosive flux does not exist for soldering aluminum. However, the residual products formed by most soldering fluxes are readily soluble in water. Warm water is satisfactory for zinc soldered joints, but alcohol would be preferred for low-temperature soldered joints to avoid initiation of corrosion in the interfacial area.

Where the residual flux products cannot be removed and the highest resistance to corrosion or electrolytic action is required, special techniques which do not require a flux, such as ultrasonic soldering, may be used. In less critical applications, some of the chemical fluxes may be successfully used.

## ADHESIVE BONDING

The metal oxide film present on the surface of aluminum and aluminum alloys forms strong, durable bonds with metal bonding adhesives. Because of this, aluminum is easily joined with adhesives. The ease of joining and inherent desirable chemical and physical properties, such as high strength to weight ratio, resistance to corrosion and formability, account for the widespread use of adhesively bonded aluminum assemblies.

The successful application of adhesive bonding requires that the assembly be properly designed and that the adhesive most suitable for the particular application be used. Chemical surface preparation results in highest and most consistent properties and best performance in most environments. The advantages to be gained by using adhesives are described in Chapter 46, Section 3.

## JOINING TO OTHER METALS

Special techniques are required frequently for joining aluminum to other metals. In many cases metals difficult to join directly to aluminum can be connected through the use of an intermediate dissimilar metal applied by cladding, dip coating, electroplating, brazing or buttering. Another technique is to employ a transition piece to which both the aluminum and the other metal can be easily joined (Table 69.54).

### ALUMINUM TO STEEL

An aluminum coating is the most common surface preparation for steel or stainless steel prior to brazing or welding to aluminum alloys. Aluminum coatings can be applied by dipping cleaned steel, with or without fluxing, into molten aluminum at 1275° to 1300°F. Small steel parts can be rub coated with aluminum or aluminum-silicon alloys using aluminum brazing flux.

The coated steel parts may be gas tungsten-arc welded to aluminum. The arc should be directed onto the aluminum member of the assembly so that the molten weld pool flows over the aluminum coating without shattering or increasing the thickness of the interfacial layer of the iron-aluminum compound.

By avoiding or minimizing the formation of intermetallic compounds, aluminum may be joined directly to steel by soldering, pressure welding, ultrasonic welding and adhesive bonding. Resistance spot welding and the fusion welding techniques can be used when the steel is silver-plated. Resistance flash-butt welding cannot be used to join aluminum directly to steel, as the brittle iron-aluminum compounds formed during the welding cycle have high melting points and cannot be forced out of the fusion zone during upset.

## ALUMINUM TO COPPER

In addition to some limited solid solubility, copper and aluminum also form a number of brittle intermetallic phases when alloyed together. By avoiding these phases aluminum and copper joints may be made by flash welding, soldering, brazing, pressure welding, ultrasonic welding or adhesive bonding. By precoating copper with solders or silver brazing filler metals, it may be joined to aluminum by gas welding, arc welding or brazing.

## CORROSION RESISTANCE

Gas welding, brazing and most soldering methods employed in joining aluminum to other materials are generally carried out with salt-type fluxes. Residues of these fluxes are hygroscopic and accelerate corrosion of aluminum, particularly when in contact with a dissimilar metal. It is very important that all flux residues be removed.

When aluminum and other metals are in direct contact the presence of moisture or any electrolyte may set up a galvanic action between the two metals and cause preferential attack. The joints should be painted, coated, wrapped or protected by any convenient method to eliminate moisture or electrolytes at the area of contact.

## QUALITY CONTROL

Control of the quality of welded, brazed, soldered, or adhesive bonded joints is essential if the fabricated part is to perform satisfactorily in service. Quality control starts with the procurement of materials and is involved in all the operations performed in producing the part from design to final inspection.

Some of the areas involved are: procurement and processing of materials, establishment of proper design and joining procedures, qualification of equipment or procedures, qualification of welders or operators, proper maintenance of equipment, establishment and maintenance of adequate inspection or testing procedures and adequate supervision of each of the above steps.

The importance of proper supervision of welding operations in the production of high quality aluminum weldments cannot be overemphasized. Although aluminum and most aluminum alloys possess excellent weldability, they do not permit as much deviation from established procedures as does mild steel, and generally require closer control over the welding variables. In addition, some types of defects in aluminum weldments may not be as readily detected by nondestructive testing. Thus close supervision of all operations is essential to meet established standards of weld quality consistently.

## SPECIFICATIONS

Codes, standards and specifications which govern the joining of aluminum have been issued by the American Welding Society. Other code-writing bodies have issued similar standards and specifications governing materials, design, inspection, testing and qualification requirements as well as quality standards. These standards vary according to the service requirements (Fig. 69.53).

**128**/*Quality Control*

*Fig. 69.53.—An M113 aluminum armored personnel carrier emerges from water*

## WELDER TRAINING

A systematic method of welder training is essential if a person is to obtain the maximum knowledge of aluminum joining. The most economical way of producing a weldment is to have a fully trained capable welder who understands the attributes of the joining processes. Many specifications require that welding be done only by qualified welders, or welders who have passed certain tests designed to prove their ability to make sound welds by a given method or procedure. To become proficient in an aluminum welding process, a proposed welder must have full knowledge of the welding equipment and must know all related adjustments for each different type of equipment, or process he intends to employ. He must also understand why he is using a particular procedure and he must practice under proper guidance until he becomes proficient and has the capability of producing a proper weld.

## INSPECTION AND TESTING

The principal methods of inspection used to determine the soundness, quality and efficiency of welded joints or weldments are described in Chapter 10, Section 1. Additional material on inspection and testing of spot and seam welds is given in the resistance welding section of this chapter.

Inspection and testing methods are classified as nondestructive testing or destructive testing. Nondestructive tests include those methods which do not require cutting or destruction of the joint or assembly. Trepanning is usually considered nondestructive. The usual methods of nondestructive testing of aluminum are

## Quality Control/129

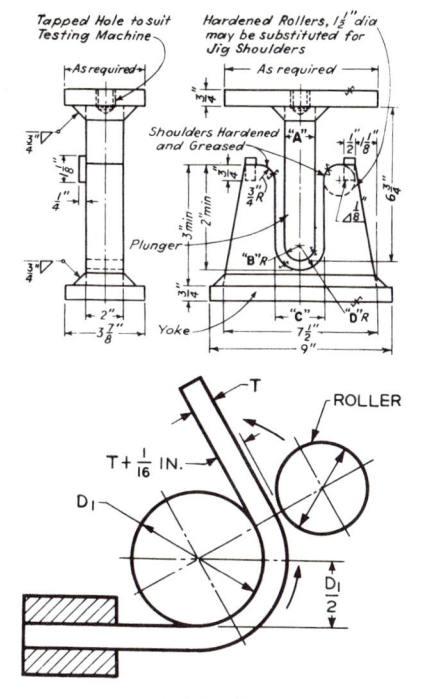

*Fig. 69.54—Guided bend test jig specifications*

visual, penetrant, radiographic and ultrasonic, leak testing and occasionally proof testing (Fig. 69.54).

**Table 69.54—General characteristics of aluminum solders**

| Type | Melting Range, °F | Common Constituents | Ease of Application | Wetting of Aluminum | Relative Strength | Relative Corrosion Resistance |
|---|---|---|---|---|---|---|
| Low Temperature | 300–500 | Tin or lead base plus zinc and/or cadmium | Best | Poor to Fair | Low | Low |
| Intermediate Temperature | 500–700 | Zinc-cadmium or zinc-tin base | Moderate | Good to Excellent | Moderate | Moderate |
| High Temperature | 700–800 | Zinc base plus Aluminum, Copper, etc. | Most Difficult | Good to Excellent | High | Good |

Destructive testing requires that the part or assembly be sectioned to provide the specimen for examination. However, in some cases a sample weldment of the same material welded with the same procedure as the production part may be destructively tested. Destructive testing methods find their widest application in the qualification of processes, procedures, welders, and materials rather than in the testing of finished products.

# BIBLIOGRAPHY

"Welding High Strength Aluminum Alloys," I. B. Robinson, F. R. Collins and J. D. Dowd, *Welding Journal Research Supplement,* (May 1962)

"Working with Aluminum? Here's What You Can Do with Dip Brazing," Paul B. Dickerson, *Metal Progress,* (May 1965)

"How to Dip Braze Aluminum Assemblies," Paul B. Dickerson, *Metal Progress,* (June 1965)

"Effects of Repeated Repair Welding of Two Aluminum Alloys," F. G. Nelson. *Ibid.,* (April 1961)

"Zinc Soldering of Aluminum," I. B. Robinson, *Welding Journal,* October 1957

"Residual Welding Stresses in Aluminum Alloys," H. N. Hill, *Metal Progress,* (August 1961)

"Gas Metal-Arc Spot Welding of Aluminum," R. A. Stoehr, *Welding Journal,* (September 1962)

"Joining Aluminum to Other Metals," Mike A. Miller, *Ibid.,* (August 1953)

"Gas Metal-Arc Spot Welding Joins Aluminum to Other Metals," R. A. Stoehr and F. R. Collins, *Ibid.,* (April 1963)

"The Automatic Welding of Aluminum Pipeline," Dana V. Wilcox, (February 1963)

"Automatic Welding of Heavy End Aluminum Pipe," *Welding and Metal Fabrication,* (January and March, 1965)

"A New High-Strength Aluminum Alloy," J. A. Nock, Jr., Marshall Holt, and D. O. Sprowls, "Aluminum 2219 . . . New Alloy for High-Strength Welded Structures," F. R. Collins, F. G. Nelson and I. B. Robinson, (September and November 1961)

"Joining New High-Strength Aluminum Alloy X7005," J. H. Dudas, Alcoa, *Ibid.,* (August 1965)

"Out-of-position Gas-Shielded-Arc Welding of Heavy Aluminum Sections," C. L. Mitchell, *Ibid.,* (September 1965)

"An Introduction to Aluminum Alloying and Designation System," Adkins and Ridout, *Welding Engineer* (June, July 1965)

"The Effect of Welding Speed on Strength of 6061-T4 Aluminum Joints," W. L. Burch, *Welding Journal,* 37 (8)

*Welding Kaiser Aluminum,* Kaiser Aluminum & Chemical Sales, Inc., Chicago (1966)

"A Fundamental Study of the Tungsten Arc," F. E. Gibbs, *Metal Progress* (July 1960)

*Standards for Wrought Aluminum Mill Products,* The Aluminum Association, New York (1966)

"Recent Advances in Joining Aluminum," G. W. Eldridge, *Metallurgia,* 61, 55-60 (February 1960)

"Assembly-Line Fabrication of All-Welded Aluminum Covered Hopper Cars," D. V. Wilcox and R. Hubbard, *The Welding Journal,* 39 (8), 783-790 (1960)

"Techniques for Welding Al-Mg Alloys," D. M. Daley, Jr., *Ibid.,* **39** (7), Research Suppl., 301-s to 305-s (1960)

"How to Interpret Fractures in Aluminum Weld Metal," W. L. Burch, *Ibid.,* **39** (4), 322-327 (1960)

"Weldability of Aluminum Casting Alloys with 5086 Wrought Aluminum Alloy," M. S. Orysh and I. G. Betz, *Ibid.,* **39** (8), Research Suppl., 324-s to 351-s (1960)

"Ultrasonic Welding of Dissimilar Metal Combinations," W. C. Potthoff, J. G. Thomas, and F. R. Meyer, *Ibid.,* **39** (2), 131-138 (1960)

"Plastic Properties of Aluminum-Magnesium Weldments," S. S. White, R. E. Manchester, W. G. Moffat and C. M. Adams, Jr., *Ibid.,* **39** (1), Research Suppl., 10-s to 19-s (1960)

"Application of 2219 Aluminum Alloy to Missile Pressure Vessel Fabrication," C. H. Crane and W. G. Smith, presented at the 41st Annual Meeting of the AWS, Los Angeles (April 1960)

"Factors Influencing the Fatigue Behavior of Welded Aluminum," J. E. Tomlinson and J. L. Wood, *British Welding Journal,* **7** (4), 250-264 (April 1960)

"Significance of Surface Preparation in Cold Pressure Welding," L. R. Vaidyanath and D. R. Milner, *Ibid.,* **7** (1), 1-6 (January 1960)

"The New 5XXX Aluminum Alloys—Strong and Weldable," R. T. Myer and D. R. Cheyney, *Materials in Design Engineering* (July 1959)

"Design of Welded Aluminum Structures," H. N. Hill, J. W. Clark and R. J. Brungraber, presented at Proceedings ASCE Annual Meeting, Washington, D.C. (October 19-23, 1959)

"Some Considerations on Design for Fatigue in Welded Aircraft Structures," J. Koziarski, *The Welding Journal,* **38** (6), 565-575 (1959)

"Ultrasonic Welding of Aluminum," F. R. Collins, J. D. Dowd and M. W. Brennecke, *Ibid.,* **38** (10), 969-975 (1959)

"Techniques for Torch Brazing Aluminum," H. E. Adkins and R. A. Ridout, *Welding Engineer* (August 1959)

*Soldering Manual,* American Welding Society, New York (1964)

*Soldering Aluminum,* Reynolds Metals Company (1965)

"Adhesive Bonding," J. C. Merriam, *Materials in Design Engineering,* 113-127 (September 1959)

*Adhesive Bonding of Aluminum,* Reynolds Metals Company (1965)

"Joining Dissimilar Metals," J. G. Young and A. A. Smith, *Welding and Metal Fabrication,* **27** (7-9), 275-281 (July), 331-339 (August/September 1959)

*Structural Aluminum Design,* K. Angermayer, Reynolds Metals Company (1966)

*Military Handbook HIB,* Standardization Division, Supply & Logistics, Office of Assistant Secretary of Defense, Washington, D.C. (1958)

*The Aluminum Data Book,* Reynolds Metals Company (1966)

*Kaiser Aluminum Sheet and Plate,* 2nd ed., Kaiser Aluminum & Chemical Sales, Inc. (1966)

*Welding Alcoa Aluminum,* Aluminum Company of America (1966)

*Welding Aluminum,* Reynolds Metals Company (1958)

*Kaiser Aluminum Weldors Training Manual,* Kaiser Aluminum & Chemical Sales, Inc. (1966)

"Investigation Toward Obtaining Significantly Higher Mechanical Properties of As-Welded Joints in High-Strength, Heat Treatable Aluminum Alloys," *ASME Boiler & Pressure Vessel Code*

"Fusion Welding of 2014 Aluminum Alloys," U. S. Department of Commerce, AD284458

"Cryogenic Temperature Up Fatigue Strengths of Al-Mg Alloys," J. G. Kaufman and F. G. Nelson, *Space/Aeronautics* (July 1962)

"Suggested Specifications for Structures of Aluminum Alloys 6061-T6 and 6062-T6," Paper No. 3341, Journal of the Structural Division, *Proceedings,* ASCE Vol. 88, ST6, Dec. 1962, pg. 1

"Suggested Specifications for Structures of Aluminum Alloys 6063-T5 and 6063-T6," Paper No. 3342, Journal of the Structural Division, *Proceedings,* ASCE Vol. 88, ST6, Dec. 1962, p. 47

"The Properties of Aluminum Alloy 2219 Sheet, Plate and Welded Joints at Low Temperatures," J. G. Kaufman, F. G. Nelson and E. W. Johnson, Aluminum Company of America (1962)

# INDEX

Adhesive bonding, 126
Aluminum, 1-132
  strength, 111, 112
Aluminum
  alloy group designations, 3
  commercial forms, 3-14
  general characteristics, 1
  joining characteristics, 2
  joining method selection, 14-18
  vacuum die casting, 3
  wrought alloys, 3
Aluminum alloy cast welding, 88-89
  foundry welding, 89
Arc cutting, 60-63
  gas metal-arc, 62-63
Atomic hydrogen welding, 57-58

Brazing, 117-120
  filler metal, 117
  fixtures, 118
  flux, 117; 118
  joint designs, 118
  clearance, 118
  postbraze cleaning, 120
  precleaning, 119

Characteristics of soldering aluminum joints, 125-126
Cutting
  gas metal-arc
    conditions, 64

Design for welding, 18-27
  butt joints, 22
  edge preparation, 25
  fillet welds, 23-24
  joint accessibility, 24
  lap joints, 23
  stress distribution, 26-27
  tee joints, 24
  joint accessibility, 24
Die castings, 69.3
Dip brazing, 119
  applications, 119
Dip soldering, 125

Electron-beam welding, 59
  electrical conductivity, 1
  joint design, 60
  technique, 60

Filler metal selection, 27-32
  aluminum filler metal, 29-33
  anodic treatments, 28
  corrosion resistance, 28
  cracking, 28
  dilution, 27
  elevated-temperature service, 28
  repair of castings, 29, 32
  selection, 28
Flash welding, 111
  corrosion resistance, 112
  schedules, 112
Furnace brazing, 119

Furnace soldering, 124

Gas metal-arc welding, 32-44
  automatic welding, 38-44
  characteristic process, 32
  equipment, 32-33
  joint design, 37-39
  power supply, 32-33
  purity, 35
  shielding gas, 33-35
  technique, 35-37
  variables, 38
Gas tungsten-arc welding, 44-49
  alternating current, 44-46
    automatic welding, 46
    characteristic process, 44-45
    joint design, 46
    technique, 45-46
    variables, 46
  direct current, SP, 46-49
    automatic welding technique, 49
    electrodes, 48
    joint design, 47-48
    manual welding technique, 49
    process characteristics, 46-47
Gas welding, 54-56
  edge preparation, 54-55
  filler material, 55-56
  flame, 55
  fluxes, 56
  technique, 56

High frequency resistance welding, 112

Joining to other metals, 126-127

Properties and performance of weldments, 72-88
  aluminum-copper alloys (2000 series), 84
  aluminum-magnesium-silicon alloys (6000 series), 82-83
  aluminum-zinc alloys (7000 series), 84
  corrosion resistance, 86-87
  ductility of butt welds, 76
  effect of temperature, 86
  fatigue strength, 85-86
  fillet weld shear strength, 84
  fracture characteristics, 87-88
  heat-treatable alloys, 77-81
  impact strength, 85
  metallurgical affects of welding, 73-76
  nonheat-treatable alloys, 76-77
  postweld heat-treatment, 81-82
  strength, 76

Quality control, 127-130

Reaction flux soldering, 124-125
Repair welding, 72
Resistance soldering, 125
Resistance welding, 89-112
  corrosion resistance, 90
  weldability ratings, 90

Seam welding, 109-111
  electrodes, 109

# 134/Index

equipment, 109
Shielded carbon-arc welding, 57
Shielded metal-arc welding, 56-57
Shop practices, 63-70
   back chipping, 68
   backup, 67
   distortion control, 68-69
   edge preparation, 63-65
   finishing, 69
   fit-up, 67
   oxide removal, 65-67
      chemical treatments, 66
   preheating, 68
   preweld cleaning, 65-67
   tacking, 67
   tooling fixtures, 68
Soldering, 120-126
   high temperature solders, 123
   intermediate temperature solders, 121-123
   joint design, 121
   low temperature solders, 121
   oxide removal, 123-124
      abrasion, 123
      fluxes, 123
      ultrasonic dispersion, 123
   preparation, 123
   techniques, 124
Solid state bonding, 112-117
   definition, 112
   friction welding, 114
   pressure welding, 113-114
      lap welds, 113
   ultrasonic welding, 114-117
      equipment, 115
      surface preparation, 115
Spot welding, 91-95
   defects, 106-107
      cracks, 106
      electrode pickup, 106
      indentation, 107
      molten metal expulsion, 106-107
      porosity, 106
   design, 98-105
      jigging, 100
      shear strength, 99

electrode force, 92-93
electrode holders, 93-95
electrode tip cleaning tools, 94
electrodes, 93-95
electrostatic stored energy welding machines, 92
equipment, 91-92
   single phase A-C slope control, 91-92
   single phase A-C welding, 91
   three-phase, 92
inspection, 107-108
schedules, 105
shop practices, 105-106
strength and nugget diameter, 98
surface contact resistance measurement, 97-98
surface preparation, 95-97
   cleaning, 95-96
   oxide removal, 96-97
testing, 107-108
welding parameters, 99
Square wave A-C welding, 49-53
   joint geometry, 53
   welding technique, 53
Stud welding, 58

Thermal conductivity, 1
Torch brazing, 119
Torch soldering, 124
   soldering irons, 124

Weld defects, 70-72
   cracking, 70-71
   inadequate penetration, 71-72
   inclusions, 72
   incomplete fusion, 71
   porosity, 71
   wrought alloys, 8-14
      cast alloys, 14
      heat-treatable aluminum alloys, 9-14
      nonheat-treatable aluminum alloys, 8-9
   wrought nonheat-treatable alloys, 4
      composition, 4
      properties, 4